The Spider's Web
and Zipper and his Father

Joseph Roth

The Spider's Web
and Zipper and his Father

Translated from the German by
John Hoare

THE OVERLOOK PRESS
WOODSTOCK, NEW YORK

First published in 1989 by

The Overlook Press
Lewis Hollow Road
Woodstock, New York 12498

Copyright © 1989
by Allert de Lange, Amsterdam and Verlag Kiepenheuer
& Witsch, Köln

Library of Congress Cataloging-in-Publication Data

Roth, Joseph, 1894-1939
    The spider's web; and Zipper and his father.

    Translation of: Das Spinnennetz, and Zipper und
sein Vater.
        I. Roth, Joseph, 1894-1939.   Zipper und sein
Vater.   English.   1989.   II. Title: Spider's web.
III. Title: Zipper and his father.
PT2635.084S613   1989   833′.912   88-31314
ISBN 0-87951-345-4

Contents

The Spider's Web

1

Theodor grew up in the house of his father, the railway inspector of customs and former sergeant-major, Wilhelm Lohse. Little Theodor was a fair-haired, industrious and well-behaved boy. He had fervently desired the distinction he was later to achieve, but hadn't dared to expect it. One might say that he exceeded expectations which he had never had.

Father Lohse was not to see his son at his peak. The old inspector of customs was only privileged to see Theodor in the uniform of a lieutenant of the Reserve. The old man never asked for more. He died in the fourth year of the Great War, and the last moments of his life were dominated by the thought that his coffin would be followed by Lieutenant Theodor Lohse.

A year later, Theodor was no longer a lieutenant. He was reading law, and he was tutor in the household of the jeweller, Efrussi. Every day, in the jeweller's house, he was given white coffee with a skin on it and a ham sandwich on white bread, and every month he received a fee. This was the basis of his material existence, for the Technical Labour Exchange, of which he was a member, rarely provided work, and what they did provide was hard and indifferently paid. Once a week Theodor drew vegetables from the Reserve Officers' Co-operative. He shared these with his mother and sisters, in whose house he lived, tolerated rather than welcomed, scarcely noticed and, on the rare occasions when he was, rather despised. His mother was sickly, his sisters were wilting and not growing any younger. They couldn't forgive Theodor for having failed – he who had twice been mentioned in despatches – to die a hero's death as a lieutenant. A dead son would have been the pride of the family. A demobilised lieutenant, a victim of the revolution, was a burden to his womenfolk. Theodor lived amid his family like some aged grandfather who would have been revered in death but who is scorned because he is still alive.

He would have been spared much discomfort were it nor for the silent enmity which stood like a wall between him and his household. He could have told his sisters that he was not responsible for his own misfortune; that he cursed the revolution and was gnawed by hatred for the socialists and the Jews, that he bore each day like a yoke across his bowed neck and felt himself trapped in his epoch as in some sunless prison. No escape beckoned to him, and flight was impossible.

But he said nothing. He had always been a silent type, had always sensed the invisible hand before his lips, even as a boy. He could only utter what he had learned by heart, the sound of which was already prepared, formed silently a dozen times in his ears and his throat. It took him a lot of learning before the recalcitrant words would yield and take their place in his brain. He learned stories by rote, as if they were poems. The printed sentences stood before his eyes as if in a book, the page number at the top and, in the margin, a nose, doodled during some idle quarter of an hour.

Every hour bore a strange aspect. Everything surprised him. Everything which happened was frightening, because it was new, yet it vanished before making any impression. His timidity taught him to be careful, to work hard, to train himself with ruthless determination, but again and again he discovered that his preparation was insufficient. He would then work ten times as hard. Thus he had forced his way to second position in his school. First came the Jew, Glaser, who drifted smilingly through breaks, carefree and heedless of books, but who in twenty minutes could turn in an impeccable Latin exercise, and in whose head vocabularies, formulae and irregular verbs seemed to sprout effortlessly.

Young Efrussi so resembled Glaser that it was an effort for Theodor to assert his authority over the jeweller's son. Theodor had to suppress a still but obstinately growing timidity before he could correct his pupil. Young Efrussi wrote down and spoke his mistakes with such confidence that Theodor began to have doubts about his teaching manual, and felt inclined to let his pupil's errors stand uncorrected. Things had always been like that. Theodor had always believed in external power, in any external power which faced him. Only in the army was he happy. There he had to believe what was told him, and others had to believe what he himself told them. Theodor would gladly have spent his whole life in the army.

Civilian life was different. It was harsh, and full of hidden traps in unknown corners. One made an effort but found no target for it, one wasted energy on uncertainties, it was like ceaselessly building houses of cards only for unforeseeable gusts of wind to blow them down. No effort was of any use, no amount of hard work was rewarded. There was no superior whose mood one could divine or whose wishes one could foresee. Everybody was a superior, all the people in the street, all the classmates in the lecture room, mothers and sisters too.

Everyone had an easy life; the Glasers and the Efrussis the easiest of all. Glaser was top of the heap, along with the rich jeweller and the jeweller's son. In the army they had amounted to nothing, had rarely even made sergeant. There, justice defeated sharp practice. And everything was sharp practice. Glaser's learning was as dishonestly come by as the jeweller's fortune. There was something wrong with things when Private Grunbaum was granted leave or when Efrussi made a deal. The revolution was a swindle, the Kaiser had been betrayed, the Republic was a Jewish conspiracy. Theodor could see all this for himself, and other people's opinions confirmed his impressions. Clever men like Wilhelm Tieckmann, Professor Koethe, Bastelmann the lecturer, the physicist Lorranz and the ethnologist Mannheim all made a point of exposing the harmful nature of the Jewish race during lecture evenings at the Union of German Law Students, as well as in their own books, which were on display in the reading room of the 'Germania'.

Father Lohse had often enough warned his daughters against any contact with young Jews during their dancing classes. He could give examples, yes, examples! At least twice a month, Jews from Posen, the worst of the lot, would try to cheat him. During the war they had been classified as unfit for active service, and were to be found as writers in field hospitals and area headquarters.

In the seminars on jurisprudence they would always push themselves forward and think up new conundrums, in which Theodor would find himself all at sea and which would drive him to new, disagreeable and difficult labours.

They had destroyed the army now, they had taken over the State, discovered socialism and that one should love one's enemy. It was written in *The Elders of Zion* – a book which was issued to the officer reservists on Fridays, along with the vegetables – that they aimed at world dominion. They had the police in their pockets and were persecuting the nationalist organisations. And one was reduced to educating their sons, to living off them, badly. And how did they themselves live?

Oh! They lived in style. The Efrussi mansion was separated from the common street by a shining, silvery railing, and surrounded by a broad, green lawn. The gravel gleamed white and the steps up to the door were even whiter. Pictures in gold frames hung in the hall and a footman in green and gold livery bowed as he escorted you in. The jeweller was lank and tall, and always wore black, with a high-collared coat which just revealed a black silk stock pinned by a pearl the size of a hazelnut.

Theodor's family lived in three rooms in Moabit, the handsomest of which contained two rickety cupboards, with a sideboard as showpiece and, as solitary decoration, the silver dish which Theodor had salvaged from the château at Amiens, and which he had hidden in the bottom of his trunk in the nick of time, just before the arrival of the stern Major Krause, who did not allow that kind of thing.

No! Theodor did not live in a villa behind silver-gleaming wrought-iron railings, and no high rank consoled him for the poverty of his life. He was a tutor whose hopes had miscarried, whose courage had been buried, but whose ambition was eternally present to torment him. Women, with the sweet rhythm of their swaying hips, passed by him, unattainable, but he was still on fire to possess them. He would have had them all, as a lieutenant, even young Frau Efrussi, the jeweller's second wife.

How remote she was, coming from that great world to which Theodor might have belonged. She was a lady: Jewish, but a lady. He should have met her in the uniform of a lieutenant, not in the civilian clothes of a tutor. During his days as a lieutenant, on leave in Berlin, he did once have an adventure with a lady. One could call her a lady; she was the wife of a cigar merchant who was away in Flanders. His photograph was hanging in the dining room, and she wore

7

violet knickers. These were the first violet knickers of Theodor's masculine existence.

What inkling had he now of women? His were the cheap little girls, the hurried minutes of cold love in the darkness of a vestibule, or in some alcove, haunted by the fear that the neighbours might come home unexpectedly, the pleasure which died away at the sound of an unexpected footstep and the glow of warmth which cooled off, raw and wet. His was the barefoot simpleton from the north, the woman with the angular rough hands and the crude caresses, chill to the touch, with sweaty stockings and dirty underclothes.

Frau Efrussi was not of his world. As he listened to her, it occurred to him that she must be a good person. No one had ever said such beautiful things to him with such simplicity and sincerity. You understand perfectly, Herr Lohse! Do you like this place? Are you comfortable with us? Oh, she was such a good person, so beautiful and so young. Theodor could have wished for a sister like her.

He was startled once, when he suddenly saw her coming out of a shop; it was as if he had had a revelation. He realised that all during his walk he had been thinking of her. It frightened him so much to discover that she lived within him that he stopped unconsciously in his tracks, accepted her invitation to ride in her car without being aware of it, and almost got in before her. He bumped against her several times, touched her arm and hastily apologised. He hardly heard her questions. He had to concentrate hard on not touching her again. But it happened again, nonetheless. He prepared anxiously for the moment when he would leave the car, but it stopped sooner than he had expected and there was no chance to get out and hand her down. He remained seated and by the time he had got out and down the chauffeur already held the parcel he was proposing to carry for her.

From a great distance he heard her say goodbye, but her smile was inescapably close before his eyes, like the reflected smile of a woman far away.

He would never reach her. Did he indeed wish to? He did, ardently. But now that he was no longer a lieutenant, his belief in his own power to make the first move had gone. He would have had to have his rank back. He longed to be a lieutenant again. A lieutenant, or at least something, not to be anonymous, a nobody, a modest brick in a wall, the least of a group of comrades, the one who listened and laughed when anecdotes were told and dirty stories bandied about. He longed not to be alone any more in the midst of so many, alone with his vain longing to make himself heard and to be done with the eternal disappointment of not being listened to and being tolerated and even popular because of his grateful attentiveness. Ah, they thought he was harmless. They would see! Everyone would see! Soon he would come out of his corner, a conqueror, no longer trapped in time, no longer crushed to the ground by the weight of his days. Somewhere on the horizon, bright fanfares sounded.

2

At times his pride overcame him, like some alien power, and he was afraid of his own wishes, which held him in thrall. But as soon as he walked through the streets he heard a million unknown voices, and a million motley colours dazzled him, the treasures of the world ringing and shining. Music drifted from open windows, sweet scent from women passing by, pride and power from confident men. Every time he passed through the Brandenburg Gate he dreamed the old lost dream of his triumphal entry on a snow white horse, a captain at the head of his company, under the eyes of thousands of women, perhaps kissed by some, flags fluttering, deafened by cheers. He had carried this dream in his heart and had fed it lovingly ever since he had first reported to barracks as a volunteer, through all the deprivations and mortal dangers of war. The painful dressings-down by the sergeant-major on the parade ground had been made less harsh by this dream, as had the daylong hunger of the endless march, the burning pain in his knees, confinement in a dark cell, the blinding, painful whiteness of the outpost in the snow, the biting frost in his toes.

His dream cried out for release, like some sickness living invisibly in his joints, nerves and muscles, filling every blood vessel, which he could no more escape than he could escape himself. And, in accordance with that unknown power which had often before helped Theodor, and which had taught him that, at the last moment, some helpful external circumstance would come halfway towards fulfilling any painful dream, so it happened that in the Efrussis' house he made the acquaintance of Dr Trebitsch.

For the first quarter of an hour of their acquaintance, Dr Trebitsch never stopped talking, and his beard, which was fair and long and fell in soft locks, edged with highlights, moved up and down before Theodor's eyes so regularly as to destroy his concentration. The words of the fair-bearded doctor pattered softly down, here and there a word or two would catch Theodor's attention for an instant and then float away again. He had never been at such close quarters with a spade beard. Suddenly, the sound of a name shook him out of his stupefied abstraction. It was the name of Prince Heinrich. With the instinct of a man who comes by chance across a prize piece from his shattered past and clutches it hastily to his bosom, Theodor cried: 'I was a lieutenant in the regiment of His Highness, Prince Heinrich!'

'The Prince will be very pleased,' said Dr Trebitsch, and his voice was no longer distant, but very, very close.

Pride, like something physical, filled Theodor's chest and puffed out his stiff shirt. They drove by car to the mess and, unlike the previous week when he had driven with Frau Efrussi, he did not feel cowed and scrawny, hunched in the corner between the side of the car and the upholstered seat. He expanded. Through his overcoat, his tailcoat and his white waistcoat his body was aware of the cool, yielding softness of the leather. He propped his feet against the seat in front. His cigar filled the coupé with the satisfying aroma of an overflowing sense of comfort. He opened the window and felt the swift, penetratingly cold March air with the delight of someone who was warm to the depths of his being. They were drinking schnaps and beer, and the evening in the mess reminded him of the Kaiser's birthday. Count Straubwitz of the Cuirassiers made a speech and they gave him three cheers. Someone told anecdotes from the war. Theodor was seated as a guest next to the Prince. He didn't take his eyes off His Highness for a moment. He ignored the guest on his other side. It was imperative that he be ready at any moment to answer the Prince's questions. Not for one moment did Theodor forget that now he had the chance to realise at least part of his dream. Was he now the unknown little tutor of a Jewish boy? Did not the Prince know him? Was he not known to all the gentlemen seated round this table? And, although the unaccustomed alcohol gradually dulled Theodor's awareness of the evening's minor realities, yet a great happiness lingered in him and a sense of self-assurance came back to him each time he handed the Prince a table napkin, a glass, or a light for his cigarette.

At the Prince's request he described the battle near Stojanowics at which the regiment had so distinguished itself. He began somewhat at random, and in a rather louder tone of voice than usual. At first things went along all right, until he noticed that he had begun his tale before deciding how he was going to end it. He paused, and the deep, attentive silence shattered him. He only knew that his previous phrase had been: 'Captain von der Heidt!' 'So this captain,' he began again, but he never finished the sentence. 'Long live von der Heidt! Cheers!' broke in Dr Trebitsch, and they all drank to the gallant captain.

It then turned out that Theodor and the Prince went the same way home, so they sat together in the car. Theodor talked as they drove. Frau Efrussi came into his head and he told the Prince about her. He could see her green eyes, and her shoulders. He peeled off her clothes and she was standing before him in her underclothes. She was wearing violet knickers. He told the Prince about everything he saw, did, and felt. 'I slipped her blouse off,' said Theodor. 'Your Highness should know that she has brown nipples, and that I bit her firm breasts.'

'You're a great lad,' said the Prince.

He used this expression again later as they sat in his room drinking yet another black coffee, yet another liqueur. They sat side by side, so close to each other that their calves touched and the Prince was holding Theodor's hand and squeezing it. And all at once Theodor was naked and so was Prince Heinrich. The Prince had a richly matted chest and skinny legs. He was slightly pigeon-toed. Theodor's head was bowed, and although it was distressing to him, he was obliged to look at these toes. It occurred to him that it would be better by far to look the Prince in the eye. The Prince was squeezing a cool, fine-scented spray from a little rubber ball.

For the first time Theodor saw himself stark naked in a tall pier mirror. He could observe that his skin was white and rose-tinted, that his legs were roundly fashioned, his chest a little arched, his nipples like two bright little dark red cupolas.

Theodor was lying on the warm, soft polar-bear skin and beside him lay Prince Heinrich, breathing heavily and audibly. The Prince bit into Theodor's flesh. The stubble of the Prince's beard was scratchy, and the tangled hair of his chest and legs tickled Theodor.

He awoke to a half-dark room, and the first thing to meet his gaze was a portrait in oils of the Prince hanging on the wall. Horribly awake, he saw all the events of the night before. He fought against them in vain. He tried to erase them. They had simply not taken place. He began to think of all sorts of unrelated matters. He conjugated a Greek verb. But his most recent experiences set about him like a persistent swarm of flies. He walked slowly down the stairs, to be greeted by an ancient and respectful servant. The world's proximity was audible already in the merry ringing of a tram bell.

Oh, how near he was to this rich world, with its million treasures ringing and shining. He was experiencing the streets, the way the women walked with swaying hips, the men striding with assurance, and he himself, so small and so inadequate in their midst.

He would be leaving the house, a man smaller than ever before. It had always been like this, that he had to retrace his steps, mortified, just as he had felt himself exalted, that he must in his loneliness take paths which led downwards just as he was about to storm the heights. He did not want to turn back, he wanted to stay here. And so he stood before the old servant and asked after the Prince.

Prince Heinrich was eating breakfast, his feet in a footwarmer placed beneath the table. 'Morning, Theo!' he said, and left Theodor standing.

Theodor came quite close to the table and studied the Prince.

The Prince broke egg after egg and threw the yolks into a glass.

'Sit down,' he said at last. And, as if it had just occurred to him: 'Have you eaten yet?' and pushed eggs, bread and butter over to Theodor.

The food strengthened Theodor. He ate in silence and a good, restorative, innocent peace enfolded him.

Suddenly, as if his tongue had declared its entire independence of him, his question flew across the table: would the Prince have any use for a secretary?

Prince Heinrich nodded. He had long been expecting the question. He wrote something on a visiting card: 'Trebitsch,' said the Prince; nothing more. And as Theodor rose to his feet: 'Morning!'

And Theodor rose to his feet and walked out into the fresh, March morning, through the Tiergarten, breathing in the blue of the sky and the first bird calls, in the knowledge that he was climbing upwards although the street was level. And he knew that one has to pass through the depths and that one should forget them. He would put aside the distracting recollections of the previous night, now swallowed up by the brilliant blue of morning.

3

Trebitsch received him and, by ceremonial candlelight, Theodor swore a long oath and set his name to a sheet of paper whose contents he had scarcely looked at. For two minutes his hand lay in the hairy paw of a man who was referred to as Detective Klitsche, and who was to be his instructor. A long and inadequate lock of this man's hair fell across an earlobe which had been shot off or otherwise tampered with. Theodor was now a member of an organisation, a society, the name of which he did not know. All he knew was a letter and a Roman numeral – the letter S and the numeral II – and that the centre of this unknown group was situated in Munich. He was to await verbal or written instructions from Klitsche. To obey orders under all circumstances was a condition, as was silence. Betrayal meant death and an ill-considered statement meant certain destruction.

In spite of his own wishes, and in defiance of his reflective temperament, things were moving too fast for Theodor. He was repeatedly stopped short by all these new experiences, and felt that he had been overtaken by events. He was frightened by the lighted candles and the resounding phrases of the oath, and by the hairy paw of his superior. He was as conscious of the nearness of death as was any traitor newly condemned. He had never been a bad sleeper; his dreams were few, but comforting. Before going to sleep, he used to paint himself beautiful pictures of the future, even if the day which was ending had given him no cause for encouragement. After that morning in Dr Trebitsch's office, he began dreaming of candles burning yellow in the full light of day. Worst of all was the thought that there was no escape, and that he could no longer return to the sheltered quiet of a tutor's life, a life of freedom. What orders were awaiting him? Murder, robbery and perilous espionage? How many enemies lurked in the darkness of the evening streets? He was no longer assured even of his life.

But what rewards could be his! Skipping the time during which I am imprisoned in the dark gaol of this existence, I throw off the heavy yoke of these days, I rise up and shatter closed doors, I, Theodor Lohse, a man in danger but a dangerous man, more than a lieutenant, more than a victor on horseback, riding through cheering crowds; the saviour of my country, perhaps. In these times victory is for the daring.

A day or two later he received his first orders: to give notice at the Efrussis and to cash a cheque, for a fantastic sum, signed by Heinrich Meyer, at the Dresdner Bank. Theodor had never had so much money about him, and the awareness of it altered his expression, his walk, the way he held himself and the whole world around him. It was a clear April evening, the girls had light dresses and lively breasts. Every window at the front of every house stood open. Twittering sparrows hopped between piles of yellow horse-dung. The streets were smiling. The lamplighter was already wearing his white summer overall. The world was unquestionably growing younger. The last rays of the sun quivered in little puddles of mire. The girls smiled and seemed approachable. There were blonde ones and brunettes and black-haired ones. But that was a superficial division. Girls with wide hips were Theodor's special delight. He loved to find a refuge and a home in women. After the consummation he liked to be mothered by the all-embracing, to lay his head between big, kindly breasts.

It was the sort of day on which it would be easy to give notice to the Efrussis. He had first come to their house two years before, to the day, and now he would never see young Frau Efrussi again. He thought of her as of a landscape once glimpsed afar off, in which one could never linger.

He could perhaps give his notice in writing – on some pretext or other. Exams were now taking up so much of his time. But that would not only be a lie, but a cowardly one, and the chance would be missed to tell the detested Efrussi the truth which he had painfully bitten back for so long.

'Herr Efrussi, I am a poor German and you are a rich Jew. It is treachery to eat the bread of a Jew.'

But Theodor did not speak like that to the dark, haggard Efrussi, whose face recalled the portrait of a stern old lady. He simply said: 'I would like to inform you of something, Herr Efrussi.'

'Please do,' said Efrussi.

'I have been teaching in your house for two years now . . .'

'I will raise your salary,' interrupted Efrussi.

'No, on the contrary. I am giving notice,' said Theodor.

'What for?'

'Because in fact Herr Trebitsch . . .'

Efrussi smiled: 'Look here, Herr Lohse, I have known Trebitsch for a very long time. His father was a business friend of my father's. He was a big man in manufacturing, and an important one. His son would have done better to stay with the business. I know Dr Trebitsch's little games. You are the third tutor he has taken from me. He is a devious fool.'

'He is a friend of His Highness, Prince Heinrich.'

'Yes,' said Efrussi, 'the Prince is known to have many friends.'

'What do you mean by that? I was a lieutenant in the Prince's regiment.'

'The Prince's regiment was certainly a gallant one. Generally speaking, I am strongly in favour of principalities, but very little in favour of princes. But that is neither here nor there.'

'But then,' said Theodor, without having grasped the implications of Efrussi's last phrase, 'but then, you are a Jew!'

'Nothing new in that for me.' Efrussi smiled. 'Trebitsch is a Jew, too; not that I have any wish to make comparisons. But I do understand you. I read the national press. I even advertise in the *Deutsche Zeitung*. So you don't want to go on teaching my son. Here is your pay for last month. Let nothing deter you from accepting it. It is yours by right!'

Theodor took it. Any hesitation on his part would have prolonged the discussion. And was it not, indeed, his by right? Had he not the better part of three weeks in the current month behind him? He took the money, bowed and went.

He didn't know that Efrussi immediately rang up Major Pauli at garrison headquarters to complain of the loss of his tutor. 'You're carrying this *agent provocateur* business too far!' said Efrussi; and the major apologised.

But Theodor has carried out his first instructions. He has taken away with him a bleeding heart. He will never see Frau Efrussi again.

And it seems to him that now, for the first time, he has honoured his long, resounding oath. This giving of his notice was a door slammed, the end of a journey, the end of a life.

4

For three days and nights Theodor enjoyed his money without a thought. He slept with girls off the streets and with more expensive ones who were lurking in the clubs. He drank wine which he did not enjoy, and sweet liqueurs which upset his stomach and the horrible taste of which he tried to dispel with cognac. He slept in grubby rooming houses only to discover later that for the same price he could have had all the paradisal pleasures of a big hotel. He joined, once, his former comrades in arms, bought them a couple of rounds and was then mocked by them. Each setback to his pursuit of pleasure stung his pride, and only fear of his fatal oath restrained him from divulging his secret and stifled the words on his rebellious lips: I, Theodor Lohse, am a member of a secret organisation.

How they would admire him, if they but knew! But almost as precious as admiration was the secret with which he lived, and his disguise. He was about to manipulate the invisible threads from which, as he knew from the newspapers, ministers, civil servants, statesmen and officials depended. And all the time he was assuming the unlikely cloak of a law student and a private tutor. He could pass a policeman and remain unrecognised. No one could see how dangerous he was. It sometimes occurred to him to reinforce his own invisibility, and he would step for a few minutes into some dark hallway and make believe that he was watching someone without being seen. He prepared himself for his new profession by carrying out missions he devised himself. He would go into one ministry or another and ask for an imaginary person. He would read the names of the officials over the porter's shoulder as he searched, and then walk contentedly away. He began to take note of things which had never interested him. He bought revolutionary broadsheets, he went into the offices of the *Red Flag* to place some insignificant small advertisement and noted how easily penetrated the place was. They should be pleased with him. Should someone give him an assignment, he would already know how to go about a number of important procedures.

He devoted the strenuous energy which he had once given to his entry into barracks life to accomplish imaginary assignments and unrequired tasks. Certainly, it was easier in the army, because one was more closely supervised. One knew the NCO in charge of the dormitory, and the lecturers, the sergeants and the sergeant-major. But here one was working in the dark. Should one carry out one's duties on behalf of Trebitsch or Detective Klitsche? It was hard to tell.

Theodor went aimlessly about the streets, filled with a restless, unharnessed zeal. He felt the need to define a visible territory for his activities, and to achieve undeniable successes. He stopped in front of a photographer's display window on Unter den Linden. Here hung a coloured photograph of General Ludendorff, a showpiece of the photographer's skill. Theodor had always made every effort to come into contact with the high and the mighty. Even in school, by means of all sorts of little services and demonstrations of respect, he had seen to it that the teacher would favour him with some personal task during break. During the war he had become, after a few short months, adjutant to the colonel. Looking at Ludendorff's portrait, Theodor stumbled on the idea of using his old methods again and establishing contact with the general. His heart thumped, his blood beat in his temples, just as if he were standing before the general in person, not merely before his photograph. He went into a café and wrote a respectful letter to 'Ludendorff, Munich,' without any more detailed address, trusting to the general's fame and the reliability of the post.

And he received an answer. He read it and grew, word by short metallic word. 'Dear friend,' wrote the general, 'I like you. Be zealous for God, Freedom and Fatherland. Yours, Ludendorff.'

Theodor read the letter over and over: in the tram, at the tram stop, in college and while he ate. Even on the street and in the traffic's whirlpool the desire to read the letter overcame him. It drew him to one of those little benches perched at the edge of a piece of lawn. He had never sat on one before, because of his revulsion for this plebeian form of seating and the members of the lower orders who used it. On this occasion he was miles away from the people with whom he was sharing the bench. He read the letter, wandered away and, ten minutes later, came back and sat down again.

Like a pious commentator on Holy Writ, Theodor was constantly finding new interpretations for the general's letter. He soon persuaded himself that the general was aware of Theodor Lohse's entry into the secret organisation. Trebitsch must have informed him. Was Theodor not a personal friend of the Prince? Between the despatch of the letter and the arrival of the answer eight days had passed. Ludendorff had therefore sent to Berlin for the information. 'My dear friend,' the general had written. This is the manner in which one writes to someone who promises more for the future than he has accomplished so far.

Theodor went to the 'Germania'. In the reading room, Spitz, the expert on German affairs, was giving a lecture on racial problems. Wilhelm Tiedemann and others from the Association of German Law Students were present. Tiedemann read the letter. In his view, Theodor could rely on it. And Tiedemann was as much convinced as Theodor was that Ludendorff must have been aware of his new friend's personality.

Everyone told Theodor so. They were all his friends. Every eye was a loving eye. He could hear the beat of every heart, and the beat of their hearts was the language of friendship. He stood them drinks. He put his arm round Tiedemann's shoulder. Everyone drank at Theodor's expense. They toasted him. He talked a lot, and a lot more occurred to him. When he left he carried with him the mighty sound of his own words.

The following morning brought him an invitation to call on Detective Klitsche. He was not to write a letter of any sort, and least of all to Ludendorff. He should never have talked about it. He was not the only person in the Association of German Law Students to belong to the organisation, and every word he had uttered yesterday had been reported to Klitsche.

'Hand over the letter!' said Klitsche.

Theodor went red. Fiery wheels spun before his eyes. He was suddenly the little first-year recruit standing on the barracks square. He stood stiffly to attention in the approved manner. He was a little first-year man with his eye on his first stripe.

He handed over the letter. Klitsche pocketed it. He ordered: 'Take your clothes off!'

And Theodor took his clothes off. He took his clothes off as if it were quite a matter of routine. He thought to himself that he had to obey Klitsche.

Slowly and indifferently he put his clothes back on again, as slowly and as indifferently as he had put them on in his room every morning.

In the streets it was spring, birds twittered, the trams rang their bells, the sky was blue, the women were wearing light dresses.

Theodor would have liked to be ill, and a little boy, in his bed. He drank in second-class drinking shops and slept with girls from the Potsdamer Platz because his money was beginning to run out, and when he had none left he found the noisy gaiety of the streets a thousand times stronger in comparison to his own insignificance. And he forgot his visit to Klitsche, just as he had buried his visit to Prince Heinrich. His way led over precipices and into chasms.

5

For the time being, his way led to the residence of the painter, Klaften.

Theodor called himself Friedrich Trattner, a comrade from Hamburg. At Klaften's he saw modern pictures, fanfaronades of tearing colours, yellow, violet, red. Looking away from the pictures, his eyes smarted as if one had been looking into the sun. Theodor said: 'Really beautiful!'

His admiration took care of everything and made people accept his identity. They addressed him as Comrade Trattner. He carried his new name with a flourish. He, who was surprised, and could be shaken, by any new situation, now invented his own: adventurous escapes from prison, sudden flight on the appearance of spies, set-tos with the police and students.

Theodor grew into the part of Friedrich Trattner. Through the person of this figure he acquired respect and stature. It was like being a temporary NCO in the army who had to be thoroughly tested out before he could go any further. This was soon got over. One was at pains to be worthy of one's new rank, but only so as to be able to be free of it.

Theodor made the acquaintance of new people: the Jew Goldscheider, who preached goodness and quoted the New Testament at every opportunity. Was he a Bolshevik or just a Jew? Goldscheider himself described his stay in a lunatic asylum. He was certainly foolish, at times incomprehensible. The others pretended to understand. This was a harmless company of poor young men without a roof over their heads. They found lodgings and a coffee at Klaften's place. The painter made his living from conventional paintings, which were generally regarded in that company as *kitsch*. Theodor reckoned they were Klaften's best work.

Theodor heard these young people cursing. They saw the great revolution almost within their grasp. They cursed socialist ministers and officials whom Theodor had always held to be communists. The fine distinctions escaped him.

Klaften made a portrait of him. Theodor was afraid of his own picture. It was as if he looked into a terrifying mirror. His face was round and reddish, his nose flattened, with faintly indicated cracks on the flat bridge. The mouth was wide, with broad, open, shovel-like lips. In reality his small moustache hid his lips, but not in the painting. It was as though the painter had shaved off his beard – and yet he had painted it in.

It hasn't worked, thought Theodor. The picture hung in the room and betrayed him. Everyone seeing the picture fell silent and looked stealthily at Theodor, who felt himself stripped of his mask, and would have run from the picture had it not been for the arrival of Thimme, a young communist.

Thimme had stored explosives in a safe rooming house, in the cellar. He wanted to set it off in the service of the revolution. He spoke of the need for a new revolutionary act and found everyone in agreement and Theodor especially enthusiastic.

Theodor was all ears and wished he were all arms. He thought of that spider from his boyhood days, which he used to feed each day with captured flies. He remembered waiting breathlessly as the creature climbed its web, how it watched for a second before making its final deadly rush, which was assault, leap and drop all in one movement.

He himself now sat like that, ready for the attack, determined to spring. He hated these people without knowing why, but fabricated his own reasons for hating them. They were socialists, without belief in a Fatherland, traitors. They were in his power. Yes, he held in his power five, six, or ten men. He held power over men again, he, Theodor Lohse, the private tutor, the law student, who had been made to look small by Detective Klitsche, who had been misused by the Prince and betrayed by his comrades. Everyone could see the fire in his eyes and the colour in his cheeks. He looked at Thimme, the young and hungry Thimme. He was a glass-blower, patently tubercular, who bore the darkness of death in his deeply shadowed eyes. He looked on Thimme as his prey, his man, his own.

He relished his concealment as if it were some nourishing food. He edged back into the darkness. He flexed his fingers in his trouser pockets and stooped forward from the waist. He assumed, unconsciously, the threatening posture of the spider.

They argued about the objective to be attacked. Some favoured the Reichstag, others the police, and others the Kaiser-Wilhelm-Gedächtnis church. Goldscheider stood with outstretched arms and begged and besought them not to touch the explosives. He had taken off his spectacles and his bearded face looked lost, helpless and in need of rescue.

Who was to make the attempt? They decided to draw lots. It fell to Goldscheider.

Theodor left. Late in the night he left the house, and strode through the dark and rustling Tiergarten to Trebitsch. He slipped through the last avenue as if he were being pursued, hugging the dark shadows of the trees. He didn't want to wake anyone. He threw a pebble at Trebitsch's lighted window. He went in, looking over his shoulder at the door. He described the immense danger he was in. Spies had followed him here, communist spies, and on the way he had leapt onto a bus. They were beginning to suspect him. They doubted that his name was really Trattner. And, as he told his tale, his fear increased. He was no longer the cunning infiltrator as he described his anxious imaginings. 'Explosives,' he said softly, and looked towards the door.

'They should not be disturbed,' said Trebitsch softly, smiling as always, and running his fingers through his beard as if they were a comb. After the attack – and it was to be hoped that it would succeed – the police would have to be briefed.

At about four in the morning Theodor went back to the painter Klaften's place. They had decided on the Victory Column. Two of them had brought the explosives in a taxi. Thimme bored a hole in the box. Thimme, Theodor and Goldscheider drove to the Column. Thimme and Theodor waited at a convenient distance. All three of them walked away, silent and grim.

Fifteen minutes after Goldscheider had lit the fuse, Theodor called the police: in a few minutes there would be a disaster. Behind the railings surrounding the Victory Column, and to the right of it, there were explosives.

Goldscheider went back to Klaften's place – the police seized him and bound him, swiftly and silently. Out of the room, handcuffed two by two, came the comrades. Beside the police inspector stood Trattner, Comrade Trattner.

They all spat at once, as if at a command, and before they could be prevented, right in his face.

Theodor wiped the spittle off it with his handkerchief. He laughed, shortly, but loud and deep. It sounded almost like a cry.

In the hallway, the dazzling torches of the police went out. From the street one could hear the ten prisoners marching in step, and the light, metallic sound of handcuffs rubbing together.

6

Sensational headlines in the newspapers: 'Communist Attack Thwarted by Member of the Technical Emergency Service!' Theodor Lohse was mentioned by name a few times. People congratulated him. He became a rare visitor to the Association of German Law Students. He no longer went to his lectures. There would be time for all that later on.

He hadn't seen his name in print since he had been mentioned in despatches. Now he came across his name in all the papers. A man came from the *Nationale Beobachter*, a thin little man who fiddled all the time with odds and ends on the writing table while he spoke. He invited Theodor to co-operate exclusively with the paper, at the same time making it clear that its budget did not, unfortunately, extend to paying a fee.

What did that matter? Theodor had received a fee from Trebitsch, rather higher than his original one. And that had been split in half because Klitsche demanded his cut. It was he who had put Theodor on to the painter Klaften! He, Klitsche, had taken himself off the case out of unselfish friendship for Theodor. Klitsche sat in his office with his coat and waistcoat off and his collar open, looking more powerful than ever. One could see his bull neck with its prominent muscles, and his clenched and heavy fists as they rested on the desk. His lank strands of hair had been pushed back and revealed the flawed remains of his ear muscles, all reddish gristle and atrophied whorls. Theodor haggled bitterly, only wanting to give him a third, but Klitsche had pushed back his chair with sudden determination, as if about to get to his feet. He did not do so, but stayed in the chair which he had pushed back, his torso leaning forward, a crouching beast; and Theodor gave him half. He then walked through the streets, stopped in front of a shop window and bought a pair of boots. He had the impression of having grown taller, of treading fresh ground underfoot.

Late in the afternoon, as the birds were singing their sweet evening songs, he spoke to a girl in a white dress. In the course of the evening they visited a *palais de danse*, and he was jealous because the girl danced three times in a row with a man from a neighbouring table. He was drinking sour *sekt*. The girl – one could hardly call her that – demanded a better hotel, and forced Theodor to book two rooms. Then he was not to come to her for fifteen minutes, after which he knocked on the door, listened, knocked again and went in. The girl had disappeared.

He had more luck with young women who went hatless, in simple blouses and threadbare coats. These were satisfied with a visit to the cinema. He was careful not to let these little distractions develop into lasting friendships, and he made a point of never making definite dates.

He was pleased with himself and convinced that willpower and talent had made possible his modest progress in so short a time.

He felt that he had happened upon the one occupation to which he was really suited. He was proud of his ability as a spy and thought of himself as a diplomat. His interest in all things criminal increased. He would sit in the cinema by the hour. He took to reading detective stories.

There still lived within him the portrait which Klaften had made of him. He tried to make a lie of it. He grew his moustache bushier. He changed his style of dress. Nowadays he wore a light brown suit, or a pale green check, with a small gold swastika pin in a silk tie with diagonal stripes.

He bought all sorts of weapons, a leather cosh, a pistol, a rubber truncheon. Like Detective Klitsche, he never went anywhere without a revolver, and in every passer-by he saw a communist spy. He knew he was not really being followed, but he would forget, especially after seeing a spy thriller. It flattered him to think of being followed, so he would believe it.

He, for whom every new hour had seemed frightening simply because it was new, who had feared the future and loved the familiar, now toyed with bold improbabilities and anticipated adventure at every step. He was armoured.

He began to be sceptical. Behind each plain fact he saw

veils which concealed secrets and the true state of things. He read politico-philosophical tracts which Trebitsch had published: broadsheets in which links between socialism, Jewry, France and Russia were disclosed. This reading fed Theodor's fantasies. Not only did he believe what he read, but from this material he construed new facts and expounded them in the *Nationale Beobachter*. Being in print made his self-confidence grow, and when his pen was in his hand he no longer doubted the truth of what he had carefully prepared himself to set down. Once he had read his manuscript over, he became certain, and struck out all the qualifying phrases, every 'perhaps', every 'probably'. He wrote essays like one who has glimpsed the corridors of power.

He knew that the *Nationale Beobachter* lay about in the reading rooms of the 'Germania', and that Tiedemann and the others read it. The *Nationale Beobachter* hung in the kiosks of the Underground, at every street corner, and from every kiosk and every street corner the red and white front page shouted the name of Theodor Lohse to the world.

He no longer envied the Efrussis their gleaming white house beyond green lawn, the silver railings and the marble steps. He thought of the lost Frau Efrussi in the way that a great man thinks of an ordinary woman who has provided him with a little adventure. He did not envy Efrussi, but he hated him, his tribe, his pride and the way in which he had, at the finish, treated him, the tutor. Theodor now recalled that in the house of the Efrussis he had adopted a modest mien, that he had in those days been governed by stupid anxiety; and he blamed the Jew for it. It was the Jews who were responsible for his long years without success; it was they who had prevented him from discovering the world earlier! At school it had been Glaser, the exceptional student, and other Jews – whose names he could not recall – had come later. They were, as the whole world knew, formidable, because they held power. But they were also hateful and repulsive, wherever they turned up – in the tram, on the street, at the theatre. And Theodor, when he saw a Jew, would pointedly finger his tie, so as to draw the other's attention to the threatening *swastika* pin. The Jews did not bat an eyelid, thereby proving their impertinence. They looked indifferently at Theodor, sometimes even sneered at him, and then swore at him when he demanded satisfaction.

He was infuriated, and sometimes, at night, he would abuse passers-by in quiet streets and, when danger threatened, disappear down side turnings. It so happened that he told Detective Klitsche and Dr Trebitsch about these adventures. Instead of praising him, as he had expected, they told him to discipline himself, because people who belonged to an organisation must not draw attention to themselves. From then on he kept silence, but hatred gnawed at him, and found its outlet through articles in the *Nationale Beobachter*. These articles became ever more virulent, until the paper was banned for a month, specifically because of an article by Theodor Lohse. Several younger readers wrote to congratulate him on his success. Women, too, wrote to him. Theodor answered them. People called on him. Boys just out of high school, members of the *Bismarck-Bund*, sent him invitations, looked up to him, watched him attentively, a silent, chosen Master. He gave lectures and stood on the podium amid the surging applause of his followers. He founded a National Youth League, and went into the woods on Sundays with his youngsters and taught them drill.

But he was short of cash, and there was no prospect of earning more: these were quiet times. No more plain-clothes men were to be seen in Detective Klitsche's office. Klitsche was not in any case assigned any. He was on the payroll and in constant touch with Munich. Theodor would have been glad of a similar posting. He did not care for Klitsche. Klitsche was an obstacle. This Klitsche had been a sergeant-major, while Theodor, after all, had been a lieutenant, and was an educated man. Sometimes he hinted as much to Trebitsch. 'Perhaps Klitsche will drop dead!' Trebitsch once said in jest. Since that day Theodor had thought about Klitsche's death. But Klitsche was fit. He proved it at every meeting, with every handshake, with his Homeric laughter. There was no hope of Klitsche being summoned to Munich, or giving any grounds for reproach.

Now and again, Theodor thought of somehow betraying Klitsche. How? Was it impossible? Didn't Klitsche associate with communist agents? Who kept an eye on him? Who knew him really well? Surely an observant watcher could catch him out?

For the time being, it was impossible, and Theodor needed money. An attempt to prise a loan out of Trebitsch misfired. He not only explained that he himself was in debt, but also suggested other, richer men of Theodor's acquaintance: for example the Prince.

'You're a friend of the Prince's!' said Trebitsch.

Yes, he was a friend of the Prince's, and wasn't the Prince still under an obligation to him?

He went to Prince Heinrich. He had to wait a long time, because it was afternoon and the Prince was sleeping. Finally he appeared, in flowered silk pyjamas, his cheeks and dimples rosy from sleep, like a child on waking.

'Ah! Theo!' said the Prince.

He sat down, put one foot on the table, let his slippers drop off and watched his toes as he wriggled them. He hummed a little tune, and yawned from time to time. He did not listen to everything Theodor said. Finally, he interrupted him. 'You can come with me to Königsberg, to the launching,' he said.

So Theodor, wearing a dazzling white sailor's cap, travelled in a first-class compartment to Königsberg. His Highness, the Prince, slept on the way, a book by Heinz Torote dangling from his right hand. The *Deutsche Treue* rowing club came to meet them, fed them and put them up. Next day they stood by the water. It was a Sunday, and it was raining, as is customary at launchings. A girl dressed in white was holding a glass of wine in her right hand and an umbrella in her left. The prince stepped up to the boat, bestowed his name and smashed the glass against its side. Everybody cried hip, hip, hooray! and the rain poured down.

In the afternoon they inspected a guard of honour from the *Reichswehr*, and made the acquaintance of the *Rhenania* students' association. Theodor recognised the student Günther as a comrade from the war. They drank together, wandered round the town, related their experiences, thought themselves fine fellows and put their arms around each other. Now there were no secrets between them, and Theodor withheld only the nature of his relationship with the Prince and Klitsche. Even so, just once, he did mention their names, and Günther admitted that he, too, belonged to Branch S II in Munich, and received missions from Klitsche. But he was sick of politics now and wanted to marry. And yes, he would go to Berlin with Theodor. He longed for it.

His fiancée was a workman's daughter, her father a shop steward at the Schuckert works. Just a plain workman, and a red.

Theodor asked if Günther were half red. He kept his hands in his pockets, stretched his fingers and listened, all ears.

'No!' But he did talk with his future father-in-law in a non-committal sort of way.

They travelled together; the Prince slept in a nearby compartment and Theodor kept silence. He watched the landscape. He looked at Günther, a straw-haired, blue-eyed youth with a silly, open face.

What was Günther to him? His name and his face meant nothing to him; someone met by chance. Like that young Thimme, for instance.

Was he fond of Günther? Was he fond of anyone? Yes, he loved his race. He lived in the service of his race. Suppose Günther were not telling the truth? Or only half the truth? Suppose he were a traitor? In touch with the communists? Betraying the organisation?

Here Theodor was on to something. He must be careful. This something pointed a way.

Detective Klitsche heard Theodor out. Could not something more concrete be discovered?

There was nothing. Neither Günther's fiancée nor Günther himself gave anything away. Once, Theodor cautiously asked Günther if his future father-in-law were not a communist.

'Yes!' Günther laughed.

They wandered through the evening, arm in arm. Theodor and Günther. Power had numbed Theodor already, the mighty Theodor; already his fingers were tying the fatal noose of hate. Theodor, clever Theodor, saw his duty done, saw himself promoted over Klitsche, over Trebitsch, over everyone. He saw himself in Munich, a man of power, taking over the leadership. Theodor, a Führer. Swiftly, he went to Trebitsch and told him of Günther's treachery. He saw dangers, described them, stirred things up enthusiastically, encouraged by the approving smile of his bearded friend. That evening, Klitsche sent messages out; sixteen members of Branch S II met together, Trebitsch lit two candles and read through the Protocol with Theodor.

Had Günther admitted that his prospective father-in-law was a communist and head of a secret organisation?

Yes!

Had he armed the workers?

Yes!

And Günther was helping with this task?

Yes!

Paragraphs eight and nine of the Statutes ran as follows: 'Anyone taking action against the patriotic organisations, whether by stealth or main force, is condemned to death by summary justice. Likewise anyone having dealings with parties of the left without the knowledge of the leaders, other than for purposes of espionage.'

The student Günther is guilty.

Lots to be drawn?

'I'll take this one,' said Klitsche.

Silence. A sigh of astonished admiration reaches Klitsche. They sing a battle song:

> 'Let the traitors pay with blood,
> Slaughter them, this Jewish brood.
> *Deutschland über alles!*'

7

A gym practice was held at Weissensee, under the orders of Lieutenant Wachtl. A hundred paces away from everyone else walked Klitsche, Theodor and Günther. Günther had been invited as a guest, had been warmly greeted and entertained with jokes. Klitsche's loud laughter could be heard. They came to a halt and decided to have a rest. A woodpecker was drilling relentlessly, a bird called shyly. Hundreds of midges were dancing in the unseasonably warm April air, the earth in the woods smelt fresh and relaxing.

Theodor would be glad to see the end of the woods. But, oh, the woods have no end! Theodor is feverish, and the top of his skull feels as if the weight of many, many trees were pressing on it. Tears are forcing their way from his eyes so that he can no longer see. He slumps down beside Günther.

He is waiting now, waiting as if for his own death. It came too soon, too soon. Theodor saw countless tree trunks before his eyes, breaking and dimming the sunlight. But the trees were disembodied, ghost trees which would not stand still but were in constant, scarcely noticeable movement, as if the whole wood were an avenue, seen through a haze and moving in a gentle wind. More clearly than the tree trunks before him, Theodor sensed Detective Klitsche behind him; saw how he lifted a pickaxe with both hands and drew himself up, how he drew in his breath; and then Theodor closed his eyes. When he opened them again, he saw Günther collapsing at his side, saw the half-open mouth of the man lying on the ground, heard the half-choked cry which died in his throat, and sensed the overpowering silence. The woods were as still as if everything were waiting for the death cry which did not come.

Just at the bridge of Günther's nose, between his brows, stood the axe. His face was white, violet shadows beneath his eyes. He was still breathing. The thumb of his left hand, which lay across his chest, twitched like a little, dying pendulum of flesh. With a final gasp he drew back his upper lip, so one could see his teeth and a line of grey-white gum.

Klitsche threw a sack over Günther, leaving the pickaxe where it had struck. He hauled him over the pine-needles, across the sandy ground, over pinecones which crackled softly. There lay a pit, and into it he tumbled Günther.

Klitsche pulled off the sack so as to withdraw the axe. The blood spurted thick and red from Günther's forehead and fell with a soft, unceasing patter among the trees, a scarlet thread dripping from the pines.

They were sticky drops, which hardened at once, even as they fell. They formed a crust, like sealing-wax. An infinite frenzy of red surrounded Theodor. He had seen and heard this red in the war, it roared and screamed as if from a thousand throats, it flared and flickered like a thousand furnaces. The trees were red, the yellow sand and the pine-needles on the ground were red, red was the sky, so sharply outlined between the trunks of the pines, and the sunshine falling between the trees was a brilliant scarlet. Great purple wheels spun in the air, purple balls rolled up and down, glowing sparks danced in and out and transformed themselves into softly coiling snakes of fire before dispersing again. This frenzy of red came from within Theodor, filling him, bursting out of him, making him feel weightless, so that his head seemed to float, as if it were filled with air. It was like a weightless, crimson jubilation, a triumph which lifted him up in a floating frenzy which was death to his gloomy thoughts, and liberation for his soul which had been buried and concealed.

Klitsche slid sideways, fell, groaned once. The pickaxe stood upright for a while, pointing stiffly skywards, as if it were alive, then fell sideways. Theodor picked it up. He repeated Klitsche's action, lifted it high and smashed it down. Klitsche's skull cracked a little. Blood and brains flowed from his scalp. Somewhere or other, the woodpecker hammered indefatigably, the shy bird twittered and the heavy mist rose from the floor of the forest.

Theodor strode briskly through the trees, brittle twigs cracking under his feet, feeling as light as the countless dancing midges.

8

It was reported to Munich that Günther had struck down Klitsche and had afterwards been killed by Theodor Lohse. This was witnessed by the sixteen members of Section S II. The dead were properly buried. A squirrel, which had been shot and dismembered, lay on their grave and accounted for any traces of blood.

Theodor Lohse's way was clear. He took over and administered Klitsche's empire, and built it up. Hot was his breath, short was his sleep, and broad was the field that he tilled. He formed a guard, drawn from forty secondary schools. He disposed of unreliable spies. He lectured three times a week, preparing himself for half an hour beforehand. He drew on Trebitsch's essays and on the *Nationale Beobachter*. He disposed of the money which he received from Major Pauli. He wrote out accounts and distributed no advances except to himself.

He gradually understood connections which he had previously only divined from articles. He went to Munich and made the acquaintance of his immediate superior, a general who never went to Prussia and lived in Bavaria under the name of Major Seyfarth. He tried to call on Ludendorff, but was not allowed to, direct access to Ludendorff being forbidden. He lost his respect for certain men whom he had once thought and called great. He talked with National

Socialists and formed a low opinion of them because he discovered that they were not party to everything, and that secrets were not revealed to them either. Theodor learned to listen and doubt. People lied to him.

This hurt his feelings. People told him to stop asking questions. This sharpened his ambition and gave him fresh courage. He wanted influence, not merely independence. He wanted to be the first in line, not an invisible link. But his eagerness overwhelmed him, poured out of him, betrayed him, people distrusted his energy, and his zeal made him suspect. All of the generals, majors, bosses, students, journalists and politicians clung to their little positions and were ruled by anxiety about their daily bread; no more, no less. Among them little people came and went, guests of the organisation, the wandering speaker Schley, the pastor Blok who seduced schoolgirls, the student Biertimpfl, who had robbed a poor relief account, the artist Conti from Trieste, formerly a sailor and a deserter, the Jewish spy Baum whose speciality was troop deployment, the Alsatian Blum, a French agent, Klatko from Upper Silesia, invalided after the plebiscite battles; naval lieutenants, foreign Germans, fugitives from the occupied territories, cashiered privy councillors, prostitutes from Koblenz, street beggars from the Rhineland cities, Hungarian officers bringing unverifiable demands from Budapest from colleagues on the run and in search of forged passports, nameless editors looking for money with which to start short-lived newspapers. All of them knew something, were potentially dangerous and had to be fobbed off.

There were witty people and stupid people, from all of whom Theodor was able to learn, and others who tried to learn from him. Many people knew him, his name was familiar to them, and he had to watch out for spies. He had to watch out generally. He would walk through the streets with his hand on the butt of the revolver in his pocket. He avoided poorly-lit neighbourhoods, never stepped out of the house without carefully looking around, he sensed an enemy in every passer-by, and in every man who shared his way of thinking he sensed a rival. He could rely only on his group of young people. He formed a guard to deal with indoor and outdoor gatherings, broke up socialist meetings, marched through the streets singing lively songs. At Trebitsch's lectures he placed his people about the hall to applaud and encourage others to applaud. Sometimes an unsuspecting spectator would shout an insult. Theodor would then blow his whistle and the guards would come at the heckler from all sides, thrash him, knock him down, trample on his back, chest, skull and pitch into him with deadly delight.

He instructed, equipped, punished cowards and praised the courageous. A little god was he. He had excelled himself. His faith was long since shattered, his hatred diminished, his enthusiasm cooled off. He believed only in himself, loved only himself and was enchanted only by his own doings. He no longer hated the Efrussis, nor did he hate the Glasers. He did not believe that the movement would succeed. He began to see through Trebitsch. He could see the senselessness of the catch phrases and the beliefs. He despised the audiences which he addressed. He knew that they swallowed everything. He read pamphlets and newspapers, not so as to pass on their meaning but to learn them by heart and to store in his head convictions to which he was perfectly indifferent. He observed that everyone worked for himself alone, but he worked harder than the others. He wanted ... He himself was not sure what he wanted.

He wanted to be a leader, a member of the Bundestag, a Minister, a dictator. He was still unknown outside his own circle. The name Theodor Lohse did not make banner headlines in the papers. He would gladly have been a martyr for fame, and have sacrificed his life to the popularity of his name. It hurt him that all his activities must remain anonymous. And as the strength of his convictions diminished, so he widened the scope of his artificial hatreds: he now spoke not only against the workers and the Jews and the French, but also against the Catholics, those Romans. His gang raided the hall in which the Catholic writer, Lambrecht, was speaking. Theodor sat in the front row. Over his head flew sentences from some alien, incomprehensible language. But one word registered, the word 'Talmud'. It impinged on Theodor's half-dormant conscience. He whistled, and forty large members of his mob dived into the audience. Theodor screamed: 'Jew! Roman!' at Lambrecht. He formed a great oyster of spittle on his tongue and launched it at Lambrecht. He hauled a grey-haired woman by her hair along the rows of seats, twisting her wrists. The woman kicked him, yelled at him. Suddenly she grew heavy and fell. The whistle sounded. Everyone disappeared. The police found only a *fait accompli* and arrested two of the injured in whose pockets they had found red buttons and who turned out to be harmless members of a bowling club.

Theodor loved Franziska, a spy, who had come to him. She brought him information about the Communist Party, her hair was cut short, her skin *café-au-lait*. He wept when she disappeared with his cash-box and his reports, and he was short of money. The postman Janitschke claimed payment for letters he had stolen. He had a withered arm but waved the other threateningly. His spy, Braune, wanted the fare to Frankfurt, his wife had had a child and he must go home.

Theodor reported the Franziska episode and had to make good the money himself; he asked Trebitsch for help. Trebitsch suggested he try Efrussi.

He waited for a long time in the anteroom. He had waited the same long time when he had first come to Efrussi, looking for a job as a tutor. The bell rang, twice, three times, the servant in his dark suit moved stiffly, his chest thrust out, his knees straight, like a wooden man. Efrussi's face was still the pale, cold, suffering face of an old, strict woman, and in his presence one became a tutor, a bygone Theodor Lohse, a rather little Theodor Lohse.

Efrussi asked for a receipt. He put the cheque into an envelope and said: 'Go to Major Pauli.' He gave the order, Theodor obeyed it, he went to Major Pauli, he understood, he knew. Efrussi's power was great, he was stronger than any Theodor Lohse, one never ceased to be his house tutor, his servant, his dependant. And the old hatred awoke in Theodor, screamed inside him: blood, blood, Jews' blood!

Only as he stood before Major Pauli did he draw himself from slump to attention, and lose his dispirited look. Melancholy became respect, and with swift determination he mustered all his strength for one purpose only: to hold himself like a soldier. The voice of the major swept away the painful memory of his begging visit to Efrussi, and the echo of his heels snapping together rang in his ears as he left and returned to his work room. No more adventures threatened him. Messengers came, and letters, which he slit open with the flat paper-knife whose cool ivory surface he loved to caress.

9

From time to time the late Klitsche's brother turned up. He was serving in the *Reichswehr*. While speaking he stood fiercely to attention, and fifteen times a minute he said '*Herr Leutnant*'. And yet somehow he seemed to fit in with all the things in this room. His eye took in the carpets, the covers, the floorboards as old acquaintances. He had lain on this sofa, sat on that chair, and he looked like the Klitsche who was dead. So like him that Theodor could neither forget the face of the dead man, nor the reason why he himself was actually sitting here, working, working, growing.

Had this brother of Klitsche's not existed, Theodor would have eased up – and although he couldn't be absolutely sure of it, he probably would have rested. He sometimes longed for a break. But then Klitsche's face would surface, or Günther's, and Theodor worked. He had killed them both, and not in vain. It had been his duty to report the one and, as for the other, he was perhaps already dead before the killing madness overcame Theodor, and this had been a task which had borne fruit.

There were, however, evenings when Theodor was compelled to consider the question of whether the dead are dead for good and all. Then he would go to the Kaiser-Wilhelm, the little bar where he was known, where they said 'Good day, *Herr Leutnant*,' and valued his custom. One or two companions from his group would butter him up and move over to make room for him in the middle, would study his mouth and, if they deduced from his first remarks that the stories would be funny, they laughed and were overwhelmed by Theodor's humour. Theodor knew many stories, he was the hero and the cynosure of all eyes: not for nothing had he been a regular and laughed there for years; he knew now that the one who told the stories was the centre of attraction. Sometimes, too, he would forget and think the stories were about himself. For he drank, and the applause set the wind in his tail so that he would sit astride the high bar stool and feel as if he were galloping.

From a great distance he could hear his friends' laughter, the music which was being played in the big room and which had been inaudible now drew nearer, they were playing the song of the nut-brown maid, and it was so sad that Theodor was almost in tears and wondered why the barmaid was smiling.

He drank another cocktail, sank from his stool and woke up next day.

How gladly he would have yielded to a different kind of relaxation! It was lovely to roam in the open air, summer lay broad and powerful across the land, and in the woods there were . . . Theodor was not happy in the woods. The dead lay in the woods, they were eaten by worms and green grass grew from their limbs.

Rest came later, one only found it on the heights, the road was long and Theodor was tired.

But something drove him towards the heights, unseen, unknown, scarcely imaginable. Within him and about him, something cried: upwards. He knew the way now, now he was a *Gruppenführer*, now he was on good terms with the journalists, knew the politician Hilper, went to the Reichstag gallery. He could picture himself speaking, he saw himself in this great hall at the head of his men, could hear his shrill whistle. He would strike down the members, drive them out and cry: 'Long live the dictatorship!' Up above, high up, beside the dictator, stood Theodor.

He recalled his old method: he made direct contact with the high up and the highest. He knew them now. Beyond his 'Major Seyfarth' stood the naval captain, 'Hartmut'. Theodor made plans: he studied the lives and the habits of Jews and socialists; he found out a lot and made up the rest. He wrote in the *Nationale Beobachter* about a connection he had discovered between a politician and French agents, and obliquely recommended an assassination. He cunningly found supporting evidence for every accusation. He exaggerated facts and manipulated them, while every event attracted his suspicion. Occasionally he would sniff out a secret connection. Journalists would draw his attention to improbable coincidences. He sent his spies out. He knew that every spy exaggerated and he would embroider their exaggerations. He invented plans for rescuing imprisoned members of the organisation. He sent the plans to Munich – to Captain Hartmut. He made money, if nothing else. He drew expenses. He would appease disgruntled spies with a comradely handclasp. There were dumb ones who went along with it. They waited.

But Section S, 'Major Seyfarth', sent reproofs and warnings, and summoned Theodor to Munich. Theodor would talk his way out. He went from 'Major Seyfarth' to 'Captain Hartmut', who was an old gentleman with thin hair combed forward over a bald head, who listened gratefully and insatiably to compliments and flattery. Theodor had his measure. From time to time he would let fall a cautious comment on the subject of Section S, but as for the Captain –

that would be another matter. He needed a free spirit, did Theodor Lohse.

He was forgetting that Trebitsch existed, that Trebitsch had to earn his keep; that he, too, had to prepare accounts; that it was his duty to keep an eye on Theodor. And Trebitsch reported that in his enthusiasm Theodor had exaggerated in this case and drawn a false conclusion in that. Oh, yes, the Jew Trebitsch had reliable eyes and ears.

Theodor was preparing to rescue a man imprisoned awaiting trial. He went to Leipzig. One of the guards had been a sergeant in Theodor's company. He wanted to win him over for the organisation. He reported good progress to Munich. And he received a visit from a man who bore orders in writing to proceed that very day, or at the latest the next, to the Luschka Estate in Pomerania, with fifty men.

10

He was powerless, embittered, vengeful. He went to Trebitsch ... Was not Theodor Lohse indispensable?

And Trebitsch smiled. He ran his outspread fingers through his beard. There was nothing he could do; Theodor set off.

The farm labourers on the Luschka Estate had gone on strike. The Freiherr von Kockwitz was calling for help.

He was old, the Freiherr von Kockwitz, and a widower. He had three sons: Friedrich, Kurt and Wilhelm. He was a hunter. A crack shot. He shot all day long. He had an arsenal of weapons in his basement. He was strict with himself and others. He received Theodor at about noon. The sun was blazing. Theodor's men had an hour's march behind them. The Freiherr demanded military order of march. Were these men tramps? Did they wander about in straggling groups? He demanded that they form fours. He pointed the way to the great barn, a quarter of an hour away. Theodor marched in bitterness, powerless, thirsting for vengeance. He knew the Freiherr von Kockwitz.

Everybody knew him. He had once shot a labourer during tree felling. He threatened Sunday excursionists with loaded weapons. In his woods children disappeared looking for wild strawberries. In summer his sons hid behind hedges, ambushing picknickers, shooting at the *Wandervogel*. The youngest son was twelve and picked off the forester's doves. Irritation with Freiherr von Kockwitz had driven his wife into an early grave. Her maiden name had been von Zick. Her grandfather was known to have been in the postal service, a young aristocrat of the mail coaches. The newspapers wrote about the Freiherr von Kockwitz. The law courts allowed indictments to wither away. Public prosecutors were invited to shoot on his estate. Investigating magistrates played poker with him. People knew about the Freiherr von Kockwitz. They hated him. They would tell Kockwitz anecdotes. Every year his labourers went on strike. Every year, the people from Rossbach had to help him out. People feared this summer work. One ate twice a day when one worked for the Freiherr von Kockwitz; barley soup and black bread.

The men lay in the barn, angry and hungry. The Freiherr von Kockwitz appeared and gave orders: 'Have your people sing! I love singing!' They sang, they worked, they ate barley soup and black bread, they went to sleep, and rose at the first gleam of daylight. They sang. Once, the Freiherr came into the fields. He was in a good mood. He had invited the magistrate. He talked to Theodor, grumbled about his striking labourers. Bunch of Polacks. Not a drop of German blood. They were being corrupted by Jews. In this part of the world there was nothing but Jews and Polacks, a rabble of reds. They needed suppressing and suppressed they would be. That night the great barn caught fire. One of Theodor's people had been smoking. The Freiherr threatened three days' stoppage of pay, but the magistrate suspected the striking labourers. Ten were imprisoned. The next day a hundred of them appeared in front of the house. The Freiherr had machine pistols brought up from the cellars. He lost his appetite, closed the shutters, boxed twelve-year-old Wilhelm's ears. He already saw his house in ruins. His sons hanged. Himself on the rack. He gave up going into the fields. He slept in his clothes, with his pistol by his side. He was afraid of poisoned food. He was just afraid.

Theodor slept in the house. Not just because the barn had burned down. Theodor organised watches. His men stood guard. The old man grew gentle, a kind old greybeard. He gave money to the church. He looked about him when he spoke. He whispered.

In this mood he was open to any suggestion.

Theodor was embittered. So they wanted to be rid of him? They wanted his name to disappear? The name of Theodor Lohse was going to blaze from every newspaper. People were not going to forget Theodor Lohse. Not in Berlin, not in Munich. People would not forget him.

One must challenge these labourers. If it came to a fight, annihilate them. A hundred men. Did they have weapons? There was an arsenal here. People would not forget Theodor Lohse. Every day, they sang:

The traitor pays with blood,
Shoot them down, the Jewish brood!
Deutschland über alles . . .

The men did less work. They drilled. They went out with their weapons. The labourers were starving. Their children were developing thin necks and big heads. The women hissed when they saw Theodor's men. They shouted: 'Dogs!'

Theodor's men fired in the air. Labourers appeared on all sides, a hundred, two hundred. They carried sticks and threw stones. They came towards the house.

Theodor let them into the courtyard. Once in, they started shouting. They pushed against the walls, window panes tinkled pathetically. Inside the windows hung mattresses to catch the stones. A worker, carried on the shoulders of his comrades, was urging them on. Theodor fired. The worker reeled. They broke in all directions. They regrouped at the gate and wrestled in vain with the triple lock. They struggled over the walls, but on the other side rifles were blazing. The workers let themselves drop into the courtyard. From the house shots echoed.

The dying groaned. The living made no sound. A great stillness spread. Silence drifted over the courtyard as if from a broad, open grave. The paving stones reflected the hot sun. High up in the air, larks were trilling. A bumblebee hummed like a great top. From far away came a dog's bark. The church bell in the village sounded.

Many escaped over the walls, pushed aside the threatening weapons and fled. Thirty dead and wounded remained. Trickles of blood drew maps on the white stones of the courtyard.

The police arrived later and drank beer in the courtyard. The blood hadn't dried. The young magistrate had a dimple in his childish chin and a swastika pin in his buttonhole.

The newspapers wrote: 'Bloody Uprising of Farmworkers. Heroic Action by the Voluntary Service Men!' The world took notice. Reporters came. Theodor Lohse spoke with them. Theodor Lohse was in the papers. A student, a lieutenant in the Reserve, had beaten back the uprising: Theodor Lohse.

That Sunday was a flag day for the voluntary services. On the streets of Berlin, white-clothed children were selling linen cornflowers.

11

Theodor heard his red blood shouting as if from a thousand throats, he saw the flames of a thousand fires, great purple wheels spun in the air, purple balls rose and fell. The overwhelming redness came from within him, it filled him and made him light. A crimson jubilation possessed him, he was uplifted in triumph.

But during the hours of evening, when the bats began to flit and the frogs to croak, when the ceaseless song of the crickets became more persistent and some maid sang as she finished her work for the day, he would grow melancholy. Touched, and tearful of soul, he would look at the red sky of evening and whistle sad tunes to himself. It was like being in the Kaiser-Wilhelm when the band played the song of the nut-brown maid.

He would recover his faith in the cause he served when the old Freiherr grew sad and began to talk of German land now fallen into the hands of the Polacks. Somewhere, Theodor heard the call of the hunting horns and the fearsome, cold and mortal summons of the battle trumpet. He was back in the midst of war and ready to sacrifice his blood if the old Freiherr gave the word: Homeland. He would fight and struggle to defend its sacred earth. The Freiherr used a long, nostalgic O and a hard, East Prussian L. He would draw in his breath before uttering the first syllable, and then release it on the second, with a sigh. Theodor often saw in the old gentleman the image of one of the last German noblemen, threatened with extinction by the new times.

It was not always like this. When it was raining and Theodor sat in the Freiherr's library, he would read the novels in *Die Woche* and study photographs of great men in the newspapers. Then he would become timid, as he always had been, and the old gentleman would lose his magic and just seem an eccentric old man, as everyone else regarded him. He understood and excused him, however, and was grateful to him for his exceptionally generous and enjoyable hospitality.

For Theodor was living better than any previous voluntary service man. Theodor was a witness in the case against the farm labourers. He conferred with the magistrate. He accompanied the Freiherr to Berlin. It was already clear that no risk whatever was involved. Moreover, Theodor was treated well. A badly wounded worker, who was being held under suspicion of being the ringleader, rapidly recovered in hospital. They even gave him wine, once his temperature had dropped. The charges against him went from housebreaking and breach of the peace to material damage and attempted murder.

The case took half an hour. The labourer was given eight months' imprisonment. That evening, the Public Prosecutor sat with Theodor Lohse over a bottle of wine in the Kaiserhof.

A week later, Theodor took his leave of the estate. He could not disguise the depth of his feeling. He thought of how the old Freiherr would soon be dead, he thought of the evenings and the sound of frogs and crickets, the dangers which had united him with the house, and to the sacred Homeland.

He then marched off, at the head of his fifty men, to the station. They sang along the broad highway. Theodor decided not to pay them until they reached Berlin. At the moment of departure, the Freiherr had not withheld the three days' pay.

But Theodor thought of doing so.

12

He went to see Trebitsch. His greeting was triumphant. Did they think he was dead? Look, Theodor was alive! More alive than ever. Had they forgotten him? His name stared out of the papers.

He shed his melancholy, forgot the song of the crickets, the song of the maids, the Homeland. He got back to work at once. He went to Leipzig. But the prisoner Pfeifer had flown without his help. Trebitsch had had him set free.

Theodor was stung by the missed opportunity. But Zange and Martinelli were still being held.

He went to Munich. He found Captain Hartmut distrustful. Trebitsch had been at work. He recognised his touch.

National Socialism was a phrase like any other. It required no definition. He was received with respect by the National Socialist leaders, before others, who were kept waiting. So they knew him, but they did not know *about* him. Theodor delicately drew aside a veil or two, to arouse their curiosity. They lived in a whirl of enthusiasm. People were flocking to join them. They were a Party, not a secret society. That seemed more powerful to Theodor. In a Party one worked with one's visor open, not buried underground. In a Party, one's name rang like a thousand bells.

He went to meetings. Everyone was jubilant. Little citizens drank beer; ate and cheered with their mouths full of cabbage and pigs' knuckles. Young storm troopers marched into the hall, lined the walls, carried the speaker along a lane cleared between the chairs, the public, and the tables. Four thousand feet were stamping. White-coated waiters darted. Banknotes rustled. It was a people's celebration. Theodor was envious.

And his work was slinking about undercover, spied on by enemies from within and without?

He went to the recruiting offices. How they poured in! Young labourers, students, office workers. Different material from Theodor's schoolboys. They were more trusting, more easily worked on, afire before they came and white-hot if they were accepted. Hitler was a menace. Was Theodor Lohse a menace? The newspapers spoke of Hitler every day. When did one see Theodor's name?

But these big, naive, uneducated men, living in a whirl of enthusiasm, needed taming. Men with so little knowledge were sufficient to themselves. They knew nothing about discussion. It was not necessary to them. When the Führer left his office, fifty men in the anteroom saluted him and twenty stood to attention. He drove in his car. It was possible that he was not aware of everything, that he was a pawn. But everybody knew him, and who noticed Theodor Lohse?

Major Seyfarth was displeased. How would he get round him? Theodor recalled his services. Theodor threatened. The major leaped to his feet. Had Theodor not sworn the oath? An oath can be broken. Theodor Lohse's power was based on two hundred bold men. Theodor exaggerated. A bare fifty schoolboys followed him. They were young and timid.

Seyfarth backed off. He had a solution. Was there not enough work for Theodor Lohse? Agitation? Propaganda? In the *Reichswehr*, perhaps? Was that not a solution? One made valuable contacts.

Theodor thought it over: the two hundred men had impressed him! Now he was afraid of them. The army promised well. Would his pay continue? Yes, and he would also get his army pay on top of it. He volunteered.

At home, he looked in the mirror. He looked no different from that Führer. Nobody pushed him around. He flashed a smile at his reflection. Uttered a word to test his voice. His voice carried. It could thunder.

He made a plan for the *Reichswehr*: he must find devoted people, become their teacher, their leader, master of life and death for a hundred, two hundred, a thousand armed men.

He joined up. The formalities only took a day. He joined with five references. Potsdam was his garrison. He wore a uniform of the latest cut. The coat was no longer close-fitting, as it had been in the old days. This was in the new spirit of the army. The silver stripes on the epaulettes were now so positioned as to reveal a narrow border of cloth. The bayonet joint was thinly nickeled. Its use was no longer outlined in the exercise manuals, but it was still good-humouredly tolerated. He drilled every morning. It was a long time since he had done so. He stood before two ranks of men. He noted the slightest variation between one body and another. He saw when someone moved, when boots had not been polished, rifles had not been oiled, packs had been put on crooked. He would order 'Knees bend!' and he was obeyed, 'At the double!' and they doubled, 'Halt!' and they halted.

In the afternoon he would give instruction. He would read from Trebitsch's pamphlets. And he said his own piece. He would make a joke. The soldiers would laugh. He thought he noticed that one was not well. He sent him home. He was a comrade. He would clap one or another on the shoulder. He talked about girls. On Mondays he would ask how Sunday had been. On Saturdays he would wish them a pleasant Sunday. He would put a good word in with the colonel on behalf of the men under punishment. He himself avoided awarding punishment and made do with reprimands. He gathered round him the men who had seen action.

He would announce lectures for the evenings. Many came. His company approved, and brought others with them. After a few weeks he was able to speak his mind. He asked how many of them would go through thick and thin with him. They all stood up, every one of them. He made one or two of them swear an oath. He gave these money, and pamphlets to distribute.

He talked little with the officers. He went into the mess. Like everyone else, they talked about the dollar. Lieutenant Schutz, son of a senior banker, had sold stocks to the colonel. There was a bull market. The colonel's good humour made the mess cheerful. They all wanted to invest, they knew what securities were, and a rising market, and margins. Lieutenant Schutz lent them all money. He also lent money to Theodor.

Theodor read the market prices in the evening papers.

13

He studied the stock prices.

His money increased: he learnt to call it capital growth. Now the road was open. The road to those shining white villas in the Tiergarten, standing among silky green lawns, behind silvery railings, with their stiff footmen and the pictures in gilt frames. Theodor had forgotten almost everything else about them. Mightiest of all was Efrussi. One never ceased to be his house tutor. Capital growth led towards the secrets of power.

He, Theodor Lohse, had always loved money. He had brought off his first coup at school. He had taken a collection for a wreath. Young Berger had died. He took two marks forty, bought the wreath for two marks ten and pocketed the thirty pfennigs. He had kept them for a whole year.

He had always been a saver. As a student, and later in the army, he had learned to appreciate the value of money. Only with Trebitsch's first cheques had he been extravagant. He had regretted it later. He always regretted having spent it.

He travelled in civilian clothes, and third class. He bought season tickets for the suburban train. In uniform, he would go on foot.

Early in the day, when they were doubling round the fields, exercising, he would see the sweet-seller surrounded by soldiers. She was selling lemonade. They were all hot and drinking it. Theodor would bite on some chewing-gum.

He smoked three times a day, after each meal. A single cigar was enough for him. He would put it out and light it again.

He watched his money growing. When he was as rich as Efrussi, he would buy himself a Theodor Lohse.

In the meantime he stood in front of the shop windows and calculated what he could buy if he were to sell his holdings. From time to time he would enquire of door-to-door salesmen how much this or that house cost. He received much information of this kind, and divided the houses into those he could not afford and those for which he had enough money.

All this almost made him forgetful of his duties. He was like a bridegroom who oversleeps on his wedding morning. His observant eye was straying to distant fields. His slumbering ears no longer marked the approaching thunder of the times. He no longer saw Trebitsch, no longer wrote for the *Nationale Beobachter*.

He walked indifferently past the food shops, in front of which hungry crowds raised their voices. One afternoon, workmen went looting in Potsdam.

The barracks were quietly busy. A strange machine-gun company reported for duty – no one knew for how long. No one knew the *Oberleutnant* in command.

People were less talkative. The colonel sat stiff and silent. His cheeks were dark-red-and-blue-veined. When he was not talking, they hung like little bags of skin over his collar. At the foot of the mess table, where the 'young people' sat, no one joked any more. People read the political pages of the newspapers and ceased to concern themselves with money.

It was a time of anxious solemnity, as if people were expecting some catastrophe to bring them a happy release. Major von Lubbe delivered a lecture on the future of aerial warfare. It was a well-known lecture, which Major von Lubbe was wont to read once a year out of the *Kreuzzeitung*.

As a captain, he had composed an article on aerial warfare. That was a long time ago. When he read his lecture, the staff officers would withdraw. Only the junior officers had to stay and listen. The major talked about Count Zeppelin. He had once been invited to Count Zeppelin's. And in fact the lecture dealt less with aerial warfare than with the personality of the Count.

On this occasion the staff officers did not withdraw. It was not appropriate in the circumstances, which required the strictest observance of military and social etiquette. But on this occasion the major did not have so much to say about Count Zeppelin. He spoke of the Count's times, comparing them with the present day and extolling German unity. And he spoke of imminent tasks. And even the staff officers listened.

In two weeks' time the dedication of a memorial was to take place. The regiment had invited all its former officers, and also General Ludendorff. Naturally, he would come. The colonel announced it in the mess; he spoke slowly, visibly shaping each syllable, and his jaws worked so hard that his dewlaps trembled.

They drilled with renewed energy. Rifles were cleaned, barrels oiled, arms drill practised. The band practised, polishing up old marches.

And the people in the towns went hungry. News of a general strike flared in the newspapers. The workers shuffled heavily and slowly through the streets in the evenings. Their women waited. The men did not come home. The hearth was cold and there was no food ready. What would they do at home? They went into the drink shops. There was enough money for schnaps, and the drunk feel no hunger. The drunks lurched and dragged their feet along the asphalt. Streets were sealed off. Police helmets sprang up. Roller-curtains hung like iron coffin lids over shattered shop windows. The shots which were not fired awaited their hour of blood.

A confidential order reached Theodor. Triple attention to duty. To Theodor this was a clarion call. His time was coming. He was prepared. He was armed for the day. It could be today or tomorrow.

He summoned his guard. The young people came. They brought fresh comrades from the *Bismarck-Bund*. They brought pistols for the shoot-out. Theodor went to the master-at-arms. All weapons were cleaned. Old bayonets gleamed. The youngsters spent a day in barracks. How the rusty old weapons exhilarated them! And how the shiny new ones dazzled them! How could they know about them? This rifle or that had been through all the wars. It had killed the enemy. A rifle butt gave off great power, and the pommel of a sabre was a thing of magic. What gallant horsemen had wielded it? The steel was dull ... from blood, said some! Patches of rust were bloodstains. The blood of the enemy clinging to the steel.

The general came on Sunday.

On Sunday, the regiment marched out, band playing. The October sun shone as if it were spring. People waved from their windows. Flags fluttered. Children ran beside them. It was like peacetime. Many forgot their poverty.

They stood before the general. The old divisional chaplain addressed them. The spike on Ludendorff's helmet blazed in the sun. A soft tinkle of medals came from the officers, a silvery, faint music. Spurs jingled like bells. The soldiers' breath lay heavy on the air like some solemn ceremonial. One could hear the quiet voices of the officers from the middle of the square. A short, harsh laugh from the general, more of a gurgle.

The general spoke three sentences, from the right of the

memorial tablet. They were hard words. He clasped his hands over the pommel of his sword. One could have taken him for a statue, a statue in full dress uniform.

Then he stepped down, inserting his monocle whenever he spoke with anyone. He spoke to Theodor. Once I wrote him a letter, thinks Theodor. What a long time ago! How young Theodor was, even half a year ago! Today Ludendorff knows him.

14

Secret orders warned them to stand by for November 2nd. Theodor had three weeks' grace. He no longer slept. His days were filled with aimless haste. In the evening he would consider his pointless activity. Through the watches of the night one decision went round and round, but without a plan: he must become powerful. The speed with which things were happening was too great for him. He would have wasted his time if, on November 2nd, he were still only halfway there, not the leader. Just a link in the chain, not its beginning. One among many, not senior to them. In that case he could expect no distinction, only humble ambitions.

Into the circle of his worries, heroic dreams would explode, he would hear the drumbeat of his mission, and crimson jubilation would sweep him to the heights. Günther and Klitsche and eighteen workers were dead, a fruitless tally for eight months of enthusiasm. He had been a misused tool in other people's hands. And to what purpose? He would think nothing of it if he reached his goal; it would kill him if he failed.

He ought to restrain himself no longer, yet he had allowed himself time, at least a year, in which to go on spinning his web; people and things were still hidden from his eyes. He had been cast aside, his keenness had betrayed him. He should have chosen his way with greater care. He was now doing what hundreds of others were doing: giving lectures, distributing brochures. It was a long time since he had been to Munich . . . who was to know if there were not new leaders, and chance might yet bring some other Klitsche to the surface.

Just one more year – and he would be rich, and money would provide him with everything that hard work did not. But before him stood November 2nd. The nearness of the day confused him and prevented him from giving due consideration to his decisions. The earth quaked beneath him, his path no longer climbed upwards.

On half-days he travelled between Potsdam and Berlin. He would read the incoming mail in his office and then go to Trebitsch, that perfect example of a man quietly certain of his aims. Trebitsch behaved as if he were standing apart. He was of the same sort as those who were hammering out the words 'November 2nd', harmless and gentle. His spade beard lent him the appearance of a worthy and a harmless man, a man of ideas, an absent-minded professor. Only an inattentive phrase gave him away. He noticed everything, just as Theodor did when he faced his company. He spoke of the 'alternative method' of handling the workers. Perhaps, in the future, it would become a question of winning over the radical left. The watchwords now were: be careful; remain calm; no provocation.

Inside Theodor, hidden from the dangers of discovery, there still lay the old, ill-defined, carefully formed wish to throw a bridge over to those others. The ringing phrases of the oath had floated away, their fearfulness was dimmed, their threat devoid of force. What happened to a man of power? Danger still threatened him – until he reached those others. Was there not danger here? The others were easier to grasp. He sensed that they were men of honour. Here it was all self-seeking, worrying about money, job, wife and child. Over there lived the diviners of gold, the crucified, who spoke of the Good and of the New Testament.

There is not much danger now. There is always a door ajar. Today Theodor can make efforts independently. To whom must he account? Who suspects him? He can answer for everything. It must be obvious that he keeps projects secret, since their success depends on their secrecy. He can risk it.

What was socialism? A word. One is not bound to believe in it. What did he believe in today? Over there he was valued. The others opened their arms. He knew those corridors.

In the night watches his plan developed, came to life and drove forward to fulfilment. Theodor had no time left. He must think about the first steps.

Is he a traitor? He is not. In truth, he only wants to overhear the others, to keep a check on his spies. He must not think too long. Reflection weakens decision. There is no time.

Day after day the headlines flared above the news. Already the Saxon metalworkers were striking. People talked of trains being held up somewhere. In the barracks they came to the second state of readiness.

15

Among the unreliable and suspect spies whom Theodor had dismissed was Benjamin Lenz. He had made double reports: to Trebitsch and to Theodor. He had been paid by both of them. Theodor got in touch with him.

Lenz, a Jew from Lodz, had worked during the war as a spy for a news and espionage agency. His appearance betrayed him: his prominent cheekbones threw shadows onto his eyes, while the lower part of his forehead and his eyebrows protruded. His black little eyes lay, as it were, in a narrow ravine, guarded on all sides and making it difficult to judge in which direction they were looking because they were so deep-set. His chin was short but broad and his nose was flat. This head, which would have suited a heavily-built torso, was perched on a skinny neck between narrow, sloping shoulders. Benjamin Lenz had small bones, slender wrists and long, nervous fingers.

He had come back to Germany with the returning armies and had drifted through many towns. He had references from the army. Policemen, although they despised his type, beckoned Benjamin towards them with understanding in their eyes. They favoured him, and he cut his cloth to suit the times, played the tunes they wanted to hear, fed false news to foreign missions, stole documents and official stamps from government offices, went spying in Upper Silesia and had himself imprisoned in company with people under investigation, so that he could overhear them, while waiting for 'his day' to dawn.

The name of his god was: Benjamin Lenz. He hated Europe, Christianity, Jewry, Monarchy, Republics, Philosophy, Political Parties, Ideas and Nations. He served the Powers only so as to study their weakness, their malice, their cunning and their Achilles heels. He betrayed them more than he exploited them. He hated the stupidity of Europe. His cleverness hated it. He was cleverer than politicians, journalists and everyone else who had power or the means of access to power. He tried out his strength on them. He betrayed organisations to their political opponents; to the French Missions he conveyed a mixture of truth and falsehood. He took pleasure in the gullible faces of the people he betrayed, who would find in his corrupt intelligence the excuse to perpetrate fresh enormities. He took pleasure in the stupid astonishment of conceited diplomats, childish and powerless counsellors, bestial Nazis, and rejoiced that they did not see through him. He seldom made mistakes, but he was not aware that Klitsche was dead and that another ruled in his place. For this reason, a long and successfully executed manoeuvre with Trebitsch, discovered by Theodor, brought him under suspicion. He had been supplying Trebitsch with false material. But he had managed to get away with it. He acted the stupid little spy. He had to have his missions explained to him several times over. He refused anything complicated. He played the part of a man whose intelligence is just sufficient to grasp his own limitations.

And he waited.

On 'his day', all over Europe, the madness which was slumbering would explode. For this reason he encouraged chaos, incited bloodlust and self-destruction, betrayed one

man to another and that other to a third. He made money.
But he lived in one small room of a dirty hotel. He ate in
furtive cellar restaurants, with beggars and robbers. He was
saving up for his brother, his two sisters, his aged father. His
father was an old army medical orderly with a little Jewish
barber's shop in Lodz. His sisters needed dowries. His
brother, who was studying chemistry, received the largest part
of his earnings. It was planned that this brother would be able
one day to open a factory of his own. Benjamin never went
near him. He never wrote to his father in Lodz. Benjamin had
no time; he was working towards his day.

Theodor had not dismissed him simply because of the
double dealing. He could smell his cleverness. He sensed
Benjamin's Jewishness. As a gun dog will scent game in any
direction, so would Theodor sniff out a Jew if opportunity
offered.

Lenz turned up half an hour late, leaving Theodor to wait.
Anyone who needed him he kept waiting. And he refused to
fulfil Theodor's wish. He always refused. Lead Theodor
Lohse to those others? What about Comrade Trattner? They
knew him, knew Theodor's portrait. Klaften had taken
several sketches of him: to the life.

Theodor had buried that Klaften episode. He asked how it
had worked out. 'Nothing came of it,' said Lenz. Thimme, the
young conspirator, had been a police spy. Goldscheider was
in hospital, Klaften was now a well-known painter. His
portrait of Theodor had won a prize in some exhibition. After
a quarter of an hour Benjamin Lenz no longer refused. Could
he read people's minds? Everything could indeed be forgotten, said Lenz, if Theodor would come as a friend. Or
seemingly as a friend.

They went.

16

There they sat, three men in a café on the Potsdamer Platz, exchanging small talk, distrust sticking in their gullets, their tongues slowed by anxiety. At a nearby table sat Benjamin Lenz.

Theodor regretted all this. It was too late. He had had no idea that it would prove so difficult. He had to make an opening. Nobody helped him. It was almost as if they were cultivating his misery.

And now it is as it once was – a long time ago – at school, when he had to say something which he had not learned by heart. The café was noisy, the hum of conversation came from the neighbouring tables, cups clinked, and yet a silence faced him, as if everyone were expectant. Only as they were walking through the streets did he recover his self-possession. He walked between two dark shadows who marked his every word.

He was not dissembling. Why should he dissemble? He could always deny things, make a frank admission instead of a trumped-up one. His true motives sounded convincing.

He described his dissatisfaction, the distrust which was all about him; admitted that he was driven by ambition.

Later, in an office, he could sense the iceberg tip of secrets.

It was late before he left, and he went to Potsdam, read an evening paper. He looked up, to see Benjamin Lenz. He was sitting facing him.

They walked through the Potsdam evening, along the old lanes which looked quite unreal, and Benjamin led the way and Theodor was unaware of being led. Benjamin Lenz spoke of November 2nd. He did not believe in revolutions. He believed there would be a small bloodbath, hardly worth worrying about, of the kind which was quite liable to happen at times in Germany; any old week, in fact.

Perhaps Benjamin was saying what he really meant, this time?

It was a nostalgic evening, the clouds reflected in violet and yellow, the evening breeze gentle and consoling, and Theodor walked beneath the rustling trees and along the road which led to the station, feeling moved in the way that he had felt during those days in the fields of the Freiherr von Kockwitz.

A warmth emanated from Benjamin Lenz, so that Theodor began to talk and ceased to weigh his words and complained of Trebitsch and of ingratitude in general. What was a man of Lohse's ability doing in the *Reichswehr?*

What was a man of his kind doing in the *Reichswehr?* came Benjamin Lenz's heartening echo. Who had thwarted him? It was a question of finding out, for one must know one's opponent.

Oh yes, how well Lenz knew it. One should keep on good terms with Benjamin Lenz.

How much did he not know, even about Theodor? He knew it all. Did he also have his suspicions about the Klitsche episode? He knew all about it. He said: 'You cannot have shed blood for no reason, Lieutenant Lohse. Others can wade through corpses because of an idea, or because they are born murderers. But you, Herr Lohse, have not believed in the idea for a long time, and you are no born murderer. You are no politician, either. You were overtaken by your profession. You did not choose it. You were not satisfied with your life, your income and your social status. You should have tried to demand more from life within the framework of your own personality, rather than choosing a life which runs contrary to your gifts and to your temperament.'

No, Theodor could not and should not have acted differently. He could have remained small and unnoticed had he not changed roads, he could have stayed on as tutor with the Efrussis, and contentedly.

On this nostalgic evening, he thought of Frau Efrussi. The soft pressure of her upper arm in the car, her smile.

The road, at the end of which power was waiting, also led to her and others of her kind. How openly he spoke, this spy, Benjamin. There are evenings, thought Theodor, when people must perforce be good, as if under a spell.

Then Günther came into his mind, Günther who had loved his fiancée; he saw his face, and the mauve tint beneath his eyes, the exposed upper jaw, the painfully snarling lips.

How sadly trains hooted in the night. Peace came from a blue sky.

Benjamin Lenz walks beside Theodor, and is perhaps his friend.

He is your companion in arms, Theodor. His cunning is useful. Two heads together will succeed. And who but Lenz can be your ally? Benjamin Lenz understands Theodor Lohse.

They walked the long way back: between them fell the soothing silence of friendship. They shook hands on parting. The pressure of their hands was an unspoken commitment.

17

From then on Benjamin Lenz came every day to the office in the Potsdam barracks. How many rifles had Theodor issued to his *Bismarck-Bund*? Had preparations been made for Marinelli's escape? How often did the couriers travel between Leipzig and Munich?

Benjamin knew everything; more than one told him. For this reason he took Theodor to the others. Theodor expected that he would find faces known in Munich: Klatko, the pensioner from the battles over the Upper Silesian plebiscite, the deserter Conti from Trieste, the CSM Fritsche from Breslau, the former police sergeant Glawacki, the bookbinder Falbe from Schleswig-Holstein.

For a whole week he went to the meetings. He went to the smoky, ill-lighted dives, which smelt like beer cellars; he listened to the voices of the speakers, some of them high and shrill, others graveyard deep. He heard the applause of a thousand listeners, stood close beside them, smelt their sweat and their poverty, saw the flickering of their pupils, saw hard-bitten faces on scrawny necks; angular fists on thin, exhausted-looking wrists; moustaches untidily combed over toothless mouths; the black gaps of missing teeth between parted lips; bandages drenched in iodine over bare arms. He saw women with thin, straight-combed, water-pale hair, the poverty of those who were pregnant, their dry necks and their thin, transparent, yellowish skin, hanging in folds. He saw mothers with big-headed children at their flaccid breasts. He saw youngsters with unruly hair falling over bold foreheads, but marked already by toil and sickness, with eyes unnaturally deep in their sockets. He saw young girls in shabby shoes, their faces pale, their eyes searching for men, their lips painted; and he heard their shrill, shameless voices. He saw how they drank, could smell the schnaps, could not understand their dialect, and smiled blankly when someone bumped into him. These people were alien to him, their faces were the faces of strangers, not from his world, not of this world. He was not sorry for them, and though he saw that they must suffer, he could not imagine what sort of suffering was theirs. He might perhaps have understood an individual case, but in this multitude there were no contours, no fixed point. Everything swayed and swam. He could not tell the manner of their loving, nor the fashion of their weeping. He watched the way they ate the bread which was in their coat pockets, how they pulled it out between thumb and forefinger, at the same time pulling it to pieces and stuffing it into their drooling mouths with the flat of their hand. But what sort of tongues did they have, what sort of gums? What did they taste? Sometimes, when they cheered, it was threatening, and much the same sound as a cry of hatred.

He had no love for them. He was afraid of them, was Theodor Lohse. He hated his own fear. Lieutenant Lohse, said Benjamin Lenz, this is the German people, whom you imagine you are serving. The officers in their mess are not the people. And Benjamin Lenz was delighted. This was the way of Europe, where one never spoke of what one did, and vice versa. Where one thought of officers and students as being the people. Europe, where nations exist which are not peoples.

And then Benjamin Lenz took himself to Trebitsch and told

him of Theodor Lohse's development and his treachery. He
had long since betrayed what he had learnt through Theodor,
had Benjamin Lenz. And he warned Trebitsch: a few days
more and Theodor would betray arms caches, Marinelli's
escape, the *Reichswehr*'s connections, the weapons of the
Bismarck-Bund.

Benjamin Lenz was happy. That evening he folded
banknotes into an envelope and mailed them to his brother.

18

How Benjamin Lenz loved these times and these people. How
he grew among them, and prospered and gathered power,
secrets, money, pleasure and hatred. His gloating eyes drank
in the blood of Europe, his half-deaf ears seemed to hear the
clash of weapons, the sharp crack of shots, the howling of the
mighty, the last groans of the dying and the overwhelming
silence of the dead.

Round about Benjamin the fruit spoiled on the tree and did
not grow ripe, the ripe hated each other and corrupted the
good, corrupted goodness itself, and dried up the sucklings'
milk. Greybeards were trampled underfoot in the streets,
women hawked their sick bodies, beggars brandished their
infirmities, the rich flaunted their wealth, painted young men
made their living on the streets, the seedy silhouettes of
workers shuffled to work like corpses long buried but
sentenced to drag on and on the curse of their earthly working
days. Others drank, howled with insane jubilation in the

streets, a last triumph before they disappeared, thieves put aside their furtive secrecy and displayed their loot openly, robbers forsook their hiding-places and carried out their trade in broad daylight; if anyone collapsed on the hard pavement, the man nearest to him would steal his coat. Illness galloped through the houses of the poor, across the dusty courtyards, hung about in the ill-lit rooms, broke through the skin. Money poured through the fingers of the well-fed, and theirs was the power; fear of the hungry nourished their worst instincts; the increase of their possessions inflated their pride; they drank champagne in palaces ablaze with lights; they clattered by car from business to pleasure, from pleasure to business; pedestrians died under their wheels, and the speed-crazy chauffeurs drove on; the undertakers went on strike, the metalworkers went on strike; in front of the brightly-lit windows of the food stores they craned exhausted necks, screwed up eyes which had sunk deep into their skulls, clenched feeble fists in torn pockets.

Self-important men spoke in Parliament, Ministers yielded to their civil servants and became their prisoners. Public prosecutors drilled with the storm troopers. Judges broke up public meetings. Wandering nationalist speakers hawked thunderous platitudes. Cunning Jews counted money, poor Jews were persecuted. Pastors preached murder, priests swung cudgels, Catholics became suspect, parties lost supporters. Foreign tongues were hated.

Foreigners were spied on, faithful dogs were put down, cab horses eaten. Officials sat behind their counters, protected by grilles, unapproachable, safe from fury, smiling and commanding. Teachers bullied out of hunger and anger. Newspapers invented horror stories about the enemy. Officers sharpened their sabres. Students fired shots. Policemen fired shots. Small boys fired shots. It was a nation of gunfire.

And Benjamin lived among distorted faces, twisted limbs, hunched backs, backs which had been flogged, clenched fists, smoking pistols, violated mothers, stranded beggars, drunken patriots, foaming beer mugs, clinking spurs, workers who had been fired on, bleeding corpses, desecrated graves, the mass graves of the murdered, exploded safes, iron clubs, trailing sabres, tinkling medals, generals on parade, and the gleam of helmets.

Oh, how Benjamin Lenz loved all this! How he must have hated, and how he must have fed and swelled that hatred! He looked upon the gruesome living and scented the stink of decay in advance. Benjamin waited. They would fall victims to him. They would tear one another to pieces and he would witness it. How Benjamin loved Theodor, the hated European, Theodor; the grim and cowardly, gross and cunning, ambitious and insatiable, greedy and frivolous, class-conscious, godless, overweening and servile, downtrodden and persistent Theodor Lohse! He was the young man of Europe: nationalistic and self-seeking, devoid of belief and of loyalty, bloodthirsty and blinkered. This was the new Europe.

19

On the night of October 20th, at eleven o'clock, Marinelli was freed. He sped to Berlin in a car which was ready and waiting, and went to Potsdam, where the driver had orders to deliver him to the barracks, to Theodor Lohse. Theodor was waiting for him. Marinelli was put into uniform the next

morning and stayed in barracks. On October 21st Benjamin
Lenz came and greeted Marinelli. He then took Theodor with
him to the Russian, Rastschuk, who was employed in a bank.

Theodor was glad to have a talk with Rastschuk. They
drank liqueurs. Rastschuk was so large and so powerful that
he quite filled the little drinking shop. He spoke very quietly,
but one heard him just the same. When he looked in the
direction of the waiter, the waiter would turn round as if he
had been called. Rastschuk was quite tremendous.

Benjamin Lenz told him about the springing of Marinelli,
his flight and his presence in the barracks. This was very
painful for Theodor, who grew hot under the collar because
Benjamin was constantly interrupting his story by appealing
to Theodor for confirmation of the accuracy of his words.
'Isn't that so, Herr Lohse?' he would ask, and Theodor would
remain silent.

What, in fact, did he know of Rastschuk? That he had been
a White Guard and was working for the overthrow of the
Bolsheviks. So Lenz said. So said Rastschuk himself. But
Theodor did not believe it. Anyway, it was too late for second
thoughts. Theodor went with Benjamin Lenz. He was his ally.

Benjamin has drawn up a plan. Theodor Lohse will learn
about the preparations for November 2nd. He will then
report to the organisation. But Lohse lays down terms: what
will he receive for this valuable information? After the success
of November 2nd he must be given a leading and eminently
visible position. Today, Theodor Lohse represents a danger.
Two weeks divide him from November 2nd.

To give the others confidence, Lohse passes on secret
orders.

Orders come for Theodor Lohse. Letters from friends in
Munich, in which there are trivial phrases: Alfred is fetching
Paul on the 2nd. This sentence means: the Berlin police are

calling on the army for help. Or: Our old friend has engaged himself to marry Victoria. And that means: The Minister for the Army has come to an accord with the organisations. And: Martin is going to the children for a week. Which means that Marinelli has gone to the *Bismarck-Bund*, with greetings from Theodor and orders to prepare the young people in the university for November 2nd.

Lenz received these letters. He took them to Rastschuk.

In exchange Theodor learnt that the Saxon Order was being brought to Berlin, that nothing was planned for Potsdam, that a hundred and fifty-two Berlin police had gone over to the communist workers.

Theodor reports this to Seyfarth in Munich. He writes: 'I could give you a lot of fresh news, if we could meet. I've no patience for writing. I'm busy.'

So the student, Kamm, comes to Berlin.

'I'm sending young Kamm to you,' writes Seyfarth. 'Show him Berlin. It's his first visit.'

Theodor, Kamm and Benjamin Lenz went about Berlin. Kamm had money, and they spent it. They drank in the Tanzpalast and in the Kaiser-Wilhelm bar, and Theodor met his old friends there, and there was a big party. They left the cafés, the dives and the dance halls, and let themselves be picked up by whispering touts on street corners and led into gambling clubs. It was late, but in those smoke-filled rooms one noticed nothing, and one heard only the flutter of shuffled cards, laughter, the rustle of banknotes, the clink of a plate.

Theodor, Kamm and Benjamin sat in armchairs, away from the tables. Kamm had no more money. He looked to Benjamin for the price of his fare home.

He was only given enough to buy a third-class ticket on the express.

'One should be unostentatious!' said Lenz.

Then they began to go into details.

Lenz demanded 'real publicity' for Theodor Lohse after November 2nd. The whole national press must mention him by name. The saving of the city, of the Fatherland must be attributed to him. Otherwise, Theodor had the means to do very well for himself elsewhere.

'You could be killed before then – the pair of you!' said Kamm, polishing his nails with a piece of chamois leather.

'Just let them try,' said Lenz derisively.

He took from his pocket the mustering plans for the Saxon Order. Lenz and Theodor saw Kamm to the station.

Kamm stood in the window and waved.

'Say hello to Seyfarth!'

'Don't forget Paul!' said Kamm.

Lenz then left. He pushed his way through the hurrying crowd of office girls, bumping into painted women standing about looking lost. It was if the night had overlooked them.

And Benjamin Lenz went to Rastschuk. They hurriedly altered the mustering plans. Lenz had given Kamm the original.

'We must work honestly!' said Benjamin Lenz.

20

A few days before November 2nd, Dr Trebitsch vanished.

His uncle Arthur had arrived from New York. He owned an agency for ships' tickets. He said 'Well,' and thrust forward his lower lip. He carried his money in his pocket, lots of money, German money. For dollars he had a chequebook.

He was of Austrian origin and had fled abroad rather than face an army medical examination. That had been thirty years ago. Now he no longer had a hair on his head. He had sons and daughters. The sons had served in the American army. The sons were brave and had given back to the armed forces what their father had stolen from them by escaping from his army medical.

Trebitsch's uncle was a widower. It was his first return to Europe for twenty years. He was called Trewith.

He was startled by his nephew's beard. He laughed loudly and a great deal and slept every night with two girls at a time.

He asked Dr Trebitsch whether he would not like to come to America. Why should anyone want anything to do with Europe? It stank and was rotten. It was a corpse.

Dr Trebitsch said: 'Yes!' His uncle cabled New York. He went to the American Consul. He took his hands out of his pockets and in general behaved politely.

Trewith suddenly loved his nephew very dearly. He was moved to tears because this youngster, whom he had seen in his cradle, now sported a long, orange, flowing spade beard, like a rabbi.

That such a thing should happen!

His brother Adolf was dead. His sister-in-law was dead. Far and wide across all Europe there was only one blood relation to be found and he had a long beard! It was touching.

Uncle Trewith stayed on and waited for his nephew.

Dr Trebitsch wired Munich for money. He went to Major Pauli, then he cleaned out his safe.

Cheques came in every day. Trebitsch telephoned everyone who had subscribed to the Voluntary Service Organisation.

Efrussi, too, sent his contribution. An association of big entrepreneurs advanced a subscription for fear of November 2nd.

Trebitsch forgot no one.

He went into the board of the *Deutsche Zeitung*, which had taken up a collection for an injured member of the volunteers. Trebitsch took away the funds.

He forgot no one.

One day before his departure he had his beard shaved off. His smooth, boyish face surprised his uncle at his hotel. Uncle Trewith wept for joy.

Trebitsch then wrote one letter of farewell, to Paula from the Ministry of Defence.

'You will never see me again!' wrote Trebitsch.

Paula rushed after Trebitsch. The post had delivered his letter to her office. The house was shut up.

On her way she met a young man with the face of a child, who paid no attention to her, although she was wearing a striking, lemon-yellow hat. This annoyed Paula, but Dr Trebitsch was a greater cause for worry. So she went on her way and saw outside a car in which was seated an elderly American, smoking a cigar.

Theodor called twice. He found Trebitsch's place locked up. Theodor came the next day with Benjamin Lenz. Lenz brought a picklock and the door opened easily. It had not been bolted.

They found the cupboards open. The drawers were open. A chair had been knocked over. There were old clothes and soiled laundry.

They telephoned Major Pauli. He knew nothing. Only that Trebitsch had taken money.

They asked at the offices of the *Deutsche Zeitung*. No one knew a thing, except that Trebitsch had taken money.

Lenz sat on the sofa and thought things over.

'He's run for it, Lohse,' said Benjamin.

At nine in the morning the bridge fell into Hamburg harbour. Dr Trebitsch was aboard the *Deutschland*.

His uncle Trewith ran below once again, and spotted a girl among the onlookers; how lovely that she had come. She had promised to the day before. He gave her a smacking kiss. Everybody saw him.

Then he ran back. The bell was ringing.

He ran so fast that his smooth, strong cheeks shook.

He stood and waved a big handkerchief. Dr Trebitsch waved too.

21

Benjamin knew a lot of people: Pisk the journalist, Brandler the film producer, Neumann the statistician, Angelli the magician, Bertuch the travel writer.

Pisk, the newspaper man, was a worthy fellow. He wrote for Jewish papers. Social sketches, sketches of ancient and modern society. When some Princess died, he would write about it.

But he also wrote about Captain Ehrhardt. He wrote about Noske's development. He wrote about Ludendorff's past. He wrote stories about Hindenburg's days as a cadet. He wrote about Krupp. He wrote about Stinnes' sons and daughters.

He wrote about Theodor Lohse. Why should one not write about Theodor Lohse? 'He is the coming man!' said Benjamin Lenz.

One of Pisk's ears stuck out. He wore his wide-brimmed hat askew, so that the brim shaded this ear. He wore his hat in cafés, too, as he did not wish to be noticed because of his ear. In this way people could not say that his good looks were flawed. The worst they could say was that he did not know how to behave. And everyone said that anyway.

But when he sat down with Theodor Lohse in the drinking shop, he had taken off his hat. That suggested a devotion which was not afraid to make sacrifices.

And Benjamin comes to the conclusion that Pisk has in mind to write a great deal about Theodor.

The *Morgenzeitung* is running articles on 'Men of the Revolution'. And in the *Morgenzeitung* it states that it was Theodor Lohse who, on a night of destiny, saved the Reichstag from destruction by the Spartakists.

There is talk in the mess about this article in the Jewish paper. The 'young people' at the foot of the table ask Theodor to tell them the story.

No, Theodor Lohse dislikes talking about himself. He says: 'Not worth mentioning.'

And although even the colonel is looking at him, and there is a pause in the meal and the colonel's cheeks are not quivering, he will not talk.

'Some other time, when it's appropriate!' says Theodor Lohse.

Pisk has conveniently left his wallet at home.

'The bill!' calls Benjamin Lenz.

And when the waiter stands by the table, expectant and leaning slightly forward, Theodor has to pay. For he is in uniform.

Sometimes Pisk says: 'Let's take a taxi!' Pisk gives the driver the address. On the way he gets out and Theodor Lohse drives on.

Sometimes Pisk has other requirements. Benjamin Lenz also has his requirements.

Theodor has now taken over Trebitsch's duties. He only has to parade three times a week.

The colonel is aware that Theodor has business in Berlin. At irregular but frequent intervals, the name of Theodor Lohse appears in reports and articles.

In Jewish newspapers the revolution is not well thought of.

But Pisk loves the revolutionaries. He lives off them. For some days past he has been wearing a monocle, and in his wallet he carries a membership card of the Agricultural Students' League.

In this fashion he is protected against street fighting and attacks.

Benjamin Lenz, too, wears a monocle.

One can see that November 2nd is near.

22

Theodor spent the eve of November 2nd in a nightclub with his fellow-officers. They held an assortment of painted girls on their knees. It was the moment to take leave of life. That is what the officers said to the girls. The idea of an early death made all the girls nostalgic. The orchestra played the '*Wacht am Rhein*'. One client remained seated. Two officers lifted him to his feet. He was fat and heavy and drunk. They held him on their shoulders, then they let him fall. He fell under the table and remained sitting there. He played with the champagne coolers.

The day dawned grey. It was raining, and Theodor waited at the station for his company, which had to take up its position in the city at eight o'clock. It was Sunday. The city looked drowsy. It was raining.

At nine some workers demonstrated on Unter den Linden. The nationalist youth groups were in Charlottenburg. Between the two lay streets, houses, police. And still the city waited for a clash.

At nine it was still raining. The workers went through the grey rain. They were as grey, as endless as the rain. They came out of the grey districts, as the rain fell from the grey clouds.

They were like the rains of autumn, endless, relentless, quiet. They spread melancholy. They came, these bakers with their bloodless faces, as if made from dough, without muscles or strength; the men from the lathes with their hard hands and their sloping shoulders; the glassblowers who were unlikely to see thirty out: costly, deadly, glistening glass-dust coated their lungs. Then came the broom makers with their deep-set eyes, the dust of the brooms and the hairs in the pores of their skin. There came the young girl workers, marked by toil, youthful in their stride but with worn faces. Carpenters came, smelling of wood and shavings from the plane. And the enormous furniture removal men, as large and overpowering as oak cupboards. The heavy-duty workers came from the breweries, stumping along like great tree trunks which have learnt to walk. The engravers came, the metallic dust scarcely visible in the lines of their faces; the newspaper compositors came, nightworkers who had not had a night's sleep for ten years or more; they had bloodshot eyes and pale cheeks and were out of place in the light of day. The pavers come, walking the streets which they themselves have laid, but nonetheless strangers to them, blinded by their brightness, their breadth, their lordliness. They are followed by engine-drivers and railwaymen. Through their subconscious the black trains still run, signals change colour, whistles blow, iron bells clang.

But towards them, with youthful faces and a song in their heart, march the students with bright caps and gold-embroidered banners, well-fed, smooth-cheeked, with clubs in their hands and pistols in their deep pockets. Their fathers are schoolmasters, their brothers judges and officers, their cousins police officers, their in-laws are manufacturers, their friends are Ministers. They hold the power, it is for them to strike the blow, and who shall punish them for it?

The marching workers sing the 'Internationale'. They sing

out of tune, these workers, for their throats are dry. They sing out of tune, but with a power which moves, a power which weeps, a power which sobs.

The young students sing differently. Resounding songs from practised throats, full and rounded songs of victory and blood, well-nourished songs without pause or distress. There is no sob in their throats, only jubilation, only jubilation. A shot rings out.

At this moment the police spring into the saddle, swords drawn and swinging, coming out of the sidestreets, with police on foot sealing off the streets behind them. Horses fall, riders lurch, the paving stones are torn up, exploring fingers dig between them, stones rain upon the breaking walls of police. Two powers are trying to come to grips, the mass of the powerful and the mass of the powerless, and the police cordons have been torn asunder while the hungry are forcing their way towards the well-fed. Above the frenzy of the people rises the singing of those who are pressing from behind. Now some are singing and some are bleeding, and sometimes a shot splits the frenzy of the songs, so that for a fraction of a second there is silence and one hears the falling of the autumn rain, and the drumming of it on roofs and windowpanes, and it is as if it were raining on a peaceful world preparing to sink into its winter sleep.

But then comes the lament of a motor horn, sounding like a wounded beast, and from far off comes the confused sound of the streetcars' bells, whistles shrill, trumpets cry like children. A dog who has been crushed howls like a human, becomes human in the hour of its miserable death, chains and bolts rattle from doors and again a shot rings out.

From the university comes Marinelli with fifty young people armed with carbines, to reinforce the students. The fire engines come. Their hoses send forth cold jets of water that falls with a painfully powerful hiss among the people. For a few moments the crowd scatters. Then it reassembles. Little groups form and develop. A shot strikes a hose. On the pavement lie firemen's helmets. The hose is torn. Police clatter up in lorries. The street paving rumbles. The windowpanes tremble. The police are at once dragged down, stamped on, bloodied, scattered and disarmed. Workmen smash carbines over their knees. Women are swinging sabres, pistols, rifles.

From the grey northern quarters more hordes come pouring, carrying household implements, pokers, spades, axes and shovels. High up above, a machine-gun stutters. Someone lets out a cry, and at once thousands have turned to flee. A thousand hands are raised, pointing nowhere. From every rooftop, guns are pointing. From every rooftop machine-guns stutter. Behind every projecting wall crouch green uniforms. Black muzzles are poking out of every window.

Someone shouts: 'Soldiers!'

The asphalt rings with the clatter of hobnailed boots. The houses are taken over and the windows have become embrasures. Riderless horses whinny in courtyards, commands ring out, weapons clink.

Theodor waits on the Alexanderplatz. His company waits. He presses himself against a closed *porte cochère*. His company crouches on the pavement. A mounted policeman informs him that the city hall and police headquarters are under attack. Theodor marches off.

It is going to be a hard fight. He will be killed. He feels like weeping. He marches at the head of his men. His ears are full of the even tread of his men. He is going to die now. He can still feel, from the night before, the delicious pressure of a woman's soft body.

A worker's commando is fighting round the city hall and police headquarters. Their leader is a man with flowing locks, with a club in his hand. Now he seizes a worker's rifle and takes aim. Theodor throws himself to the ground. He lands in a filthy puddle. Dirty water splashes up. He fires from this position, at random. His men are running forward. He can see nothing, only the bulk of the pavement, and above it the flatness of a square stone. An explosion startles him. Human bones spin through the air. The bloody stump of a leg falls from a height. Then a boot with a foot in it.

It is burning. One can smell the fire and see the cloud of smoke fighting against the rain, rising. Theodor jumps up. Runs. The Jewish quarter is burning. Pots and pans are hurtling from the windows of dirty houses. People are leaping, too. A Jewess is gasping beneath the weight of a soldier. She lies sideways across the pavement. An old woman hobbles across the street. Her haste is laughable. The strength of her crippled feet is all too feeble. Her face is the face of a fugitive and her movements are halting. Children crawl in the mud. They are wearing yellow shirts and there are bloodstains at the edges. The blood flows away with the rainwater, along with horse droppings, feathers and straw, all flowing down the thirsty drains in the gutters.

White-bearded men hurry with flying coat-tails. Someone grasps Theodor by the knees. Someone whining for mercy. Theodor kicks out with his foot. The whiner falls back into a stream of blood. Red flares up. Flames lick the windows. Smoke breaks out of falling rooftops. Men with iron bars cry: 'Kill the Jews!'

Everyone is killing and being killed. He sees a head in the mud. A dying face. Günther's face. Theodor stares at it and suddenly receives a hard blow on the head. Blood runs down his temples. Red wheels spin and he falls. He sees the workers' leader. His mane of hair. The flying club. Theodor draws his pistol. The man leaps sideways. He swings his stick.

Theodor sees his white face. He still has not cocked his pistol, and already it is flying from his painfully struck hand. The man comes nearer and he can see the whites of his eyes which are full of hatred. The man yells: 'You killed Günther!'

Theodor runs. Behind him he can sense the hot breath of his pursuer. At his shoulder he can smell his enemy's breath, behind him he can hear his enemy's hastening steps. On soundless feet runs Theodor. He runs through silent, burnt-out, murdered streets. He runs through an alien world, through a long dream. He hears shots, drumbeats, cries of pain. All sounds are muted in the layers of some insulating substance. Now comes a turning. Does safety lie over yonder? Double the speed, gallop faster on winged feet! Now he looks back and there is no pursuer behind him. He falls into a doorway. Before him lies a lost rifle. He picks it up and runs on. The dead still live! He hates the dead. He finds himself among soldiers. Now he recognises his own men. Cheerful greetings come to him. The butt of his rifle bumps against corpses. He smashes it against dead skulls. They burst. He stamps on the wounded with his heels, their faces, stomachs, their limply hanging hands. He takes his revenge on the dead, who will not die.

Evening falls. A damp darkness lurks in the streets. It is a victory for law and order.

23

It was a victory for law and order. Two ministers fell. They knew too much about the secret organisations. Two new ministers were appointed. They knew more. But they were friends. They belonged to the Democratic Party. So they seemed to be democratic. Yet they were honorary members of the *Bismarck-Bund*. And they were in touch with Munich. And they feared the workers.

'To take preventive measures' was the technical term for the ensuing policies. Spies, whom everyone knew, infiltrated secretariats and party headquarters. The police would announce a 'weeding out of secret nests'. Spies would leap on some harmless and insignificant speaker at a meeting, and the papers would state that some long-wanted Bolshevik spy had at last been caught, but that it was difficult to discover his true name. *Agents provocateurs* would arrange raids on working districts, loading two or three hundred men onto wide, rattling trucks. 'Aliens', which meant citizens from former German territories, were quartered on the aerodrome in barracks, guarded by police and sorted into trucks which took them to the frontiers. In these barracks lived thousands from all over the old Reich, with their children, wives, grandmothers. Dirt led to illness. Illness ensured a high death-rate. Before the trucks came, each day saw several deaths. Soft-spoken, drunken men went through the Jewish quarters, demanding money from all those who were about to emigrate. They were paid. The Jews who did not pay were thrown into prison as Bolshevik spies for examination by the police. This went on for a couple of months. Then the Jews, whose tickets for the passage had expired along with their American visas, would be returned to the frontier. The National Citizens' League was allowed to carry arms. Its members used them. German princes put on uniform and drove through the towns. Old generals shuffled about wearing decorations and spurs. Striking workmen who stood outside their factories were stabbed, shot and beaten up by the National Citizens' League. The newspapers would announce that the workmen had threatened passers-by and could only be dispersed by armed force. Wandering preachers drifted through the streets. They spoke of a national renewal. All the citizens in their businesses, all the importers, the factory owners, the civil servants talked about this national renewal. The socialist newspapers expected fresh attacks at any moment. The police arrived too late and took evidence.

It was a victory for law and order.

Benjamin Lenz proved how useful he could be. The journalist, Pisk, brought out a report on Theodor Lohse. Other newspapermen asked for interviews. They dragged up all Theodor Lohse's past achievements. They invented new ones. Theodor Lohse, overwhelmed by fame, lived surrounded by journalists. Rich Jewish establishments invited him. He even went to the Efrussis once. What a long time ago that had been! How much he had achieved! Now he stood in the Efrussis' house, with politicians, bankers, writers: a guest, just as they were. Now he could approach Frau Efrussi not only as an equal, but as a hero, in uniform, and as a famous man. But now her voice had a very distant sound. She no longer smiled. Her kindness had vanished, no warmth was in her: she nodded to Theodor, who could scarcely feel the tips of her cool fingers, and her expression was almost one of scorn, as if to say: Well, look at Theodor Lohse!

Theodor was able to forget about Frau Efrussi when he was talking to Fräulein von Schlieffen, who was living with her aunt in Potsdam, and who danced very well. Theodor was no dancer, nor a specially good seat on a horse. Fräulein von Schlieffen, however, rode every morning. And although every officer in the garrison was at her beck and call, she gave Theodor preference. She was twenty-six, an orphan, from a famous family, but penniless. Her father had ended his life as a modest Counsellor of Embassy in Sofia.

The daughter had been raised by nuns. Her aunt had always looked after her. Now the time had come to look about for a husband. In earlier times this would have been easy, but under the Republic, as one grew older, one was more likely to remain single. In these modern times money was more important than connections. Of what account was her name? No von Schlieffen could previously have married a bourgeois. Now it could be done. One was still blonde, those two tiny, premature lines at the temples were scarcely visible, one could still display fine white teeth. Yet those legs were already distinctly thicker and, on many nights, sleep was not to be found for the longing of one's heart and body for a man. There was none so unassuming as Theodor Lohse. No other man with such fame, success and ambition still retained such shyness with women. He was over thirty, at the best age for marriage. He had a future. A woman who wanted to move out and up could make good use of his ambition. Elsa von Schlieffen had reached the age when one thinks sensibly, and she came of a family which believed in careers.

'Why don't you marry?' asked Benjamin Lenz.

'Marry!' said Lenz, threateningly.

90

The time had come to take leave of the army. For all the people in Munich cared, one could spend a lifetime in the *Reichswehr* and end up as a staff officer. Trebitsch's post was already filled. It was time to look around. What use was a day's popularity? Fame was short-lived! Tomorrow brings a fresh story and the newspapers are ungrateful. People forget. One is forgotten.

Benjamin Lenz wants to sit at the fountainhead, he has no need for affable friends, he needs men in high places. Benjamin needs no small lieutenants. He wants his information at first hand; insight into an important state industry.

Theodor must marry. This simpleton of a Theodor, in the hands of an ambitious woman, will rise to the highest office. 'Exploit the way the wind is blowing!' said Benjamin.

Clearly, he could no longer be a soldier. How he had grown up. A year ago he could still have lost his life as an officer.

And what did a year ago matter now?

A miserable time, ham rolls and coffee with skin on it at the Efrussis, vegetables once a week and *The Elders of Zion*. The elders of Zion were not as they were described in that book. They were not striving for power in Europe. They understood. They had money. Money was the greatest power of all. But it was not easy to come by. Theodor's capital had not been growing for a long time, and Benjamin Lenz said: 'Sell out! Anyone who has no inside information on the stock exchange is fleeced. They're as bad as the gypsies!'

Benjamin liked to see Theodor without spare cash. Benjamin willingly lends his friends money, cash down. He is a noble fellow, is Benjamin Lenz. He is delighted when he can help Theodor.

Munich would gladly have left Theodor in the army. But he was no longer dependent on them, as in earlier days. He notified them that he was sick. He was a neurasthenic.

Neurasthenia is not susceptible of diagnosis, said Benjamin Lenz.

Theodor retired from the army. The mess laid on an intimate farewell party. He informed Munich of his resignation and requested further instructions.

To him it felt as if he had pushed aside the last obstacles.

24

A week later he became engaged to Fräulein von Schlieffen. Benjamin advanced money for presents, flowers and the reception.

Benjamin's resources seemed inexhaustible.

Fräulein von Schlieffen danced no more, nor was she seen out riding. Suddenly she lost all her sporting inclinations.

She stayed at home and sewed monograms onto blouses, bloomers, handkerchiefs.

Theodor came to Potsdam every evening.

The first snow fell. There was a fire in the grate.

Once, Theodor brought his sisters along.

They sat in silence, curtsied to the aunt, and went.

They were bemused by the sound of the name: Schlieffen.

Theodor's mother never dared ask after his fiancée.

At home, it was a long time since Theodor had been the one who was put up with and looked down on. How good it had been of God to keep Theodor alive.

If only his sainted father were alive! thought his mother. She, too, was sewing monograms. With red silk she sewed rhyming proverbs of varying connotations.

The mighty Hilper was now Minister of the Interior. He knew Theodor. Did Theodor know him? His press secretary was that little reporter from the *Nationale Beobachter*.

They all liked Theodor. He was a likeable person, and modest despite all his achievements. He also had contacts. He seemed to get on well with the press, and he was well-connected socially.

Nothing was known to his discredit. He had never been entangled in litigation. His past was blameless. He was even trained in the law.

Why should Theodor not receive an appointment?

Hilper decided to find him a place. He even promised to do so.

Now Theodor went from office to office. Counsellors shook his hand, not knowing for what appointment he had been selected, though they knew the selection had been made.

At one moment the journalist, Pisk, brought his friend, Tannen. The name Tannen was a pseudonym. But Tannen was a chatty man, a smiling man, he smiled a professional smile such as jugglers do when they take their bows.

Tannen slipped little paragraphs into the newspapers. He reported that a new post had been created in the Secretariat for Public Safety, a sort of liaison post between the Ministry of the Interior, the Secretariat and the police.

The journalist, Pisk, went to the Minister and enquired.

'I've heard nothing about it!' said Hilper. For Hilper was a straightforward man, a headmaster from Westphalia and no diplomat.

'But it would be a brilliant idea all the same!' said Pisk.

And then Pisk mentioned that Professor Bruhns, the astronomer, was celebrating his sixtieth birthday.

'Has he distinguished himself?' asked the Minister, who was a classical philologist and knew nothing about astronomy.

'And how! He's one of the top meteorologists,' said Pisk, 'and he's published a two-volume work on Saturn.'

'Indeed!' said the Minister. 'Good of you to let me know. Should I write to congratulate him, or send a representative?'

'A representative, Your Excellency,' said Pisk.

Pisk did not give a damn about it, but he must find bridges, bridges towards the subject of Theodor Lohse.

'Did you know,' asked Pisk, who avoided categorical statements, 'that Lohse is to marry?'

'Ah!' said the Minister. 'Whom?'

'A von Schlieffen!'

'Schlieffen? Good name!'

'A good match, actually,' said Pisk.

'Rich?'

'Supposed to be well off.'

'*Donnerwetter*!' said the Minister, who had married a poor girl while he was still a professor.

'Smart youngster!' said Pisk.

'And modest!' added the Minister.

And then they talked some more about Professor Bruhns.

And Pisk wrote: 'The report about the new post in the Secretariat for Public Safety has been confirmed by responsible sources. During the past weeks a former officer has often been mentioned as the coming man.'

The wedding was in January.

25

For the first time, Benjamin Lenz went to a wedding. He did not so much go as glide in a car to the church door. For the first time he wore a morning coat and top hat, and later he sat at a table with officers and old ladies, and drank wine which he had paid for himself.

It was a splendid wedding. Theodor wore mess kit. Comrades similarly attired glittered, clinked and rattled. In Potsdam, people looked out of their windows and stood in front of the church, despite the cold.

The colonel made a speech, and Major Lubbe spoke, too, mentioning Count Zeppelin once, but only from force of habit and without particular relevance. Elsa made Theodor give a speech of thanks, so he had to stand up and hold forth, and the upraised eyes of his bride quite confused him. A great love for all those present flooded his heart, and a couple of times he stood up to shake the hand of Benjamin Lenz, who was seated opposite.

Benjamin was enjoying himself. This was the true European wedding. Beside him sat the widow of Major Strubbe, talking about Kattowitz, where she had lived her loveliest years. Benjamin was not listening. His profound gaze was fixed somewhere far away. He was thinking of Lodz, of his father's dirty barbershop. He could see the single, blinded mirror in the shop. How simple and how wise were the sayings of the old Jews in Lodz, how sharp was their wit, how measured their laughter, how good their food tasted, the food of the Jews, beaten, scorned, living in exile with no helmets and no means of shining or showing off. This was the true European marriage, of a man who had killed senselessly, worked without purpose and who would now beget sons who in their turn would become murderers, killers, Europeans, bloodthirsty and cowardly, warlike and nationalistic, bloody but churchgoing, believers in the European God who was worshipped through politics. Theodor will raise children, students with caps of many colours. They will fill schools and barracks. And Benjamin saw the Tribe of Lohse. There was work to do. They will murder one another.

And Benjamin listened to the telegrams as Major Lubbe read them out. Congratulations came from Pisk, from other journalists, from Hilper, the Minister, from counsellors and from Efrussi. Then Major Lubbe paused, breathing audibly, and read out a telegram from Ludendorff.

And every time someone spoke, they spoke paper words, European words. It seemed to Benjamin as if he had himself ordered this wedding, and that the Europeans were presenting him with a ridiculous slice of their lives, for his entertainment.

Entertained he was. By the parson who, with an air of resignation and as if he were letting something dreadful happen to him, kept pouring more and more wine into his glass and becoming more and more silent as his watery eyes sent heavenward their humble and beseeching looks. The colonel was noisy. He must have a weak bladder, for he was always pushing back his chair, disappearing, and returning after a few minutes with a fresh joke, at which the officers' laughter was short, sharp and indifferent. The eyes of old Frau Lohse, who sat on the colonel's right, slid here and there like small, shy animals. When the colonel spoke to her she smiled, and when he spoke to old Frau von Schlieffen Theodor's mother was thankful that she did not have to look at the colonel, but looked instead at her son, at Theodor and his bride. Frau von Schlieffen wore a stiff Potsdam coiffure, her hair was scraped back hard and showed her yellow ears which looked like old leaves, while the sight of her bun was painful to the beholder.

How Theodor joked; he kept telling his bride anecdotes, since he simply had to speak. And even if he said something trivial, Elsa laughed, because she simply had to be amused. He felt proud. His bride was beautiful, but now and again he thought of Frau Efrussi, and deep down, in his most secret depths, he debated the question: was she better and more beautiful than Elsa? This Jewess irritated him. Everything irritated him. Although he should in fact be delighted. He was taking a von Schlieffen to wife. On his account she was surrendering her titles of nobility, giving up that old, resounding name in favour of a name which was commonplace, even if it was frequently mentioned and had connotations of fame. The first months were taken care of, a quiet home was rented. Benjamin, faithful Benjamin had exchanged the share certificates for currency. Today or tomorrow Theodor would enter his home. The day after that, and the days and weeks which followed, he would spend there. The days and weeks lay before him full of happiness; his nerves needed a rest. 'You must rest, my love,' said Elsa. He must rest.

In the front room he unpacked the presents. Outside the windows lay the night, the lamp shone redly in the bedroom. Elsa embraced him, hugged him, he caressed her, smelt her hair, stroked her neck.

Next morning, Benjamin Lenz sent flowers and a big picture. 'In memory of bygone days,' wrote Lenz.

It was a portrait of Theodor by the painter, Klaften. Elsa hung it in Theodor's study.

26

Benjamin Lenz had paid for it in dollars. Not too many dollars.

Theodor put up with his portrait. He was no longer afraid of it.

He wore a modern suit with padded shoulders and a single button on the jacket. He didn't feel at home in this outfit. He couldn't find the pockets, which were placed high and on the slant.

He forced his wide feet into narrow shoes made of thin leather. He froze, and his feet hurt, but he found them smart.

He should have gone to Munich. He had to talk with Seyfarth. 'Don't go,' said Elsa, 'they'll come to you.'

He was worried that they might not come. But he showed no trace of anxiety.

'My love,' said Elsa, 'I just have to admire you.'

And he allowed her to admire him.

He lost his way a little. He began to believe what she said, to believe what she believed.

She went to church. 'I'm used to it!' she said. And he went with her, because he was jealous.

She refused to enter a train compartment if there were Jews sitting there.

He would take her to another compartment.

They had to travel second class in the suburban railway. He bought no season tickets.

In Berlin she often felt tired. She wanted to take a taxi. And they took one.

She would look lovingly at Theodor's portrait. And Theodor realised that his anxiety at the time had been exaggerated. It had been the excitement. Yes, he liked the portrait. Klaften had painted it when he still thought Theodor was a fellow traveller, Comrade Trattner.

'When did he paint you?' asked Elsa. 'Do you know this Klaften?' And she was proud.

Theodor was waiting for his opportunity. He wanted to outline his career to his wife.

Once he did talk about it. He picked a suitable evening. The wind was blustering in the chimney. Elsa was sewing bright flowers onto a cushion. Theodor began to tell her about Trebitsch. He was a very dangerous Jew. Theodor had been the first to spot this. No one had listened to Theodor's warnings. Unluckily. Theodor did not mention the Prince.

But he did describe the painter, Klaften. And Thimme, the young communist. He allowed Thimme, the *agent provocateur*, to blossom. He made him out to be older, and a leader. And it had not been a question of the Victory Column. The whole of central Berlin was supposed to have been blown up. The explosives had been placed in the canals.

'Were you in mortal danger?' asked Elsa.

'Nothing to speak of,' said Theodor.

'Tell me about the farmworkers,' Elsa begged.

Theodor told. There had been no farmworkers. They had been vagrants, Bolshevik agitators, every one of them armed to the teeth. On that occasion Theodor had cleaned all the undesirable elements out of Pomerania.

'I really have to admire you,' said Elsa.

Theodor then told her about Viktoria, the bestial woman, the dangerous spy who had fallen in love with him and given the whole game away to him.

Elsa thought about this for a little and said: 'That's not actually very pretty!'

'My dear child,' said Theodor, 'people of our sort can hardly credit it!'

'And she was his own wife!' Elsa concluded.

'His very own wife!' Theodor repeated.

And they kissed each other.

27

Once every week, Theodor went to Hilper. His case was making progress.

Elsa had thought up a position for Theodor. It was to be called: Head of Security.

No such job existed. But the very sound of the title gave Theodor no rest. He kept thinking: Head of Security.

He was appointed, sworn in, congratulated. He assumed his duties. Ten police officers waited in the anteroom for instructions.

There were meetings. Between the police and the Secretary of State. Between the Secretary and the Minister. Between all of them. Theodor drove in a car.

The waiting policemen set to work. Since they had as yet nothing to do, they filled out questionnaires. They wrote down lists of communists who had been expelled, in triplicate.

Whenever Theodor came into the anteroom, they were bent over rustling papers.

Then work came their way. Theodor found his feet. He resumed his old activities. He sent out spies. And because the police were in any event carrying out arrests, Theodor had still more arrests made.

Lenz gave him tips. This was the address of the organiser, Rahel Lipschitz. Arrest her! The next day Stock, the pacifist, was to speak. Arrest him! The socialist students were holding international evenings. Speakers were to come from England. Arrest them at the railway station!

Theodor had arrests made. He himself conducted cross-examinations. Minor offences took on the aspect of high treason in his hands. He needed a press officer.

Pisk became press officer. He sent out horror stories to the press. Scattered among all sorts of articles on foreign affairs, he would slip in little notes of warning.

The press resounded with the dangers through which the Reich was steering. Underground agitators were at work. But the authorities were on guard. Details of arrests would end with the phrase: The cross-examination was continuing late last night.

The obstinate prisoners admitted nothing. The police struck them. A policeman would pull a man forward and twist his wrists backwards. This was a 'security measure'.

If the suspect answered Theodor's tricky questions, the policeman would reduce the pressure. If he would not answer, the pain was intensified. 'Answer,' Theodor would say.

All the prisoners would realise that there was a connection between their answers and the pain. And they would answer.

The prisons were bursting. The police were no longer arresting burglars. The magistrates let them go. If they did put a burglar in prison it was so that he could spy on the others.

The prisons filled up. Huts were built to take the overflow. It was a cold winter. The wind keened and blew clouds of dusty snow. The snow fell through the joints in the hut roofs, melted and froze again on the floor. The straw was damp – too damp to rustle – and smelt of wet earth. Through it crawled children with faces like parchment and ribs cracking together. The prisoners in the huts were forbidden to light candles, although the electric light bulbs were old and unserviceable, and the men sat together in the dark and sang. In faltering voices they sang songs of blood.

Sometimes Benjamin Lenz would go, with a permit from Theodor Lohse, to inspect. He took his soldiers with him. He handed out cigarettes to the men, and on little bits of paper he would give them advice and plans for escaping. Some of them did succeed in escaping from the huts. They came to Benjamin Lenz. For one or two of them he could arrange forged papers. But most of them had wives and children and were forced to wait for their transport. They waited for a long time. They were waiting for death.

Once Thimme came to Theodor. They swapped reminiscences of the old days with Klaften. The young man, Thimme, liked Theodor, and said so. 'I took to you at once!' said Thimme.

This man is dangerous! thought Theodor.

I must watch my step, thought Theodor. But he did not watch his step. After a few days he grew to like young Thimme. He was a gifted man, a sharp youngster. All he wanted was a job.

And it turned out that Thimme knew of hiding-places. The drinking shops in Moabit, in the cellars of which explosives and weapons had lain. Nowadays no more weapons were found there. But Thimme had the knack of finding them. He would uncover them the night before they were to be used. He knew ways in. He had keys. He was useful.

Theodor did not watch his step. Within the satisfying quiet of his house, within the fixed terms of reference of his post, which was a goal and yet not a final goal, a small peak leading to higher peaks, Theodor Lohse became easy-going, as he always had been until danger or a threat to his purpose made him watchful and sharpened his commonsense. Thus he became what Benjamin Lenz wanted him to be. He could no longer function without Benjamin. Theodor needed him in his work, just as he needed his wife at home.

28

At home he was aware of his own importance. Here, his word was law, and here what he merely dreamed came true. He was always served his favourite dishes, without having mentioned them. He found his clothes brushed, his trousers pressed, no buttons missing from his shirts. No papers went astray, his weapons were in their proper places – he loved weapons – and Elsa cleaned his pistol. She, too, loved firearms.

Nowhere was he so powerful as at home. If he was in a mood to be masterful, then he could indulge it. If he felt a longing for warmth, it was at hand. Nobody here doubted his wholeness. In the evening he would complain of tiredness. Elsa said: 'You're overworked.' He would talk about what he had accomplished. 'You have a sharp eye,' said Elsa, and he would consider himself a fine judge of men. 'I'm fond of Lenz,' said Theodor. 'He's a loyal friend,' answered Elsa. And he believed in Benjamin's loyalty. He loved to hear the song of the nut-brown maid: Elsa would play it, without being reminded, before they went to bed.

She liked neither the song nor Benjamin Lenz, nor did she believe in Theodor's wholeness. But it was necessary to give way in small matters, so as to have one's way in large ones. A von Schlieffen only married a commoner because she hoped that he would be able to achieve the highest government offices. This required, above all, eloquence. And she taught Theodor to speak.

He almost forgot his wife. He began quietly and then increased the power of his voice. He never spoke in his room. He spoke in their big salon. A thousand people listening attentively to him would strike him almost physically. He spoke well when he spoke with enthusiasm. His eyes glowed with a strange light. He believed his own words. His convictions came from his own speeches, grew with the ring of his voice and were confirmed by it.

He spoke of the need to save the Fatherland, and he won back the faith of his young people. All his experiences were erased. He honestly hated the enemy within, Jews, pacifists, plebs. He hated them as he had hated them in the old days before he had known the Prince and Trebitsch, Detective Klitsche and Major Seyfarth. Elsa, too, hated the enemy within. Elsa was patriotic. She talked about the nasty smell Jews had. And Theodor seemed to think that he remembered Trebitsch speaking Yiddish. Only about Benjamin Lenz did Theodor know nothing precise. Nor did he wish to. He numbered Benjamin Lenz among his friends, like the Jewish journalist, Pisk.

And always, after talking like this with his wife, his rage against the enemy within would mount next day and he would reach for his bloodthirsty work with renewed energy. These people who stood before him, under arrest, what were they in Germany for, anyway? If they disliked their condition, why did they stay? Why not emigrate? To France, Russia, Palestine? He put this question to them. Some said: 'Because Germany is my home.'

'Is that why you are a traitor?' asked Theodor.

'It's you who's the traitor,' they answered.

They were delighted to have a row with someone. And they paid at once for their insolent answer. The policemen at their side squeezed the bones in their wrists.

Sometimes men were brought before Theodor who had been beaten till they bled, red blood ran down their faces. Inside Theodor rose the old crimson flames, red Catherine wheels of fire spun before his eyes, jubilation sang within him, raised him on high, and he rejoiced, felt himself light and borne upwards as if on wings.

There was one man living whom he wanted to see: the man who had pursued him. Theodor could still see the man's flying hair, his white face alive with hatred, his arm raised high; he could hear the swish of the stick as it came down, feel the pain in the hand which it had struck. This man, who had seen Theodor as a coward, seen him, Theodor Lohse, as a coward on the run, was still alive. He sent his spies out in vain to find this man. They questioned everyone under arrest about his hiding-place. Every time a fresh arrest was made, Theodor hoped to come across the spoor of his enemy. It was pointless in most cases to torture these people. Either they knew nothing or they gave nothing away. Some gave false information, and when they were faced with their own lies, they would laugh. Or they would claim they had made a mistake. Hope could only come from one source, from Lenz. Lenz knew the man.

'In a manner of speaking, he is Günther's brother-in-law,' said Lenz, 'and this is a kind of vendetta. He wants to kill you, but I believe I am on his trail.'

Again and again it was a false scent. Every morning came Benjamin's call and fresh hopes. Every evening disappointing, painful news.

Lenz described him precisely. He was the brother of the girl whom Günther would have married, Lenz said. Sometimes Benjamin said: 'On account of whom Günther died.' And, when he forgot himself: 'On whose account you killed him.'

And this expression was disagreeable. Theodor would see the upper lip painfully drawn back, the white gums, the cross-eyed look.

But Lenz would also describe the man's dress and his habits. He had already almost laid hands on him. But one bolt-hole always remained open, through which the wanted man escaped.

'We'll find him,' Benjamin Lenz assured him.

But he did not find the man, Theodor's mortal enemy.

'There's something on your mind,' said Elsa, 'and you won't tell me.'

'My work,' said Theodor. And he began to talk about the political aims of the Fatherland.

29

The night refused him sleep, and its overwhelming stillness swelled Theodor's fear of the unknown, fearsome enemy. Was he out of the country? Was he living somewhere in Theodor's neighbourhood? Was he perhaps living in Theodor's building, disguised as a hall porter? Did not the waiter in the little coffee shop facing his office have the face of his enemy? The long hair, the pale expression of hatred. The powerful, ponderous tread. The broad shoulders.

Was that man living inside the uniform of the official driver who looked after Theodor's car? Might he not be lying in wait round any corner which Theodor turned? Might he not have placed a bomb in this house, under the bed?

Theodor put the light on, walked up and down the room a couple of times, looked through the window at the quiet night in the streets and the flickering lamplight and listened to footsteps in the far distance.

Later, as dawn was breaking, Theodor fell into a heavy slumber. Daylight brought fresh hope, fresh fear, and grim hours of waiting. This was the one thing which Theodor could not talk about at home. He would have had to tell everything, from the very beginning. About Günther, about Klitsche. That would have been no tale to tell, but a confession, a fall from the heights attained by such a struggle; self-exposure, suicide.

And that left Benjamin.

Benjamin listened, consoled, promised, gave the latest gossip, gave advice, found out what had transpired at secret conferences, learnt the secret plans of the government, photographed documents, sold them, brought others to Theodor.

He was a busy man.

The workers rose in the working districts, and the unemployed demonstrated, since they were no longer earning anything. The long and painfully restrained fury of the masses burst into flame again. Groups of the unemployed came in from Saxony, not by train but on foot, wandering along the broad State highways, through a wind awhirl with snow, forerunner of spring.

Indeed, spring came. It was already to be sensed on the streets, for the snow was melting and its edges were covered by a grey crust. But the hungry, the refugees, the escaped prisoners and the workers who, before their arrest, had already undertaken the flight from their homelands and had hoped to disappear without trace into the great city; the women, whose men had been killed, the Jewish emigrants from the east who dared not board a train – they felt the spring as a triple scourge. They had made friends with the stinging frosts of winter, with the crunch of snow and its soft flakes, but the bitter wind which carried with it the coming rains of April, which bit through their clothes and dried the pores of their skin, this was more than they could withstand.

They fell down in the streets, and fever shook them; with chattering teeth they awaited their last hour, and then lay rigid in the streets. In their pity, refugees, new arrivals, buried the corpses in the fields at night, when the peasants were not watching.

Spring strode over Germany like a smiling murderer. Those who survived the huts, escaped the round-ups, were not touched by the bullets of the National Citizens' League nor the clubs of the Nazis, those who were not struck down at home by hunger and those whom the spies had forgotten, died on the road, and clouds of crows cruised over their corpses.

Diseases lay hidden in the folds of the wanderers' clothing, their breath was diseased. The policeman who encountered them on their way inhaled the disease from their curses, and if they were not outnumbered and murdered they would die in a few days anyway. Soldiers perished in their garrisons. Patrols sent out onto the highways would creep along the side roads to avoid meeting the Great Sickness, and still would not escape death.

But in the cities they spoke of the national rebirth, and

Theodor gave lectures. Now, more than ever, they were threatened by the enemy within, and the neighbouring states on their frontiers were ready to march. High-school boys were drilling. Judges were drilling. Priests were swinging clubs. Before God's altars and in the beautiful great churches of the land, wandering preachers were holding forth.

Theodor was kept busy by all these high-school boys, students, leagues. He spoke in the evenings at public meetings and he spoke his way upwards. Already he counted for more than the Commissioner for Police, more than the Secretary of State for Public Security, more than the Minister.

He stood on the podium, and the ring of his own voice uplifted him. His wife sat in the front row. Entrances, doors, windows were guarded. Here he forgot every danger, even his enemy, the lurking one, the unknown. 'I really do admire you,' said Elsa, and she sat in the front row and gazed up at her husband, who had come far and was going farther. Head of Security – thought she – President of the Reich, Regent for the Kaiser to come. Dazzling celebrations in white halls, marble staircases, gleaming gold, full evening dress clinking spurs, music, music.

New elections had been called. Who knew if another, even more brilliant post might not be free.

The newspapers wrote: 'Theodor Lohse'. Reporters from foreign countries came. The 'great world' knew of Theodor Lohse. His photograph was in the big American papers.

'One of the top men,' they called Theodor Lohse.

Why not the top man?

30

Once Theodor went into his office late in the evening and found Benjamin Lenz with the safe doors open.

Lenz was photographing documents.

As he saw Theodor he drew his pistol.

'Quiet!' said Benjamin.

Theodor sat on the table, staggered.

'Quiet!' said Benjamin.

'Spy!' screamed Theodor.

'Spy?' asked Benjamin. 'You were with me on the other side of the fence. You betrayed mobilisation plans. I have witnesses. Who murdered Klitsche?'

'Let's go,' said Benjamin Lenz, and escorted Theodor to his car.

'And sleep well!' called Benjamin as the chauffeur pulled out.

And Theodor drove home.

His wife was still at the piano, before going to bed. The windows were open and mild March breezes were drifting through the curtains.

'You will have great tasks before you now!' said Elsa.

'Yes, my child.'

'We must be prepared!'

'I am prepared!' said Theodor, and thought about murdering Benjamin.

Benjamin Lenz went to his brother that night. It was a long time since the brothers had met.

'Here's money for you, and a passport,' said Benjamin. 'Get out today!'

And Lazarus, his brother, understood.

They did not know each other at all. Lazarus did not know what Benjamin did, nor how he came by the money and the passport, but he understood.

Lazarus understood everything. Someone would make a small, unimportant remark, but a whole world lay behind that small and trivial phrase.

One could say a single word to any Jew from Lodz, and he would understand.

Jews from the east needed no explanations.

Lazarus had soft brown eyes. His hair shone. He studied so hard that he made new discoveries.

'Can you interrupt your studies?'

'I must,' said Lazarus, and was instantly ready. He only had one bag. And the bag was packed. Almost as if he had expected this departure from one minute to the next.

'Are you a doctor yet?'

'For a year now.'

'What are you working on?'

'A gas.'

'Explosive?'

'Yes,' said Lazarus.

'For Europe,' said Benjamin.

And Lazarus laughed. Lazarus understood everything. What was Benjamin by comparison? A minor intriguer.

But this young brother, with his gentle eyes and their golden lights, could blow up half a world.

The Paris train left at twelve-thirty.

Benjamin stood on the platform.

'Perhaps I may follow you,' said Benjamin.

Then Benjamin waved. For the first time, he waved. And the train slid out of the station. The platform was deserted, and a man was sprinkling water from a green can.

Somewhere, many locomotives were whistling on the tracks.

Zipper and his Father

1

I had no father – at least, I never knew my father – but Zipper had one. This earned my friend my special respect, as if he had owned a parrot or a St Bernard. When Arnold said: 'Tomorrow I'm going to the Kobenzl with my father,' I would wish that I too had a father. I could have held his hand, copied his signature, been scolded, punished, rewarded, caned by him. At times I wanted to urge my mother to marry again, because even a stepfather would have been worth having. The state of things, however, did not permit it.

Young Zipper was always showing his father off. His father had bought him this, forbidden him that, promised him this, denied him that. His father wanted to speak to the teacher, to arrange a tutor, to buy him a watch for his confirmation and to let him have his own room. Even when his father did something disagreeable to his son, it was as if it had been at Arnold's request. His father was like a mighty, but at the same time a serviceable, spirit.

From time to time I would come across Arnold's father. For a whole quarter of an hour he would treat me like his own son. He would say to me, for instance: 'Do up your collar, the wind's round to the north-west and you could get a sore throat.' Or: 'Show me that hand of yours; you've hurt yourself. We'll go across to the chemist and have something put on it.' Or: 'Tell your mother to send you to the barber. No one should have long hair in high summer.' Or: 'Can you swim yet? A young fellow must be able to swim.' It seemed then as if young Zipper had lent me old Zipper. I was grateful to my friend, but had at the same time the painful feeling that I had to give him back his father, just as I had to return his *Swiss Family Robinson*. In the end, things you borrowed were not your own.

Nevertheless, every so often I would spend quite a bit of time with Zipper's father, if only to share him with Arnold. The three of us would, on occasion, attend particular events; we climbed important towers, visited menageries, freak shows, Lilliputians, the Tanagra Theatre, and watched the fast runner who could sprint from one end of the long Lastenstrasse to the other in ten minutes. Old Zipper claimed that it was really eleven minutes and forty-five seconds, for he was much preoccupied with time. He had a timepiece which he justifiably referred to as a chronometer. It was a big gold watch with a lid. The dial was painted in lilac enamel, the black Roman numerals were trimmed with gold, and an unlikely, scarcely visible hook beside the ring would activate a chime. A clear, silvery bell would strike the hour and its quarters. 'This watch,' said Zipper's father, 'can as easily be used by a blind man as by a man who can see. He must of course reckon the minutes himself,' he would add, wittily. 'This watch has never yet been to a watchmaker. It has already gone for forty-one years, day and night. I acquired it in Monte Carlo under unusual circumstances.

These 'unusual circumstances' afforded young Zipper and myself much food for thought. This father, a man like any other, with a round black hat and a stick with an ivory handle, had once, in Monte Carlo, of all places, had an unusual experience. We observed with respect how old Zipper would compare his watch with the clock at the

Observatory, verify the sun's position at noon, check the electric clocks downtown. Sometimes, sitting at table with everyone eating in silence, he would set off the mechanism and the company would listen wonderingly to the mysterious sound.

Zipper's father loved surprises. He was given to practical jokes; false matchboxes out of which small mice would spring, exploding cigarettes, small rubber bubbles which moved about, ghost-like, under the thin tablecloth. He occupied himself with a number of small matters which grown-ups usually despise. But he was also interested in more important things, such as geography, history and the natural sciences. He thought little of the classical languages but attached the greatest importance to the modern. 'Nowadays,' he would say, 'every young man must learn French and English. If I had had a better youth, I would have become a polyglot. I'll grant you Latin. One may possibly require it if one becomes a doctor or a pharmacist. But Greek? A dead language! After all, one can read Homer in translation. The Greek philosophers are way out of date. If I had had my way, Arnold would have been sent to a modern secondary school. But his mother! And she still claims she loves her son! Loves him and leaves him to study Greek grammar!'

There were a number of other differences of opinion between old Zipper and his wife. She respected teachers, priests, the Court, and the generals. He was a denier of the eternal verities, a rebel and a free-thinker. He made honourable exception for genius; Goethe, Frederick the Great and Napoleon, various inventors, explorers of the North Pole and, particularly, Edison. He respected science, but only those of its practitioners who were far removed from him by death or by significant geographical distance. His reverence for medicine was only equalled by his mistrust of doctors. He claimed never to have been ill and that he had as much need for a doctor as his watch had for a watchmaker. Even so, from time to time he found himself in a situation which he described as a rest-deficiency. He would then declare that the healthy person – especially the healthy person – occasionally required a rest and even an increase in temperature. He had several methods for taking his temperature. No one else knew better how to shake down the mercury. His cures were remarkable, and unknown to medical science. They seemed rather to bear witness to his own leaning towards superstition, and they contradicted his one solitary belief: in common sense. He ate onions when he had a headache, put spiders' webs on open wounds and trod water to cure gout.

2

The Zipper family lived in a lower middle-class district, whose houses suffered from their rooms being too small, their walls too thin, and too much bric-à-brac.

There was one uncommonly noble room in the Zipper house. It lay behind their bedroom. It was also accessible from the hall, but that door was kept locked. It was opened once a year, at Easter, when old Zipper's brother from Brazil came for a visit. For us two, young Zipper and myself, this elegant room, known as the salon, was opened on Sunday afternoons, if we promised to keep quiet and 'not to break anything'. For a lot of breakable material was assembled there. I can remember an inkwell of pale blue glass with a silver lid, a little tub of the same colour containing sand for blotting and a blue glass pen-holder. These made a set, which stood in the midst of the heavy, ruby-red wine glasses on the sideboard, along with the silver jug and the sterling silver fruit bowl. Inside the glasses, which were always a trifle dusty, lay mother-of-pearl buttons, children's rings in soft silver, tie-clips, wooden containers for needles, brooches with glass jewels, black, flexible, tacky spangles which fell from Frau Zipper's best black evening dress whenever she wore it and which she picked up with the idea of eventually sewing on again.

The salon lay in an eternal half-light. Heavy red curtains allowed the sun hardly any access, just one narrow ray which drew a thin column of silver motes between the window and the round table. The room smelt powerfully of mothballs from cupboards which were always closed. A heavy dampness reminded one of autumn fields, All Souls' Day and the scent of incense in cool chapels. On the walls hung portraits of Frau Zipper's parents and grandparents. Old Zipper possessed no pictures of his forebears, as he came from a 'simple' family which had never had portraits of its members painted. He himself, however, seemed to wish to become the founder of a line worthy of respect. He often had his photograph taken, and all these pictures were enlarged. He hung them on the walls of the salon. Here, one could admire Herr Zipper, with hat and stick, on a garden seat, with jasmine background; there, at his writing table, reading a weighty tome. To the right hung the picture of Herr Zipper in the uniform of a sergeant – a pay corps sergeant – in the infantry. To the left, Herr Zipper top-hatted, white gloved, on his return from a wedding or a funeral. Here he was much younger, a bridegroom, holding a bouquet of flowers in a white paper bag. There he was a properly serious father, Arnold as a baby on his knee.

119

Young Zipper was photographed even more often than his father. Arnold as a six-month-old, stark naked, smiling on a bear-skin rug; Arnold as a one-year-old in his mother's arms; Arnold at four in his first long trousers; Arnold at six, with his first school satchel, his slate and its dangling sponge; Arnold at seven with his first school report; Arnold at eight, seated at the feet of his teacher and surrounded by his schoolmates; Arnold in Spanish national costume and as a cyclist; as a small rider in the Hippodrome, and as a driver in a funfair; Arnold on a donkey and on the coachman's box; Arnold at the piano and holding a violin; Arnold with bow and arrow, Arnold with sword; Arnold as a little dragoon and as a little sailor; Arnold at all ages, in all sorts of clothes and in every situation; Arnold, Arnold, Arnold.

Why, I asked, was Arnold's older brother never photographed? He was named Caesar, after a brother of his mother who had died early. It seemed that this name had proved a burden to the boy, had set him tasks for which he was not born. He had either to be a genius or a scoundrel. With a name like that, who could ever satisfy his parents?

And, indeed, he afforded them no satisfaction, at least not his father. Caesar was seldom seen at home. His life was on the streets: one found him outside the entrance to Cavalli's Circus, outside suburban cinemas and in the little lane where every house was a brothel. And he was all of fourteen. I can clearly remember his red, uncouth face, on which the features had been roughly and provisionally sketched. His shallow forehead was knitted with deep lines, and looked as if it were preoccupied with false worries. I remember the contrast between his disillusioned mouth, the shape of a sad old sickle, and his light green, bestial, madly glittering eyes. At fifteen he was sleeping with all the serving wenches of the neighbourhood, from every corner of his face he was sprouting a black beard, and his eyebrows were growing together over his nose. He 'did not want to learn'. Old Zipper took him away from the grammar school and 'gave him' to the secondary modern. Here he had a fight with a schoolfellow, broke his nose and, when a teacher tried to intervene, gave him a thick ear. Old Zipper took Caesar from the secondary school and placed him in the town school. Here there were several Caesars, and the teachers could cope with thick ears. Caesar Zipper caused no particular problem. He spent two years in each class, but it was no use. When he left school, he could just about read and write.

It was as if Caesar did not belong to the Zipper family. For a start, he was never to be found in the house, except at meal times. He would sit at the end of the table, the door to the kitchen at his back, opposite old Zipper, who would throw filthy looks at his graceless son between courses. Caesar did not react. He stared at his plate, hummed softly, drummed his heels on the floor and his fingers on his chair, knowing that his father's fury was mounting. Indeed, he seemed to enjoy the sound of old Zipper coming to the boil. The latter restrained himself, but now the *Mehlspeise* was approaching, a dish with which old Zipper always found fault; and suddenly he blew up. He flung the salt cellar at Caesar, who had long been expecting it and who, with the practised eye of long experience, caught it and put it down on the table. There was then the sound of a chair being pushed back, and old Zipper rose to his feet. He stood there, stooping, his napkin in his left hand, his right hand behind his back, searching for the back of his chair. For a moment his hand clawed the empty air. I can still see that right hand. It looked like an animal, or some sort of hairy spider blindly reaching for a prey which was not there. It was frightening, that hand, more frightening than the face of the old man, which was too harmless to be frightening even for a moment.

At this instant precisely, Caesar opened the door to the kitchen. One could now hear the simmering of the pots on the stove, catch the aroma of the dishes, and hear Frau Zipper snuffling and clearing her throat. With his left hand on the door handle and his right held out before him as a shield, Caesar stuck out a long, red tongue at his father. This tongue was some-how shameless, naked, as if it had been peeled of its skin. It stuck out towards his father like a wound or a flame. At the same time a gloomy rumbling came from Caesar's insides, like a small earthquake. The next moment he was gone.

This scene was repeated several times a week – whenever old Zipper had invited me to a meal. Arnold already knew all its phases, and no longer took the least interest. It seemed, indeed, that he took a certain pleasure in letting it pass him by. Now and again I saw him trying to suppress a mischievous smile, but revealing it during this brief, wordless scene, accompanied only by dreadful gestures and inhuman sounds as father and son raged at one another. I cannot now recall a single occasion on which Caesar or old Zipper finished their *Mehlspeise*. There were always some ugly remains on their plates. Wreckage left by a storm.

But, just as sunshine follows a storm, so did old Zipper begin to make jokes as soon as his misbegotten son was out of sight. The ruins of the interrupted meal still lay before him. He seemed not to see them. He was thinking already about the afternoon and what we might do during the rest of the day. Had we finished our homework? Had we seen the new merry-go-round, which some Italian had put up in the last few weeks? One more, among so many. Did we know that Andreas's marionettes were putting on a new show today? Had we read in the paper that this year the summer holidays would not start, as they usually did, at the end of June, but in the middle of the month?

For, as I mentioned before, old Zipper's preoccupations were of this sort. Now and then he would go to the clothes cupboard, open it slowly, as if it were an altar, and extract his violin from its black case, which looked like a coffin. Within it, along with the violin, were buried Zipper's youth and hopes. For old Zipper had at one time wished to be a musician. It was said that he had nearly become one. He had, as he used to say, 'an uncanny sense of pitch', and, without instruction, without notes, without any basic training, he had, one fine day, simply begun to play, 'inspired by some spirit'. In the days immediately following, he played everything he heard. He played minuets and waltzes. He went to 'all the latest operettas' and next day would play all the hits 'by ear'. Nowadays he could only play one piece, namely '*Weisst du Mutter!*', a song which did not make him the least bit sad, but which reduced me to tears. The more entranced, nostalgic and remote Zipper's expression became, the merrier were his spirits. He would draw out his notes into the unfathomable, would draw them out like elastic, and his fiddle would lament and howl and jibber, whether or not this was called for, and whenever the spirit moved him he would insert a tremolo. It made my hair stand on end, but Zipper's father would reveal his good mood by the merry way in which he would keep time with his foot and by the contented pauses he would insert, which were not in the score, during which he would glance round with the gratified air of an artist acknowledging applause so distant as to be audible only to himself.

In any case, it was music which old Zipper honoured above all the arts, and, indeed, above all the spiritual forms and manifestations of life. For him it took the place of God, whom he denied. It took, perhaps, the place of love, of which he was deprived, and of luck, which had escaped him. Small wonder that he had wished to make a musician out of at least one of his sons. It was with a certain expectation that he had admitted to himself that Caesar was a slow, reluctant learner with an aversion to books, and therefore had 'a poor head'. Aha, thought old Zipper, he will make a musician! The name, Caesar Zipper, might have been made for an artist. Caesar a virtuoso, Arnold an academic! But it turned out that Caesar was not capable of progress in music, either, and after three years of expensive study with the best teacher in town he could barely scratch out his scales. 'Not so much as a waltz can he play!' grumbled old Zipper. 'Even if we can't make an artist out of him, and one has to admit that not everybody is capable of it, he should at least be able to play in company if people feel like dancing. A young man should make himself popular and agreeable!' But by no means did Caesar make himself popular.

One day old Zipper came home an hour earlier than usual from his morning constitutional. What had happened? It was one of the merriest days of spring, Easter was approaching, his brother was expected from Brazil, and the entire Zipper household was in that state of happy excitement which is induced by unforeseen expenditure, a laundrywoman in the house and the expectation of a stranger. The sun was shining and the sparrows were chirruping. Old Zipper, however, strode relentlessly and with bowed head through one room after another. What had happened?

As he was out walking he had met Caesar's music professor. He had learned that his miserable son had not been to his 'lecture' for months; that he had probably squandered the fees which were regularly handed over to him. When Caesar returned home, unsuspecting, his father grabbed the violin from his hands, raised it and smashed it down on his thick skull without a word.

Old Zipper carefully picked up the remains of the violin

from the floor, tied them up with some strong string and placed them in a sack.

'Until my dying day,' he swore, 'I shall keep this broken violin.' It lay in the fire-proof chest made by Eisner & Co, alongside the insurance policy and the marriage lines.

3

Thinking about old Zipper today, I am astonished that at the time I did not notice his great sorrow. He was never himself conscious of it. There was something of the tragic clown about him. But I found him funny, as children always find clowns funny. Old Zipper with his thin, light, tea-coloured nautical beard surrounding his wide, round face, a superfluous luxury, like a frame round an indifferent picture. Old Zipper with his brown, good-humoured, serious eyes; old Zipper with his eternal round, stiff hat, which he would put on if he went to an open window and if he went a step out of the house to buy a newspaper; old Zipper with his black stick made of 'genuine mahogany', this same old Zipper who, today, whenever my memory calls him back, fills me with nostalgia. He makes me sad now, as I describe him. He had a great deal of bother in his life, and probably no pain. It is for this very reason he is so sad, as sad as a room which has been emptied, as sad as a sundial in shadow, as sad as a stripped railway coach standing on a rusty line.

There was, however, one person to whom he, the gentle one, the harmless one, caused great pain, surely without knowing it. There was Frau Zipper.

They did not suit each other; no, they did not suit each other. But, in the way of things, one never thought about their not suiting each other. This is the usual way of it when we look at older married couples. They present a *fait accompli*, and there can no longer be any doubt about their common interests. They have children, grown-up children. Nothing remains of the arguments which, in the early days of their marriage, they bore like weapons into battle against each other. Both have blunted their cutting edge and exhausted their ammunition. They are two old enemies who, for lack of weapons, have called a truce, which almost looks like an alliance. And one sees no more of their old enmity.

But, at moments of which onlookers are unaware, they use their last remaining weapons against each other, or they use other weapons, the weapons of peace, in their household warfare. They still retain, from the days when their enmity was young, ways of showing hatred which are not yet used up: a smile which strikes home exactly where the other is most sensitive; a phrase recalling a desolate scene long past which, brought again to the surface, reopens old scars; a way of looking at each other which can freeze both; sudden movements which reawaken clouded, dormant enmity, just as a flare fired in wartime above a dark area will illuminate it in all its horror.

So it was with the marriage of the two Zippers. Frau Zipper's appearance will always remain in my memory. She lay behind a moist veil. It was as though her tears, ever ready for shedding, already lay over her eyes. She wore long blue aprons, which made her look like a second-class nurse. She moved through life in soft slippers. She never raised her voice. She often sighed and blew her nose. When she raised her handkerchief to her face, one saw her hard, dry hands, the fingers of which were disproportionately strong, as if artificially grafted onto a hand too weak for them. When, on special occasions, she put on her black spangled dress, she looked even yellower than usual, and somehow frozen, as if she had just been taken out of an icebox. She seemed stiff – not out of pride, but out of resignation, powerlessness, unhappiness and regret – even as she sat on her chair. She combed her thin, colourless hair over her broad, high forehead, a sort of compulsive beautification, a measure taken against her own will, as if someone had done her hair while she lay in a deep trance and she hadn't looked in her mirror. Only Frau Zipper's mouth, now drooping and morose, betrayed – on the all too rare occasions when she smiled – a long since faded charm, a vanished beauty, a fullness, and, for a fraction of a second, a soft dimple, no longer a dimple but rather the ghost of one, would appear in her chin. Her smile, her rare smile, was like a faint memorial to her dead youth. Within her pale, moist eyes flickered a faint and distant light, soon extinguished again, like the blinking of a distant lighthouse.

She never smiled in the presence of her husband. She never shared his little jokes, never joined in any conversation which he might try to begin. She answered his questions with a yes or a no. How she must have hated him; despised him, even! He might have sensed the hatred behind her silence, as one senses ice under a covering of snow. She irritated him. Because he was not clever, he began to despise her. Whenever Caesar disappeared after a row, she would come out of the kitchen with a sigh. Old Zipper would assume a falsely cheerful tone of voice: 'Has your dear son given any indication of where he is going?' The Zippers had a housemaid, but the old man 'wanted to see no strange faces at table'. Frau Zipper had, therefore, to bring the dishes to the table from the kitchen door herself. When she placed the soup tureen in the middle of the table, old Zipper would say: 'A little nearer, if you will, Madame. Let us not play at Versailles!' Sometimes he would say: 'This table napkin is at least two weeks old! Someone else must have used it! There are traces of egg here, and I do not eat eggs. Haven't for years!'

On days when I was invited, he seemed to attach special importance to starting a conversation. He tried to break his wife's silence at any price. He even forced himself to say something friendly to her. But his good humour slid off her like a drop of oil from a frozen glass. When Caesar or Arnold made a spot on their clothes, did not pay attention, spilt a glass of water, old Zipper would say to his wife: 'Look at that now, how your children are behaving again.' For ten years or so he had taken tea after every meal. It had to be a special canister of tea, not too full, so that Zipper could hold it by the upper rim without burning his fingers. If, however, the canister was not quite full enough, he would wittily ask: 'And what is the price of a *full* one, Madame?' If the tea was too clear, he would send it back to go on steeping. If it was too dark, he would ask for warm water. He was served it in a metal jug, the handle of which was so hot that he had to grip it through a handkerchief, and although he knew, or must in any case have learned from experience, that the handle was impossible to hold, he would still always reach his bare fingers towards it, then rear back in alarm, shake his hand in the air like some white bird, and glare at his wife in the reproachful manner one uses towards someone who has trodden on one's corns. Old Zipper never missed a chance to enlarge on the subject of tea, its preparation, its sundry variations, its health-giving properties and the dangers inherent in it. I myself heard at least sixteen times how he once had tea poisoning. 'It was, however,' he concluded, 'not anything like this sort of tea.' And with that he would look at his wife.

When I recall Frau Zipper, I realise that she lived in a kind of haze, a dim, grey, religious light, suitable for martyrs who patiently suffer pain and sorrow for ludicrous ends and for ludicrous reasons. I cannot say if she loved her children. Perhaps she was indifferent to them, or hated them as she did their father. She seemed to exist for pain rather than for love. As far as the children were concerned, Arnold came to love his mother late. To begin with he attached himself more to his father, who, indeed, gave him more fun. Old Zipper had taken the whole of their education on himself, although he often used to call his sons *her* children. They were sons, and he had resolved to make 'real people' out of them.

He began with 'training for manliness'. Spartan methods impressed him, but the Athenian no less. He only knew of Sparta and Athens what, as a self-taught man, had come under his nose. History in general he knew from anecdotes, the world from illustrated encyclopedias, and life from the correspondence columns of the newspapers. What he did not know he looked up in the encyclopedia or the Wednesday supplements. Many questions occupied his mind. He was interested in the distance between the earth and the moon, between the moon and the sun, between the sun and Mars. He was interested in the Milky Way, the burning of Moscow, the Crimean War, the last epidemic of cholera in Vienna, a system for winning money at Monte Carlo, the dangerous properties of flies, the origin of sunburn, the height of the Himalayas, the first aeroplane, the private life of Count Zeppelin, the first performance of *Die Räuber* and the last Indians of Bolivia. He had the eternally unquenched thirst for knowledge of the simple man who has worked his way up the hard way and suffers from the delusion that knowledge is education, that education gives power and that power brings success. He swore by hygiene. He plunged his children into cold water every day. When they were three, he bought them little bicycles. Caesar was already independent by the time he was eight, but Arnold went on acquiring bigger and bigger bicycles. He was given roller-skates, ice-skates, snowshoes, sleds and skis, tennis rackets and duelling swords. At five, he learned to dance. He learned national dances. He danced the *Mazurka*, the *Krakowiak*, the *Kasatschok*, the *Csardas*, and he learned to click castanets. Old Zipper allowed him to appear as a dancer at a charity show. The old man sat in the front row. Half the audience had free tickets. He dragged in distant relatives and indifferent acquaintances. He had Arnold photographed on stage. He came out himself to take a bow, five minutes after he had been clapping.

He took Arnold to the Hippodrome every Sunday and had him taught riding. He employed a 'teacher of dramatic art'. Arnold learned to declaim. He frequently had to recite verses to his father. The old man had odd literary tastes. He loved one poem by Rudolf Baumbach: '*Die Reise ins Paradies*'. Although he despised the Kaiser, he enjoyed hearing a poem by a contemporary lyricist which had as its theme the Kaiser's birthday. Each verse dealt with one hour of the day, and the work the monarch accomplished in it. Old Zipper loved '*An der Quelle sass der Knabe*', '*Habe nun, ach, Philosophie*', '*Der Turner, der schaut zu Mitten der Nacht*', '*Durch diese hohle Gasse muss er Kommen*', '*Der Gott, der Eisen wachsen liess*', and '*Die Lorelei*'. Arnold recited all of these 'fluently', as old Zipper put it.

But if Arnold ever got stuck, old Zipper would clasp his hands to his brow and ask: 'What is going to become of you?' The same question was asked if Arnold fell from his bicycle or his horse. What was to become of him? According to his father's wishes, anything was possible: Arnold might become a circus artist and an actor; a professor and a poet; a researcher and a horseman; a diplomat and a magician; an adventurer and composer; a Don Juan and a musician; an adventurer and a prime minister. Arnold could become anything; anything that old Zipper had *not* become.

4

Why was it that old Zipper had amounted to nothing – or at least had amounted to nothing in his own estimation? Because he had been forced to devote the greater part of the energy which God had bestowed on him to making a bourgeois out of his proletarian self. For that is the way of the small man. When Zipper, the carpenter's son, was young, he was supposed to become a carpenter, too. He became an apprentice. He made oak tables, cupboards, cradles, chests and coffins. In the end he came to study under a great cabinetmaker in Vienna.

In small towns it seems as if one were destined from birth for a certain trade, profession or business. One is a municipal policeman, another a sexton. One is a clock maker, another deals in food. One becomes a rich merchant, one a poor glazier. But the father of the rich man was already rich, and so was his grandfather. The oldest inhabitant cannot remember any forebear having been poor. The son of a carpenter never becomes a sexton. The son of a delicatessen owner never becomes a floor walker. Zipper, the son of a carpenter, would have remained a carpenter but for his coming to the great city.

He did not confine himself entirely to his trade. He used

some of his energy to cross the frontiers which had circumscribed his life. The spirit of enterprise was in his blood. He was also a bit fickle. He no longer worked in a simple shop with three companions, as he had at home with his father, but in a big coffin factory with three hundred workmen, most of whom weren't carpenters.

Each day, precisely seventy coffins were turned out. Where a lot of people live, a lot of people die. It was a depressing business. At first Zipper was constantly preoccupied with death.

He changed his trade, but stayed with wood, and apprenticed himself to an instrument maker. He learned to build the various parts of a violin. It was this opportunity which revealed to him his talent for music. He did not intend it to be long before he could make a complete violin. He prayed for a stroke of luck, particularly since he had fallen in love with a girl whose parents, the owners of a prosperous delicatessen business, would only marry their daughter to a man of means. He took tickets in the lottery and won, whereupon he visited the parents of his beloved and spoke of opening a music shop. He became engaged. A small music shop would not suit him, he wanted to start with a big one. That required more money than he had won. Because he believed in his luck and felt like an adventure or two, he took a train to Monte Carlo. And it was there that those unusual circumstances occurred which led to the acquisition of his chronometer.

He lost the greater part of his money, came back, and married. There was not enough left for even a small music shop. Through the good offices of his father-in-law he became a traveller for a paper firm. How far that was from working with oak! All day long he had to call on big firms in the city centre to collect orders for printing. In the meantime his young wife sat in a small delicatessen selling herrings on credit. After Zipper had 'worked his way in', as they say, his wife gave up the herrings. One could never grow rich in the paper business but one could live a long time. Gradually Zipper developed a liking for his trade. It was not hard work. It enabled him to amble slowly about the liveliest streets of the city, to talk to the directors of the biggest businesses, to take opportunities here and there of learning things he wanted to know about. He made contacts to which he attached great importance. Theatre cashiers, variety agents, circus directors swam into ever nearer orbit. At the right moment he would make these people small presents; visiting cards, for instance. Where other people had to pay, he was let in free. Where others had to wait, he would come first. And even when one could go in without waiting, it pleased him to behave as if only he had this privilege.

He adapted his clothes to his profession. It seemed as if he had been born with a delicate taste in his choice of material for his suits, his shirts and his ties. He felt that he owed it to his career to cast his eye from time to time over the fashion magazines. He was determined to be a success. And yet no great riches could be expected from a humdrum paper business. So Zipper, fortified for his business calls by the elegance of his attire, would propose 'projects' to various influential people. His proposals were concerned with the improvement of the trams' braking system, the development of tourism, or the reorganisation of the advertising business. He had many bright ideas. He was always pregnant with plans. Gradually, since none of them caught on, he grew sad, like a gardener who has sowed unfertile seed and who sees summer and autumn pass by without yielding a harvest. He paid less and less attention to his finances. He had various methods of appearing more elegant than he could really afford. He would wear white ties with a black suit. He could look like a gentleman rider, a flunkey, a Sunday fisherman, a sea captain setting foot ashore after long years afloat, or a circus manager, and God knows who else. As his hair began to grow thin, he discovered and blended all sorts of tonics in order to preserve it. With a combination of turpentine, quinine, sulphur and salt he created a hair ointment which he used successfully himself, and the secret of which he sold to a hairdresser – for an undertaking to cut his hair once a month for two years. For this was not a matter of necessity to old Zipper, but rather an opportunity to differentiate himself, even in the matter of haircuts and shaving, from other mortals, who paid their barbers cash.

It was his ambition to have 'contacts'. On the whole, he succeeded in winning the favour of those people whom one generally least needs in life. Since he was convinced that one must have friendly connections, he wasted a lot of time – which in any case he always had in abundance – cultivating them. He knew the district inspectors of the police and one or two people from the fire service. He was on greeting terms with customs officers, magistrates' secretaries, clerks to the justices, men who collected taxes, solicitors, notaries. He even knew the public executioner. He boasted of his ability to attend executions, but never actually did so – I suspect that his soft heart would not allow him to go. Nevertheless, at accidents, fires, popular assemblies, arrests, demonstrations, processions, official celebrations and other occasions, he always managed to turn up where it was forbidden to go. He, who thought nothing of the Kaiser and was given to making derogatory jokes at his expense in the coffee houses, would march alongside the torch-bearers and the veterans' band on the eve of the Kaiser's birthday.

When some important person was being buried, his scepticism did not deter him from sitting in the same pew as the chief mourners. Every summer, when the Kaiser travelled to Ischl, old Zipper would be found among the generals and mayors, almost next to the stationmaster – whom he knew – on the platform. Long after his chronic varicose veins prevented him from taking part in manoeuvres, he would go to the villages in which they were taking place. He knew all about the movements of troops. Thanks to a contact with one of the porters at the Reichstag, he had a seat next to the journalists' box when the House was sitting. He attended all the important trials and had cards of admission for his entourage.

Unfortunately, his business affairs went from bad to worse. For he paid less attention to the customers who gave him business and a chance to earn money than he did to those who, in exchange for small favours, gave him small perquisites. Others he would give presents and shower with printing samples in vain: 'One must give tit for tat,' he would say. Business went downhill. His wife owed money, the piano was only half paid for, the instalments on the encyclopedia, and on the collected works of Darwin, Häckel and Schiller, remained in abeyance. The collector came and threatened seizure. But Zipper only smiled: seizure? Was there in the whole area one single bailiff who would impound him?

5

One evening in summer, at nine o'clock, just after dinner, about the time when the householders of the neighbourhood were leaving their houses (the women without hats, the children holding the women's hands, their dogs off the lead and the men without jackets) to go and stroll in the nearest park or along the quays, Zipper suddenly said to his wife: 'I've let the salon.'

That evening the Zipper family did not go for its airing. Everyone in the room – including me who had dropped by to pick up Arnold – thought old Zipper had gone off his head. Frau Zipper stood up and moved to the back of her chair, as if behind a fortification, to escape an attack. As she saw that her husband was still sitting quietly, she stayed where she was without moving. She looked him in the eye, seeming to have grasped the situation quicker than any of us. All at once she began to nod her head, as if she were confirming something she had thought of, confirming a question which had been put to her by someone invisible, and inaudible except to herself. Yes, yes, yes, yes, her poor head kept saying, and her hard, bony hands lay motionless on the back of her armchair. Yes, yes, yes, yes, nodded her head, and nothing else in the room stirred. Arnold sat quietly, Caesar had already gone out, I lurked in the corner of a sofa, and at the head of the table sat old Zipper, while facing him, stood his wife, nodding her head.

'Why are you nodding like that?' asked Zipper. She did not answer, at least her mouth did not answer, but her pale, moist eye did, and let fall a tear. I remember how it gleamed, that tear, on her yellow face.

'My friend, Secretary Wandl,' Zipper began, 'is separating from his wife. That is to say, I mean, only from bed and board. He's looking for somewhere to stay. Where is he to go?

'"Come and stay with me," I say to him, "I have a salon free, though I can't give you a bed, but by now I should think you'll be happy not to have to look at a bed, what?" At which, of course, he laughs. "As for the price . . ."'

'Yes. What is he paying?' interrupted Frau Zipper. It was the first time I had heard Frau Zipper interrupt her husband. She was thinking, poor woman, of the unpaid bills, and was already consoled for the misfortune her husband had just announced. She already saw its other side, and it began to look like hope.

Zipper then said: 'Naturally we haven't discussed the price.' At the time I failed to take in that 'naturally'. Why was it so natural for Zipper not to speak of the price? Ah, what a noble fellow old Zipper was!

At this point the second tear fell from Frau Zipper's eye. It emerged still and shining, rolled quietly and slowly in the silence, and was lost at her lips.

The evening began. Frau Zipper removed herself to the kitchen, Arnold and I worked on a mathematical problem, Herr Zipper read the newspaper. The old clock, which hung in the leased salon, struck the hours, the window was open, one heard the voices of people talking, and from time to time a dog barked, a child cried, a bluebottle buzzed round the lamp. Everything was just so. It might have been an ordinary evening. But there was something more: the breath of a stranger; the wingbeat of an unknown oath; the inaudible signal of a decision. We were all as shattered as if we had just learned that the world was coming to an end that night. What was it that seemed to me so dreadful about the Zippers having let their salon? Was it because I had so often played in that cool, musty room? Had I grown fond of it? Was I losing a tiny bit of my homeland? Was I seeing the disappearance of that narrow bar of sunlight, that pillar of dust between the table and the window? Was I thinking nostalgically of the blue glass set?

It was as if someone had died. Old Zipper rustled the paper – and each time he turned a page it made me jump. Arnold was drawing like an automaton, taking in nothing. We wanted to laugh, but could not. All at once we catch each other's eye, and lower our heads again over our exercise books. From the kitchen comes sobbing. Frau Zipper is probably crying. Arnold goes out, and comes back after a couple of minutes. He says nothing. 'Where have you been?' asks Herr Zipper. 'Outside!' says Arnold.

Finally, Herr Zipper stood up, walked up and down the room a couple of times with his hands behind his back, sat down again, folded up the paper, ran the flat of his hand across it so as to iron it out, looked at his chronometer and said: 'It is seventeen minutes past eleven.'

Upon which I went home.

6

Secretary Wandl moved into the salon. Everything was left just as it had been before. The door from the hall to the salon, formerly opened only at Easter, on the occasion of the visit of Zipper's brother from Brazil, was left open. The piano remained. When Secretary Wandl wasn't at home, Arnold had to practise. Secretary Wandl was a good-humoured man. Although no one had demanded it of him, he paid a respectable rent. Frau Zipper paid for the encyclopedia, Darwin, Schiller, Häckel and the rest, for three months. There was Emmenthaler again every evening, salami and beer. After many years, Zipper went again to the coffee house in the afternoons.

It was a noisy coffee house, where most of the guests played cards. Cigar and cigarette smoke hung coldly above their heads, cold, heavy, solid, in spirals, lumps and blocks. The men sat in shirt-sleeves, the waiters stood behind them, watching them play. Cards were shuffled with magical speed. They were thrown onto the table and clattered, as if they had fallen in water. The players called each other names, in a bewildering sort of foreign bad language. It sounded as if they were quarrelling violently, but in fact they were laughing. Chalk ran squeaking over dry slates. Damp sponges lay in saucers, odd-looking creatures. The soft click of billiard balls drifted across from the far end of the saloon.

The room was half-dark. It was the half-light of a grotto, of a conspirators' den, of a masonic hall. It stimulated my imagination. When one stepped out of the coffee house and into the bright sunshine it was as if one had been woken in the middle of a dream. Sitting inside, time had ceased to exist. It is true that a clock hung over the cash desk. It even ticked, and every evening it was wound up by Franz, the head waiter, but it had no hands. What could be more frightful than that clock? It went and went and in its hidden workings time kept its steady pace, but one did not see it. One knew only that the hours were passing, but how many, one never knew. Still, the people sitting there kept looking towards the clock, imagining perhaps that then they would know the time. They could hear the tick, and this clearly comforted them.

There Zipper sat and played cards every afternoon from three to six. He played and lost. He didn't lose a lot of money, but enough to start him buying cheaper cigars and, finally, a pipe and the cheapest tobacco. 'A pipe,' he declared at the time, 'is much healthier than a cigar, not to mention a cigarette. Above all, one can see what one is smoking. Some people find the smell disagreeable,' he added, if his wife was at table. Occasionally he would bring a cigar home, a *Trabuko*: perhaps someone had made him a present of it. It lay in his cigar case, alone and lonely, and the case itself was withered and faded, with drooping cheeks. And the cigar would still be wrapped in a piece of newspaper. Zipper smoked it in the evening. He would take three puffs, look at it, take another puff, set it down, turn it round, look at it from all sides as if he were searching for some wound, put it back in his mouth and fall silent. He would carefully put the butt into his old yellow amber holder and smoke it until it was reduced to a most miserable specimen. He would push this out with a pencil, separate it from the ash, crumble it and shake it into his tobacco pouch.

Things went from bad to worse for poor old Zipper. But the lower his income the greater his social honours.

He already belonged to three charitable associations and several social clubs, and in each one of them he held some position. He was Honorary Treasurer here, Chairman or Vice-President or Secretary there. He had to 'sacrifice', as he put it, a couple of nights each month for meetings, celebrations, annual reports. The older, the shabbier, the more colourless his black suit became, the greyer and dirtier his white tie, the more often he put on formal dress.

Sometimes he had his big days, when he had to make a speech. Two weeks ahead of time he would prepare his speech, and for two weeks he would learn it by heart. The same turns of phrase would appear in every speech, but old Zipper was so firmly convinced that he had set down particularly original thoughts that he was afraid he would forget them. He would pace back and forth in the room in which they were all sitting, reciting his lines loudly, penetratingly and solemnly. Frau Zipper had to rehearse him. Although she had long had the discourse by heart herself, she held the manuscript in her hand and followed every letter with her finger. 'Pause!' she would say, whenever Zipper hurried from one train of thought to the next.

'My honoured audience!' each speech began. And on each occasion Zipper memorised this form of address as well. By now we all had the speech by heart, except Caesar, whose head was proof against all impressions. There were times when, quite of its own accord and despite my attempts to resist it, the speech would unwind inside my brain like some unending thread from a spool.

Frau Zipper and Arnold went to Zipper's big evenings, and sometimes he took me along too. We would sit in the social room of some coffee house, in the basement, and from afar we would hear the clink of cups, the buzz of the guests' conversation, a bar or two of music from the merry world above. Each time the door was opened these rich sounds would roar with full force into that deep room. It was as if one blocked one's ears in the middle of a busy street, then freed them momentarily, then blocked them again. We sensed that, up above, lovely, lively, important events were taking place. Down here, however, sat Frau Zipper, pale in black spangles, with stout gentlemen and stout ladies all about her. Arnold stood in the background of the room, rather pale and tremulous, and on the podium, harshly lighted, stood Herr Zipper, top hat in hand and the script of his speech inside the top hat. He still had not mastered it. Frau Zipper whispered it soundlessly, every word, before her husband uttered it.

She whispered and nodded.

7

After matriculation – for alphabetical reasons Zipper was presented on the last day – old Zipper had a private talk with his son: 'I myself have never studied, as you are aware. Nevertheless I have become a man. I would have studied, though, if unfavourable circumstances had not prevented me. I can't allow you enough to live like a wealthy young man. But you won't starve, and you can study what you like. I recommend you to take law. In any case, get your doctor's degree. Personally, I care nothing for titles and visible honours. But the world has not yet progressed that far.'

So Arnold Zipper became a lawyer. I was studying philosophy. But we would still meet now and again during the week and, just as before, I would often eat at the Zippers'. The old man's affection for me remained unchanged. Nothing occurred in the Zipper household which I did not learn about within twenty-four hours.

One Sunday, a hot summer's day, the Crown Prince was shot in Sarajevo.

Frau Zipper was inconsolable. One might have thought that it was her brother who had been shot. Herr Zipper, on the other hand, found here a brilliant opportunity to exhibit his rebellious attitudes. As his wife was reading the details in the paper, her handkerchief at one eye, her lorgnette at the other, Zipper said: 'One should only speak well of the dead. The Crown Prince was a swine. But perhaps he would have been less awful if it hadn't been for his wife. Two years ago she had a suit made to measure for her younger son at Weinhorn's. The cutter went out to them a dozen times if he went out once. When the suit is ready the cutter takes it out personally, whereupon that Sophie says: "You must take this back, I specifically ordered shorts, I hate children in long trousers!" And nothing! Not a red kreuzer of a tip! That's what these people are like! The Serbs can fry in their own fat. The Hungarian landowners are afraid the price of their pigs will fall. Rag, tag and bobtail, the lot of them! When I was with the Eighty-fourth he came to the manoeuvres on one occasion. A swine! Evil shone out of his eyes!'

'The poor Emperor!' lamented Frau Zipper.

'The Emperor will be delighted that the fellow's dead!'

'Ssh!' said Frau Zipper. 'Don't talk so loudly.'

'I'm not afraid. I speak my mind to everyone!'

Zipper's mind changed, however, during the following days, when the demonstrations began. He himself paraded before the Serbian Embassy. He came home and held forth: 'We'll show them a thing or two! The Crown Prince was a swine, but what's that to do with the Serbs? We would have dealt with him ourselves. They'll see now that we're not to be messed about with. The police are really splendid! They draw their truncheons and in no time everyone's blown away. The whole square cleaned up in five minutes. It was Inspector Hawerda on duty today. "You people did a good job today!" I told him. Nice fellow, Inspector Hawerda. A bit of a sabre-rattler, but at bottom that's what the people want. "Duty's duty!" said Hawerda. One has to agree.'

In the end Zipper was disappointed that we didn't immediately march on Serbia. Of all the people I knew at that time, he was the only one not surprised by mobilisation: 'I've said all along that it can't be solved without war.'

And Zipper, Zipper, Zipper the revolutionary, said to his wife: 'Unpack my uniform, you can never tell. Varicose veins are of no importance in wartime. I'm an old soldier and, whatever the Emperor may be, I've taken the oath.'

Perhaps Zipper would have been against the war had his wife's viewpoint not altered. Her patriotism ended on the day the first men reported.

'Where there's a will, there's always a way to settle things amicably,' said Frau Zipper.

'Don't you shove your oar into world politics,' shouted the old man. 'Arnold, you'll volunteer tomorrow!'

Then, for the first time, I saw Frau Zipper spring to her feet. For the first time I heard her hiss. She stood up, facing her husband. She picked up the chair. She must at that moment have had the strength of a thousand mothers.

'No!' she cried. 'As long as I live no son of mine will volunteer. Not Arnold, not Caesar. Go off to the war on your own. I don't need you! Go, go off to your Emperor! You, you!'

She tore her hair. For the first time I saw the blood rise to her cheeks. She became beautiful. For the first time in twenty years she was beautiful.

Zipper fell silent. Arnold didn't volunteer and the old man didn't report.

But every time I came across Herr Zipper, he said the same thing: 'We are retreating. We are leaving the Galician plains to the Russians, we are dividing our forces and we shall form two fronts. We'll take the Russians from the north and from the south, do you see, in a pincer movement!' He curved his forefinger and middle finger, spread them and closed them again. 'Meanwhile, we'll take Paris in the west. The French will give up, because if they do hold on longer the Italians will go for them in the south. Then the Kaiser will throw his entire army eastwards. The Tsar will be annihilated in three months. The whole trick today is to envelop the enemy. To envelop him with as few troops as possible! We also have to maintain the correct balance between attack and defence.'

Zipper read every paper every day. He even neglected his cards. In his regular café he was one of the fiercest patriots. Some of the others began to make fun of him. He was furious, and threatened to report them. People drew back. He would not speak to the doubters. He no longer spoke to his wife. He even dropped his little jokes. What a long time it had been since he had allowed his chronometer to strike! What a long time since he had last been to the circus! Nowadays he went only to the theatre. He even neglected his influential friends, and he looked down on police inspectors. What did they do? They stayed at home. They malingered. They kept their hands in their pockets.

Secretary Wandl had been called up, to the Field Post. His rare postcards formed Zipper's evening distraction: 'I'm anxious to know where this Field Post mob is to be found!

That's a really clever system. Only numbers – and the people out there know where everything belongs. And nothing ever goes astray. Organisation is a marvellous thing. The post never worked so well in peacetime!'

The salon stood empty. Frau Zipper hung out a notice: 'Room to let to serious gentleman.' Herr Zipper took the notice down. He brought it into the house, holding it on high between finger and thumb, like some revolting worm, and said: 'My wife hangs this notice out, now of all times. Now she's looking for a serious gentleman. In the first place, all serious gentlemen are under arms, and the cripples are already accommodated. In the second place, Wandl will be coming back. What do we say to him if his room is let? It is remarkably inconsiderate to let a uniformed man's room behind his back!' Herr Zipper threw the notice out of the window.

One day I saw him wearing a black, iron watch-chain. He was also wearing three iron rings. On each of them was engraved: 'I gave gold for iron.'

On one occasion he went with Arnold and me to hammer nails into the 'Iron Man'.

'Here,' he said, 'I'll buy a nail for you!' And he bought me a nail, because I had no money. He himself hammered in no fewer than five.

Every week he turned up with some new badge. He wore the black and yellow cross, the silver cross, and an edelweiss in his hat. One of the welfare societies to which he belonged organised a collection of old clothes and warm woollens for our soldiers for Christmas. Zipper accompanied the truck himself, a big supply truck. He stopped in front of every house, went into the hall with a bell and received the presents. He went round for a whole week, the whole of so-called 'Warm Wool Week'. He came home late every evening. His paper business went into hibernation. From just one patriotic association, under the patronage of the Countess Windisch-grätz, did he receive a monthly contract. He was noticed, too, in the Military-Geographical Institute. It looked for a while as if he might earn something for supplying paper for the project 'Our Heroes in Winter'. But someone else came along and made the deal.

So Zipper earned less and less. In 1915 he finally gave in and allowed the salon to be rented – but only to a member of the armed forces. This was *Oberleutnant* Mauthner from the War Ministry. This officer, an antique dealer in civilian life, paid absolutely no attention to the war. At the War Ministry he was in charge of the office which issued permits of entry. In the evening the *Oberleutnant* changed into mufti and repaired to the coffee house, where he would meet his business friends. As time went by, it was discovered that Zipper's salon merely served the *Oberleutnant* as a *pied-à-terre*. Herr Mauthner actually lived with his wife and children in six rooms outside the city. In Zipper's salon he established Fräulein Mima from the Rathauskaffee. But he did pay well, and after all he was an *Oberleutnant*.

Arnold and I finally ended up in the army. A month later Caesar, too, was in uniform. Arnold could, should and must be an officer. Zipper, therefore, in no way bestirred himself on behalf of Caesar. Caesar lived in barracks, and came home only once, the day before his infantry company left for the front. He got drunk, lay for eighteen hours on the sofa and shouted in his sleep. 'Some hero, your son!' said old Zipper. In the evenings old Zipper came and collected us at the Recruits' School. He would drink a glass of beer with our sergeant. One day – it was a foggy November evening and the light from the streetlamps, reduced by wartime regulations, looked as if it were wrapped in cotton wool – we had been standing waiting for old Zipper outside the school for five minutes. He didn't come. Suddenly a sergeant appeared in front of us, a small sergeant. We saluted. The sergeant laughed. It was old Zipper. He had volunteered.

Oh, how splendid he looked! He wore a special uniform, his gold lace gleamed, his tea-coloured nautical beard had disappeared and only his grizzled little moustache, itself much reduced, remained. In the smart uniform one could see clearly that old Zipper had a paunch and that he waggled his hips as he walked, also that his feet turned out.

He allowed us to salute him a couple of times on the street. We went with him to a tavern and he told us old stories about his regiment. He was now in the Home Guard and, because he understood some Czech, he ended up in the Russian censorship section a few days later. His job was to examine letters addressed to Russian prisoners of war. He couldn't read them, however. He started learning Russian. Meanwhile the letters piled up on his table. He distributed them to his clerks and conscientiously learnt Russian.

He had himself photographed: behind his desk, on which lay the letters he could not read, twenty separate packages of them; with cap, cape and sabre; with Arnold, the recruit; with Arnold and myself; at home with Arnold; in the street with Arnold. All these pictures hung in the salon.

Eventually we set off for the front, and he went with us to the station. He began waving before the train even pulled out. In fact the train was on the wrong platform. There was a lot of shunting back and forth. Each time I thought old Zipper must have gone home, he reappeared. Because he was a sergeant, he could press on into the most distant goods yard, whereas everyone else had already had to leave the main platform. I had never seen old Zipper in such high spirits as then, when we were perhaps going to our death. As our train finally pulled out, he appeared for the last time, a paper in his hand, and ran beside the coach. He shouted after us: 'Victory at Lublin!'

Arnold and I looked at each other, and began eating a sausage.

Two months later Caesar lost his left leg.

Old Zipper informed Arnold of this event, adding: 'He is being given a splendid artificial one.' And his mother had added a line or two. One could see how her hand had trembled. I can clearly recall her handwriting. The characters lay about like bundles of thin webs, over and under each other. 'Keep fit and well!' wrote Frau Zipper.

But Arnold caught a shrapnel wound, was sent home on leave and promoted to lieutenant. What could be lovelier for old Zipper? He had himself photographed as a sergeant, with his son as a lieutenant beside him. Arnold sent me the snapshot. There stood old Zipper, his hand on the lieutenant's shoulder, staring into space. He had grown older. His cheeks hung loosely and one could see the veins on his hand as it rested on his son's shoulder. Arnold wrote that things were not going too badly. His mother was receiving money for all three of them who had joined up. Caesar was being taken care of, since he had lost a leg.

A little later I went on leave. I saw then how Frau Zipper would get up at midnight with a footstool and a half-darned stocking, her spectacles, a saucepan and her marketing basket, to go to the shops and queue till morning for meat and milk. Zipper still addressed his wife in the third person, but he would get up at three to relieve her. As a war casualty, Caesar could have procured any sort of food without having to wait. But he only came home from hospital once a week, on Saturday afternoons, stumped across to the drawer in the sideboard where his mother hid her purse, emptied it and took himself off to the tavern.

He had become gloomy. His shallow forehead seemed even shallower than before, and consisted only of a tiny area knitted with a thousand wrinkles. A sad, stupid smile was always at the corners of his mouth, a hint of complacent apathy, like the beginning of an oath or of the change from man to beast.

He was given an artifical leg which didn't fit, so he threw it away. He broke crutch after crutch. When his mother came to visit him in hospital, he hid in a cupboard. He was sent to the lunatic asylum. He had an outburst of fury, was locked into a padded cell, wept, became gentle, ceased to speak. He began to eat newspaper. The asylums were becoming crowded. There was no more room for him. It was proposed that the Zippers should take him home.

He now seemed to have become completely catatonic. He sat in a velvet-covered armchair which they had brought out of the salon and ate the war news which old Zipper had read.

Once, however, he laid his hands on a paper which his father was intending to read that afternoon. Old Zipper tried to take it away from him, whereupon Caesar lost his torpor. He jumped up, fell down, got up again and laid waste with his stick all the furniture, glass, and mirrors. An ambulance was sent for. Caesar lapsed into delirium and died a few days later.

In that one hour, during which Caesar went mad and Frau Zipper fainted, old Zipper's hair turned white. He buried his son and was suddenly an old man. He began to speak to his wife again, and to call her 'Du'. The letters he sent Arnold at the front rang like cracked bells. His writing was as smooth as ever, with big, round characters, his signature was still enveloped in its old ornamentation, which resembled a big knot, or a butterfly. The phrases with which he began and ended his letters were still the same. Every letter began: 'My deeply loved son!' – every letter ended: 'Nothing else of importance, your loving father.' But the letters were about the bitterness of the times. They gave off a harsh, relentless fog, rising as if from the fields of autumn. These letters smelled worse than death. They were like the life of those who were living the war.

Old Zipper had been awarded a Long-Service Cross. He asked permission to wear civilian clothes off duty. 'I have only one wish,' he once wrote to Arnold, 'and that is to see you once more.'

I thought of the old man from the days of peace, who had climbed towers with us, visited the Lilliputians, watched the fast runner, the travelling circus, the lion people, the women without nether limbs; I thought of old Zipper, who had acquired his watch under unusual circumstances in Monte Carlo, setting its secret chimes to work; I thought of how mice jumped out of matchboxes and how the tablecloth moved in a ghostly manner. I saw how the man we had known was coming to an end. He was changing into someone new, and quite unknown. Was this still our Zipper?

The last time I went on leave I paid him a visit. He was in civilian clothes, it was a Sunday, and I met him at his front door. His moustache was white, his hair was white, he was leaning on his stick with the ivory handle, and his back was stooped. He had shrunk by half a head. He stopped once or twice on the steps, not to catch his breath, as I had thought, but to think. He said very little. When we came to the top step he went into the kitchen and said: 'Fanny, come here!'

Out came Frau Zipper. And so I learned for the first time that her name was Fanny. Her hair was as colourless as ever. Her face was as thin, her hands as hard as ever. But when she smiled the last trace of a dimple had gone from her chin.

In the corner by the window, in the room where we had sat so often when the world had been at peace and the Zippers at war, stood a chair covered in red velvet, which had come from the salon.

'Caesar always used to sit there,' said Zipper, 'those last weeks.' Frau Zipper went back into the kitchen.

'When is this war going to end?' asked Zipper.

'Not yet, I believe,' I said. 'We are waiting for death.'

I went back to the war. And the war was not over. Old Zippers and young Zippers were serving. Millions of Zippers were firing and dying, and hundreds of thousands were losing their reason.

Letters kept coming for Arnold. They were all the same. Arnold wrote home. I always added a line.

Sometimes, as I inspected the pickets, I saw before me the Zippers' room – and it seemed to me to be a room of peace.

8

In spite of everything, the war came to an end one day. The monarchy fell to pieces. We came home.

I hadn't seen Arnold for six months. He'd fallen ill and had been posted to railway station duty. Thanks to various unhelpful circumstances, I didn't come home until December 1919.

By then Arnold was in civilian clothes. It was obvious now that he could no longer take his doctor's degree. He had to find work quickly. The winter of 1919 was awful. It was so damp the snow hardly lasted a day. The wind ripped through the streets like a wet murderer. The streets were dark. Italian officers were wearing warm woollen scarves, puttees, stiff yellow cartridge pouches. They strolled about victoriously, winter's allies, everybody's allies. From America came corned beef and clergymen with Christmas trees for poor children and newly released civilian prisoners. From Russia and from Italy came the returning prisoners. Many who had been waiting for them died and made room for them. The Bourse was busy and the currency became valueless. A million young men were looking for jobs. Among them was Arnold.

Until this time I had only seen Arnold in the shadow of his father and his home. I had only known him as my schoolfellow in the corner of the third bench, who was always half a head shorter than 'the whole class', distinguishable from the others by his freckles, which reminded me of toasted breadcrumbs, who was sometimes industrious and sometimes lazy, like the rest of us, and who recited poems 'fluently', as his father demanded. At that time Arnold had been a student like many others. He loved a girl who wrote to him at the university, his name was often on the blackboard by the porter's lodge, his surname (not many names began with Z). Then he became a soldier. And, like everyone, he concealed his individuality. Perhaps until then he had had none. I saw him grow up, grow older, celebrate birthdays. But I didn't see how he acquired a face. I wasn't aware of ever having studied him closely enough to see him precisely. Eight months previously, I had seen him in a uniform which, like the uniforms of most young officers at that stage of the war, was slightly inconsistent with regulations, inconsistent enough to change the heroic into the coquettish. Because vanity was, in those days – and not for the first time in history – stronger than discipline and careless of death. Arnold, for instance (and this was forbidden to infantry officers), would wear his cap without a badge and tilted to one side of his head. He was not immature enough to be content with his military existence and his rank as an officer; nor did he impart this air of cheeky self-satisfaction to his dress, because he was pleased with his uniform. But he did belong to those men – I noticed it later in many of them – who will 'catch' a fashion just as people with delicate bronchial tubes catch influenza.

I know that Arnold Zipper first really struck me when I met him after the war. Although it was only six months since I had seen him, he seemed so changed in his civilian clothes that I felt I was meeting him again after many years. He was wearing a dark blue suit made of cheap, dyed army material. It was one of those suits one sees in poor districts hanging on poles outside little shops, suits which, when one has put them on, seem to abhor the human frame which, in its turn, withdraws, leaving a vacuum between the body and the material which is meant to clothe but in fact merely covers it. Beneath the movements which Arnold Zipper made in this suit, I could detect the original, more delicate and less disjointed movements of the unclad body. It was as if the movements of the sleeves and the trousers were a fraction of a second behind the actual arms and legs. There thus arose a scarcely perceptible awkwardness in Zipper's conduct – which meant, somehow, that I began to observe him more closely.

A blue and white striped collar which Arnold was wearing with a shirt of the same colours but a different pattern, perhaps in the hope that the striking colours would make one overlook the difference in design, first drew my attention to the dimple in his chin, which often reminded me of his mother and which gave him the expression of a *bon viveur* and a good-hearted fellow. I was struck by his small, white teeth, the teeth of a rodent, which lent his face a merry, almost playful expression when he spoke. When his mouth was closed his face became saturnine. His forehead was smooth and high, giving him an air of frankness and innocence. His glance was light and easy, sliding off its target as harmlessly as a cork fired from a child's popgun. Through these eyes Arnold regarded the world. He knew its surfaces, its smoothness and its roughness, its brightness and its dulness. And he sometimes had the gift of sensing what he couldn't see. On the whole he held his tongue, but he was too careless not to give himself away. He was sensitive, but not attentive enough to avoid hurting people's feelings. By comparison with his father, he seemed to me unremarkable, in fact rather ordinary.

Although he had little money, he didn't live with his parents. He only ate with them. For a long time I didn't know how he made ends meet. In another age his abilities would have earned him a living. In the first months after the war, however, only one of those remarkable combinations of circumstances which we call 'luck', or that extraordinary power which drives the genius and the brute forward like a tank, could help. Arnold Zipper was no genius, nor was he a brute. On the contrary, he was delicate, kind-hearted, gifted and shy.

From December to March he survived by disposing of surplus army material, as I was soon to discover. He operated between buyers and sellers. This was then the custom of the country: the 'disarmed' officers, who had no profession, or were unable to exercise it, dealt in military surplus. Zipper was not among the more enterprising ones.

He hated this business. Before entering a coffee house – for it was in the coffee houses that deals were made – he would hesitate a hundred times. Others would go in with the victorious cheerfulness of the professional salesman, confident that they would find their prey, talk him over and bend him to their will; a confidence which makes commercial travellers as irresistible as courageous lovers, or generals on the offensive. But Zipper was timid, and as a result he attracted misfortune in the way some people fall sick because they are afraid of infections and of catching cold. Zipper's sensitivity was such that he took any harmless chance look from a waiter as a reproach. He would wait in the card room of the café until the buyer rose from his game. How often, however, the buyer spotted Zipper as he came in, signalled him to wait, and then, in the heat of the game, forgot or seemed to forget all about him! For there was also a method of wearing down the vendor, checking whether he was under such pressure that he would wait patiently, or whether he was so independent that he would go away if the buyer didn't make his move quickly enough. Others might come as guests to the coffee house in which they wished to do business – simply sitting down at a table from which they could observe their prey, and ordering a coffee. But Zipper couldn't afford these 'expenses'. His difficulty was that he had to come into a coffee house as if he were looking for a business friend, then wait until the said friend had finished his game, yet at the same time wait in such a way that he would be taken neither as an undesirable, nor as pushy, nor as pitiful. He had to give the impression that at any moment he might order a coffee, and at the same time adopt such a casual air that the waiter would assume that the only reason he didn't order was that he had already had enough and had no wish for more.

It was tiring, standing about, and he couldn't sit down, because if he took a table he would have had to order. For Zipper there was nothing worse than these half and quarter hours he spent waiting in the dim light of the card room, in which the yellow lights were already on although the sunlight came through the front room. (The players required this false evening, just as the frequenters of brothels required drawn jalousies.) Zipper waited. He walked back and forth. He stood and riffled through a newspaper and made as though he had found some announcement which particularly interested him. At the same time he couldn't let the man for whom he was waiting out of his sight. Indeed, he must try from time to time to remind him that he was there. If at last he succeeded and the man he wished to see rose to his feet, his energy, the very energy he needed to persuade the obstinate client to buy, was drained by the wait. If only Arnold had been blessed with the harmless, optimistic pleasure in talking which had distinguished his father! But young Zipper had a duller temperament, a sharper mind and a thinner skin than his father.

If, in spite of everything, Arnold earned enough to be able to go to a coffee house every evening – a different one from his customers – to smoke cigarettes, and sometimes to take a tram out into the country, it was thanks to the fact that many of his old comrades in arms were among his clients. These comrades, merchants by chance, had light fingers, humane hearts and a certain solidarity with Zipper. They gave him his daily bread, as they say. But, when all his acquaintances had done their bit, Zipper had to look for a new line of business.

The Zipper family had nurtured the hope that Arnold could go to Brazil, to old Zipper's brother, who hadn't written since the war. Many had set off on that road without having an uncle in those parts. The fatherland had become so small that the oldest folk, who had never left their own districts, began to long to wander to the most distant parts, to uproot the world around them from their memories, their hearts, their very lives. To Arnold this seemed the only escape. When he searched his heart he was forced to admit that nothing could be more tedious to him than an ordinary, regular job at home. Perhaps he would have to work harder in foreign parts, but at

157

least they were far away. He read a lot of travel books. He had been reading them since his childhood, but never before had he felt the wish to travel. He first felt the desire to go to Brazil when he returned from the war, saw again the house in which he had grown up, the father who had raised him, the mother who had wept over him, sensed the shadow of his brother, who had only become a member of the family after his death. When Arnold saw this country, of which he was a citizen, in which one had to belong to a party, to express an opinion, and to go on serving some 'common weal' which one neither saw nor grasped but only read about in the papers, then for the first time Arnold wanted to set out for Brazil.

He was, however, too sensitive to emigrate in the expectation of receiving assistance from his uncle, as his parents had wished. Of all the stupid rules through which people are led astray, one of the stupidest was Arnold's conviction that 'everyone is his own man!' He had achieved, quite on his own and without assistance, this American ambition to amount to something, to follow the principle of the American millionaire's son, which drives him, at the age of twenty, to begin by selling matches and to trudge all over again the road his father has already put behind him. An unnatural urge, in some ways comparable to that which drives a Jewish civil lawyer to be the first to reach the top of some unclimbed Alpine peak, without the benefit of a guide; or a circus artist to perform his act on top of an aeroplane although it is mortally dangerous even on a trapeze; or a stonemason to work on a skyscraper without a safety harness. Arnold possessed this drive. He wanted to go to Brazil alone, and he dreamed of surprising his father with a cable from on board a steamer. Perhaps, basically, this was an inheritance from old Zipper, this love of causing surprises, a pleasure of the petit bourgeois. In those days there were many agents offering emigration to remote, romantic places. There were young people's clubs which thought of a group journey to Australia as a Sunday excursion, and held that nothing was impossible for them since they had escaped death. Arnold joined one of these clubs. He thought it better to go, since he had been paying his weekly subscription. His life acquired a new purpose. Concealing something was an occupation. But, after a short time, the club treasurer disappeared with all the funds. He was probably the only one to reach Brazil.

In the meantime Zipper's father had already written to his brother. Relations were resumed, as if between states. From old Zipper's Brazilian brother came a registered letter with money. They were to wait, wrote the brother. He was thinking of starting his yearly visits again, as before the war, and he had it in mind to come soon.

9

In the height of summer, old Zipper's brother came from Brazil.

I had never seen him before, because when he came I wasn't invited. The family only saw him once a year, and wanted to have him to themselves. His visit cost money, and they wouldn't let him know that they were short of it. The Zippers could only just feed him, and he must have eaten like ten men, according to the descriptions Arnold gave me. From these I was able to paint myself a wonderful picture of Arnold's uncle. Firstly, he was a farmer; a man, therefore, to stir the imagination. A slave-owner. A man who probably corraled wild horses. A man likely, perhaps, to find a goldmine, if he had not already done so. A man without a jacket or waistcoat, with a wide belt and a big Panama hat. The fact that the brother of that worthy citizen, Zipper, was a farmer, seemed to me even less probable than the story of the unusual circumstances in Monte Carlo.

And yet, so it was. Arnold's uncle was a real farmer from Brazil. This time I was to see him.

He arrived on a hot day, it was in July or August. That afternoon both old and young Zipper went to the station.

On the following day I lunched with the farmer.

He was almost as I had pictured him. I looked in vain at his face for any trace of family resemblance to old Zipper. But he was not at all like a brother, he was like a remarkable story, a story from Brazil. He was about three heads taller than old Zipper. His head was shaven smooth, his neck was so brown and dark that it might have been cooked, and he had a strong red nose and small, light eyes under short, bushy brows. His glance was as quick and sharp as an arrow. His eyes were like bright lights on a dark evening. His chin was remarkably square. Broad and solid, it reminded me of some sort of lectern, or of a flat stone covered with skin. As a matter of fact, the entire man made one think of stone. He stook like a wall, and his silences were mural. He was more human when he drank. He sent Arnold out for a few bottles of wine. He had himself brought a few with him. In the anteroom stood his remarkable trunk. He had only brought one trunk with him. It was an old brown leather hold-all, the top and bottom folding in like an accordion. On the sofa lay his hat – he never took it off in the hall. And it really was a big, broad-brimmed Panama hat. 'Pleased to meet you!' he said in a foreign-sounding German, as he gave me his hand, which was, as I'd expected, huge, warm and dry. He then asked about the war in the tone of voice one uses to ask about the harvest or some interesting event. He had had more important matters to deal with back home; the cattle, the harvest and the men took up a very great deal of time. Had he been rich and carefree he might perhaps have come over to fight on one side or the other. He showed real admiration for Zipper's iron rings. He considered taking back to Brazil an ashtray made out of a shell case which Arnold had brought home. A couple of times a day he would look at the velvet chair in which Caesar had sat. He did not sense that Zipper's heart stood still, he did not see how Zipper's eyes grew big and his look became distant (a look which was wandering in the distant fields of sorrow) when he slapped the chair, turned it about and said indifferently: 'So Caesar lived here, and a chair was all the room he needed. The last time I was here, the whole town couldn't hold him. No wonder he went mad in this chair.'

Each day, when the paper came, the farmer asked: 'Are there any pictures today?' For he believed that our paper would appear with pictures one day and only text on the next, because the photographer had fallen asleep. 'Your Virginias have gone downhill,' he would say as he smoked, and he would stub out an expensive cigar, for the butt of which old Zipper would have been grateful. An uncontrollable desire for pleasure drove him to all the places where there was music or dancing, or to the theatre. For the hours he spent in the house he bought a gramophone, which he promised to leave with the Zippers. After a meal he would lie down on the sofa, even when I was present. I then saw how his eyes would wander round the room, fastening on people and their surroundings, as if he were looking for something whose image he wanted to take with him into sleep. Last of all his look would settle on the red chair, would become drowsy and contented, and his eyelids would close.

I noticed that the farmer used a number of unusual expressions, that in a certain way he had a style of his own. If something pleased him, whether it was a man, a woman, an event or an object, he would say it was 'jolly'. He might say the soup was jolly, that I was jolly – for he seemed to have taken to me – or that the shell-case ashtray was jolly. If something didn't appeal to him he wouldn't say, as I anxiously waited for him to do, that it was 'not jolly', but that it was 'out of the question'. A theatre would be out of the question, meaning that the auditorium displeased him because it had too many pillars, and the stage would be out of the question because the curtain had an old 'painting' on it. He called any picture a 'painting', to distinguish it from a photograph. Moveable furniture, namely chairs and tables, he called 'vehicles'. He called Frau Zipper 'Sister-in-law', and Herr Zipper 'Brother'. He called Arnold 'Zipper Junior'. He said that he could never remember first names and that they were superfluous. He had, for simplicity's sake, given his own sons (he had three) the same name. They were all called William.

'Now, isn't that a remarkable fellow?' said old Zipper of his brother. 'He's full of energy. Neither I nor the other brothers were like that. He went over when he was fourteen. I wanted to follow him, you know, and if Monte Carlo hadn't intervened, I would be a farmer today, like him.'

I thought of the quite unusual circumstances, and looked at old Zipper talking with his toothless, weak, soft mouth which sprayed out his words. I looked at this white-haired, stooped Zipper and compared him to his brother, who was only a year younger than him. The farmer did not belong to this continent, to this *Mittel* Europe where the war had started, where it had burst open like an old boil. Old Zipper would never have made a farmer in Brazil, he was a *Mittel* European burgher.

When the farmer had been there for a week, the Zippers began speaking of Arnold's prospects. Arnold had no wish to be present.

'I don't want my uncle to help me,' he said. 'Haven't you looked at him? A brutal, narrow-minded egoist. If he took me across, he would exploit me worse than a stranger. I hate this blood of ours. I don't want anything to do with this family. I will never go to Brazil with my uncle. I'll make my own way. I certainly won't go under.'

But it never occurred to the farmer to take Arnold with him.

10

It was late at night. One could hear the crickets in the gardens. We came out of the coffee house. We often met there. They closed the place too early. There was a police closing time, which we hated. We came late and drank a *moka*. It seemed to us at the time that we had a lot to say to each other and that it was inhuman to close the coffee houses at all. Even nowadays, long after having grown accustomed to police closing times, I can't explain why, at that time, we felt we could only talk together in a café. Perhaps because we had just come out of the war. However dark, impoverished and gloomy the city might appear, we were returning citizens and felt at home in it after many hundreds of evenings and nights in the trenches, in the mud, in the marshes, in village huts with old newspapers in our hands, after the nights of attacks and barrages. They threw us out, they closed the coffee house, stood the chairs on top of each other, the waiters gathered at the cash desk to settle up. We would slink out, like homeless dogs.

It was a warm summer night. We walked back and forth, each accompanying the other, and when we arrived at one of our front doors we would sense the gloom waiting upstairs in our rooms, our beds, our sleep, our dreams. We would turn back and walk to the other's door. Only when pale morning showed behind the houses would we part, midway. At this hour we felt less nervous of our houses, which we had so longed for during the war and in which we no longer felt at home after our return. We fell asleep easily at dawn, since we had no wish to see how the day began.

On one of those nights Arnold told me what his uncle had said about his prospects: 'Even if you gave me a million, Sister-in-law and Brother, I wouldn't take your son. I have money, he could live with me, he could at least eat. But I wouldn't take him. Brazil is a dangerous country. Anyone who can pull it off there has long since gone there, has long since grown up there. But I wouldn't have a grown-up European on my conscience. If I can help him with a loan, if he wants to set himself up here in this country, I'll help him. But against his word of honour and a signature; for I give no presents of a fortune and I'll spit in the eye of the man who thinks a loan is forever. Ask him, let him say what he wants.'

'Well, did you make up your mind?'

'No,' said Arnold. 'Can I ever make up my mind? Sometimes it seems to me that I could perfectly well become a peasant. Then it seems to me romantic and absurd. Back to nature? Can I go to sleep and wake up with the hens? Can I do without one single evening in the coffee house, talking with you or with someone else? Can I marry and have children who will lead cattle into the meadows?'

'But you'd have to do all those things in Brazil, too!'

'In Brazil, yes. Just as I could sell newspapers in the street in New York, but not here!'

'Why not here?'

'Because people know me. Because it would be comic and I would be a figure of fun.'

I made no effort to persuade Arnold. But I didn't understand why he felt he couldn't sell newspapers here. Why would he have been a figure of fun? No occupation, whatever its nature, is to be laughed at, unless one is already laughable oneself, I wanted to say to him. But I didn't say it. I felt it was pointless. I felt that Arnold, like everybody else, was obeying specific rules when he decided to take an opportunity or to let it go. On that night I was aware of the law of the world. I could hear the swift, precise, inexorable and smooth movement of the wheels which sets in motion the mechanism of Fate. I thought that old Zipper's son was subject to an unknown law, as his father had been and as his descendants would also be. I pictured to myself the evening on which the farmer had taken all hope from the Zippers. A silence must have followed, like the silence which had followed the breaking of the news that the salon had been let. Arnold's parents must have been convinced that they had lived in vain. Their son was to have brought them light and warmth in their old age, and he came to them to eat a bowl of soup.

On the following day I met old Zipper. He was sitting in a park, reading a newspaper through a big magnifying glass, since his spectacles were no longer powerful enough. Sitting there in his shabby black suit, which was almost as green at the shoulders as the foliage which surrounded him. Sitting in the corner of the bench, you might have taken him for a beggar, had it not been that he had acquired a certain notoriety on account of the paper and the magnifying glass. I sat down beside him.

165

'Now', he said, 'Arnold will have told you that my brother wants nothing to do with him. You are the friend of his youth, you know him as well as I do, even better, I should say. Do you think he is capable of going to Brazil on his own? Don't you believe that he is gifted, above average? If only we hadn't had this war! What could Arnold not have achieved? My business was going along all right,' (he had forgotten that the shrinkage of his income was due less to the war than to himself) 'and I would have kept it going for a while longer. My brother said he should become a peasant. My Arnold, a peasant! Why not a carpenter, like my father? I thought our family was moving upwards, not downwards.'

He continued for half an hour in the same vein. Finally he told me 'in confidence' – and he took my hand and swore me to silence – that he himself was looking out for a job for Arnold. He was 'digging out' old contacts. But Arnold mustn't know that his father was 'making preparations'. One day, Arnold would find a splendid career ahead of him!

Old Zipper then went off. His paper was sticking out of his jacket pocket, dappled sunlight played on his back, and not only did he stoop but he was so weak that he jerked from side to side, as if heavy weights were pulling him first to the right, then to the left. He saluted the park gardener, a distinguished personality, one of the personalities with whom he had always considered it advisable to maintain cordial relations. Indeed, the gardener broke off from his work of trimming the edges of the grass, came to the iron railings which separated the flowerbeds from the grass, and leaned on his shovel. Zipper talked with the gardener. The old man was probably pleased because he knew that I could still see him and that this would show me that he was a well-known character. He was the only person, among all those strollers in the park, who was allowed to walk on the grass. This privilege probably filled him with pride, even now, when he was trying to find a job for Arnold.

He knew Councillor Kronauer at the Ministry of Finance. (Who didn't know him? There was no one whom Kronauer hadn't helped at some time or other.) He was one of Zipper's oldest customers. What did the revolution matter to Councillor Kronauer? He was second to none in his knowledge of the law, of Orders in Council, of income tax and corporation tax, of reliefs and supplementaries. He remained at his post and dug himself into it like some great old tree in a park. He dispensed kindness, help, influence. Old Zipper hadn't wasted his time with him. Arnold was given an appointment.

'In an age in which civil servants with ten years' service behind them are dumped on the street, Arnold gets a posting,' said old Zipper. 'Even a republic cannot be governed without real professionals, and the best proof of it is Arnold's case.'

'That's very jolly!' said the farmer. The next day he went off.

They rarely spoke of him in the Zipper household. He had disgraced himself. He had turned Arnold down! Not to take a genius like Arnold with him to Brazil – this betrayed the farmer's lack of education.

'Basically,' old Zipper said about his brother, 'he has never had time to learn anything or to think anything over.' And the farmer was dismissed as a topic of conversation.

Their talk now consisted of praising Arnold. Zipper seemed to have completely forgotten that it was he who had found Arnold his job. They acted as if young Zipper had received a summons from on high to regulate the country's finances.

A month later Arnold started his job.

He was a minor civil servant with a small salary. His father, however, already saw in him the Minister of Finance. Arnold showed none of his father's optimism.

'How can a man who was in the war, and who wasn't a civil servant before it, be expected now to sit at a desk for eight hours a day?' he asked. 'I sit in a room on the fourth floor with two other men; both of them are my father's age. You have no idea how they hate me! One day recently I came into the office in my new pale grey suit. One of them, Herr Kranich, went at once into all the other offices and told everybody how a young man in a pale grey suit had now been taken into the service. Whenever I went out a few of them would be standing whispering in the corridor, watching me. Others would open the doors of their offices as if by accident, take a look and close them again. In the end Kronauer sent for me and told me that, out of respect for the hard times of the civil servants who were fathers of families, I shouldn't wear new suits on duty. Moreover, I should wear the prescribed uniform.

'You can't imagine how that uniform disgusts me. Yet another uniform! Just as I've got rid of the old one! I tried to move my desk a little nearer to the window. Not that you can see much, it gives onto a court and has bars across it, and there are more offices opposite. The court is depressingly clean, it's absolutely forbidden to throw pieces of paper, ashes or cigarettes into it. But the desk of the man who sits by the second window must be level with mine. I went out for five minutes. When I came back, my desk was where it had been before. The two old men had pushed it back. They have soap, nailbrushes and face towels in a cupboard. They wash their hands before they go home. I'm not allowed to wash my hands there. I'm just glad to be out of it, and I go home with dirty hands. As a result of this I leave work before they do. I say: "Good evening!" – they don't answer. I go on my way. From the top of the stairs one of them calls: "Herr Zipper!" – What's up? I'm to collect the key next day from Room 25 on the second floor instead of from the porter, should I arrive early by any chance. Work begins at nine, I arrive at five to. Both of them are there already. I tried once to come in at quarter to nine. The next day they were there at eight-thirty, and at work.

'I have nothing to do with their work. They're not my superiors. But when I'm ready with a report one of them will come over to my desk and say: "Very good, Herr Zipper." They dare not criticise me, but they've discovered a more cunning method: they discourage me by praising me. At times they'll start a general discussion about the youth of today; that every young man thinks, just because he's been in the war, that he's cleverer than his elders. On one occasion I couldn't help saying to them: "It was exactly you people who sent us to war!" And I thought of my father. Do you remember one day when he turned up in uniform in front of the Recruits' Barracks? And speaking of my father: I simply cannot eat at the house any more. He asks a thousand questions. He's always wanting to know if people are satisfied with me. I have to fill him in with the precise details of my day's work. He seems to imagine that I drew up the tax regulations. And do you know what I actually do? Addition and subtraction and division and multiplication, with decimal points.

'It's unbearable! I must look for something else. But when I've finished work I want to get home as fast as possible. There's a tram at six-twelve, and the next one comes at six-twenty. Often one of the old men will say something of no importance very slowly – and when I've finally got out of the building I have to wait eight minutes for the tram. Those eight minutes are longer than the whole day.

'I don't want to even see the street until the day is over. Then I go home and put on my newest suit, my best shoes, my best shirt. Then I play something, just a couple of tunes that have stayed in my mind, and finally it's evening. He comes in while I'm playing, it almost seems as if I call him in. I don't give a damn for my upbringing, and I'm grateful to my father for only one thing, that he helped me to discover music.

'In the evenings I go out into the streets. I'd be ashamed to in the daytime. When the day has been taken up with work, it's spoiled and dirty, and I can do nothing with it. Besides which, I'm as tired as after a retreat, after a three-day march. I'm hungry all day, as if I were living in the open air. It's the hunger of exhaustion. People in advanced old age, lying in bed all day, also feel this kind of hunger.

'Eventually one can adapt oneself to any activity, even a senseless one. The army was senseless, too. But at least one could see a superior officer, and he took the place of sense. One was punished or rewarded every day, every hour. One had an order, and that took the place of a goal. But in the civil service you can't see where an act originates, why it was drawn up, or for whom. I must confess that sometimes a kind of stupid pride takes hold of me. I begin to make particularly elegant letters and figures. I write away for half an hour at something I could do in five minutes. Do you understand that?'

'I do understand,' I said. 'I think the war has corrupted us. Let's admit that we were wrong to return. We know as much as the dead, but we have to pretend to be stupid because by chance we stayed alive. These streets, this administration, the taxes, the mail, the dances, the theatre and illness and the old folks' home and all the rest of it, all seem to us ridiculous. We still know, perhaps, just two things which make us certain we're alive. We can obey and we can give orders. But we prefer to obey orders rather than give them. We've played this as a sort of national game. Because, since we were dedicated to death, the military preparations for death were just a game. We were as far above it all as the serious men who pass the time in trains playing dominoes are above the pieces with which they play. But it did interest us, or at least it diverted us. Today I think that that world, the military world, which in any case is only any good for those who are dedicated to death, was a carefully arranged, comfortable world. It spared us life, with its struggles, worries, plans, thoughts, hopes and disasters. In the army there was no hope, no plan, no thought. At two-thirty you have to fall in for parade. You know quite precisely what the Colonel looks like, what he says, what his orders mean, how he will punish you. It's all in Standing Orders. If the Colonel has had a stroke or been hit by a bullet, then the Major stands there. In his absence, the Captain. If no one is there, then it's up to you to say everything and do everything which the circumstances demand. How well this world is organised! There can be no doubt, no uncertainty, no conscience, no care. If there is no bread, you go hungry. You're allowed twenty-five cigarettes a day. At six in the morning you march off. At half past four they wake you. At five they bring you black coffee.'

'Stop it!' cried Zipper. 'Anyone would think you were advising me to join up again. It's too late. There isn't a war in sight these days.'

'I advise you,' I said, 'to find yourself a woman.'

'Should I fall in love?'

'Perhaps even that: fall in love. In any case, a woman is a help. She helps you to have the illusion that you still have a goal in this world. She wants dresses and shoes, a home and food and sometimes a child. If you have something to worry about it makes it easier to believe you also have some reason for living.'

'I was in love just once,' said Arnold. 'Truly in love. Did

you know Erna Wilder? She was my neighbour. When we were children we would meet in the mornings going to school, and again when we came home. Her parents and mine once went on holiday together. We went to some spa in Silesia and we shared a villa. Our fathers were friends in business. Things weren't too brilliant with Wilder, but they were better than with my father. We could only afford to stay at that spa for a fortnight, although the Wilders stayed longer. But in my memory those two weeks seem like six – I experienced so much there. I was fifteen years old, she was thirteen, I believe. All day long we played together, because we were much of an age. There was a mountain, which they called 'Gloriette'. A winding road climbed to the top. There were benches by the side of the road and couples would sit on them. During the day we didn't see them, or we looked past them. We had more important things to do. We caught stag beetles, collected acorns, caught butterflies. But when twilight came, Erna changed. If we passed a courting couple, she would press herself against me for a moment, then run away, wait till I caught up with her and laugh softly. It was dark, I no longer knew what she looked like when she began to laugh. It seemed to me that she changed into an unknown woman; this wasn't her voice, she didn't laugh the way she laughed in the daytime. Then I would want to take hold of her and to feel that it was still her, laughing in the dark. I reach out and feel her breast and I'm startled and she runs away.

'The next morning we meet in the park, and it's as if the previous night had never been. We go back to looking for stag beetles.

'I once noticed the way an older gentleman looked at her on the spa promenade. Then she wanted to turn back, although we were on our way to the meadows. She said she wanted to look at a concert programme. In front of the pavilion, where the band is playing, stands the gentleman, and Erna laughs. He winks an eye, she turns scarlet. I think I fell in love at that instant. I could no longer play with Erna in the same way. I kept trying to go up the 'Gloriette' with her in the dark, I longed to be able to touch her breast again. But I never succeeded.

'Once there was a ball in the spa assembly rooms. I stood there and watched her dancing with the officers. Next day she was greeted by many gentlemen. She had already changed. She no longer skipped across the street as she had the day before, but walked like a lady. When she came to a stream, through which she had often paddled in her shoes, she would hesitate for a moment before deciding to cross it, after finding the narrowest point. I had to cross first and give her my hand. I loved her. I had sleepless nights. And then we left. I was jealous, touchy, discouraged, and I hated my parents because they had no money. I dreamed up idiotic fantasies. An orphanage catches fire, I save all the children, my name is in the papers and she comes to me, asks my forgiveness and says: "You can touch my breast if you like."

'Then, after the holidays, I saw her again. But we never spoke again, although I often followed her home and she must have noticed.'

'And what is she doing now?'

'I was told that she became engaged during the war, but that the engagement was called off. She's in a drama school now, she wants to be an actress. I think she is right, remembering the way she could laugh in the dark.'

'How long is it since you saw each other?'

'It must be ten years. I don't know if I'd even recognise her.'

That evening we did not go together to each other's doors. It was a cool, foggy night. Arnold very soon took his leave. I had the impression that he was ashamed.

We had talked so much together that we had no more to say to each other. He must have felt that walking the same road together in silence would have been painful. Besides which, he had touched on an old tale for the first time in many years. Sometimes when we do this it is as if we have released a spring long blocked up, and we must wait until the flood, which for the time being overwhelms us, has died down.

Perhaps Arnold had a wish, or a longing, to see Erna again, and wanted to consider the best means by which he could meet her. Perhaps in her, or at least with her help, he hoped to find his strength and a goal. Perhaps, too, his memory of her was the pleasantest and easiest escape from the little life he led, and he wanted to be alone with this memory, just as one sometimes wants to be alone in a cemetery!

11

After Arnold started working at the Finance Ministry his visits to the coffee houses became a passion rather than a habit. It was among his fulfilments rather than his necessities. If in his earlier days – and especially after his return from the war – he had found it difficult to spend an evening alone, he was now possessed by a real horror of solitude. Not that he had any wish to be part of a community. He just wanted to sit in the coffee house, nowhere else but in his coffee house.

He had a few acquaintances, perhaps one or two friends. These were writers, painters, musicians, sculptors. I knew of no more attentive reader, no more conscientious citizen, no more ardent theatre-goer and no more devoted listener to music than Arnold. He was interested in all the arts. Among his pleasures was being near those who practised them. He certainly envied them. For it seemed to him that they alone had achieved something in life and had a right to be there, to be looked up to, to be esteemed and to hold power. Their utterances seemed to him to be so important that he just listened to them, without taking part in their conversation. Perhaps he found some comfort in sharing their evenings, although his days seemed so very different from theirs. On the other hand, perhaps he was cleverer than I imagined, and took comfort, when he saw the artists, in the fact that they talked about the same worries as the rest of the world. They, too, had no money. They, too, could not travel. They, too, drank coffee and dunked their croissants. They, too, played sixty-six and tarock and dominoes.

Arnold didn't play, but he was glad to look on. After a time he became for many of the players an indispensable spectator. One relaxed to some extent from the excitement of the game when one looked up from one's cards and saw Zipper. The permanent melancholy of his face – the origin of which nobody knew and I alone probably understood, knowing as I did the Zipper household, the breeding ground of his melancholy – his constant passion for sharing the alternation of luck good and bad, his attentive silence, his keen look, always following the movements of hands and cards, must have been as restful and gratifying to the players as is a tense, transported listener to an author reading his own work. It flattered the players when Zipper watched them. It was as if he were giving them his silent approval. When they stood up from their game, it was only with reluctance that Arnold would leave the table. It obviously pained him. He felt empty. He had then to go to another table, where they were no longer

175

playing, just talking, and conversation was far less easy to follow than cards. He also felt less at home at a table where they talked than at one where they played. For while the rules of a card game definitely require the presence of a spectator, the rules of conversation do not. Arnold's sensitive ear picked up a hundred times, even though no one ever put into words: what is this fellow Zipper actually doing here? For it was known that he neither painted, wrote nor composed, and yet everyone who painted, wrote or composed knew him. He never dabbled in politics, as did every other guest in the coffee house on the quiet, nor did he do newspaper work. Yet Arnold belonged to this coffee house and to no other. He went about among the writers – who were always on the lookout for a 'theme' – the raw material of a novel – on offer, but in vain. Writers, however, are not inclined to believe that a man who watches card games is literary material.

They grew used to Zipper. All of them had already asked themselves so often what Zipper did, that in the end they were all persuaded that they had found the answer. They liked to have someone around who was not of their profession, but who was nonetheless so close to it that there was no need for an interpreter to make themselves understood. When they talked, he formed a public for them. And as they talked more than they wrote, it was useful for them to have a reader who would listen.

And Arnold listened. The coffee house drew him every evening, as the tavern does the drinker and the gaming rooms the gambler. He could no longer live without the sight of the small, round white tables and the square green ones; without the stout pillars which once, in the youth of this coffee house, must have underlined its brilliance and elegance, pillars which were now blackened by smoke, as if by decades of sacrificial fires, and on which hung newspapers, like withered fruit, in shrivelled, yellow, clattering binders; without the niches dark with overcoats on overloaded stands, the lavatory in the corridor with its endless comings and goings, in front of which one met and greeted acquaintances, where one could stand for half an hour without noticing how the time flew by. He could not live without the blonde cashier at the counter, who knew everyone by name and distributed their mail to the regulars, whereas letters and cards which came for the ordinary 'passing trade' were displayed in an impersonal, official, cool window; without the waiters, who never changed, never died, never asked the guests what they wanted but just brought their usual order; without the carbide lamps, which at that time had taken the place of gas and electricity and looked like will o'the wisps domesticated and brought into human service. And these lamps sang, and their music was also indispensable to Arnold. When they burned down, they flickered and threw scalloped shadows onto the tables. A waiter would then stand on a chair and breathe new life into them with bellows. Flies buzzed, cards were slapped, dominoes clicked, newspapers rustled, chessmen fell with a dry tap onto the floor, billiard balls rolled quietly over green baize, glasses clinked, spoons clanked, shoes shuffled, voices murmured and water dripped sentimentally from some distant, dreamlike tap which was never shut off – and above all this sang the carbide lamps. Sometimes the coffee house resembled a winter encampment of nomads, sometimes a bourgeois dining room, sometimes a great anteroom in a palace and sometimes a warm heaven for the frozen. For it was warm, with an animal warmth, reinforced by glowing coals in three fat stoves, through the bars of which came a red glow, so that they looked like entrances to a hell devoid of terror. Only on entering this coffee house was Arnold finally free of his day. Here began his freedom, for, although the revolving doors never ceased moving, Arnold could be certain that inside this coffee house he would never encounter anyone who reminded him of his work or indeed of any work whatever. There was nothing here to remind him of his work, of the district from which he came, nor of his father's friends. Only thin, yellow curtains shut out the street beyond the windows. But these curtains seemed so thick that one could imagine even stones and bullets bouncing harmlessly off them. This world had nothing to do with the bitterness and meanness of the day. Even if the sun still stood in the heavens, it had no business here.

Only a theatre or a concert could prevent Arnold from spending the whole evening in the coffee house. He would then arrive at eleven o'clock instead of his usual seven.

Arnold had inherited his love of the theatre, like many other things, from old Zipper. But whereas old Zipper preferred operetta, his son was drawn to plays. If old Zipper obtained free tickets thanks to his connections with the cashier, his son received his straight from the director. Where the old man had been fascinated by backstage and by stage machinery, the young one studied the work of the directors and the actors.

If Arnold attended the theatre with passion, it was in no way because he imagined himself standing on the stage. He was not so childish, and not ambitious even in his dreams. He just wanted to breathe the air of the theatre, in the same way that he entered the coffee house not to play cards but to breathe the air of the coffee house. He was a member of the public, with a professional's inside knowledge. If he met an actor, he felt the need to see him act. If he saw an actor on stage, he had to meet him. If he knew an author, he had to read him. If he read a book, he wanted to know the author. If he talked to a painter, he would visit him in his studio. These inclinations and passions of his were almost scientific. He was more interested in the manuscript than in the printed book, preferred a work in progress to a finished one, was more interested in the motivation and origin of a work than in the finished product, more interested in the model than the portrait. It was as if his unhappy nature were trying to discover 'how it was done'. For he had the sensitivity of a creator and a craftsman's interest in technique. Yet he could create nothing. He lived, as it were, in an anxious dream, in which one tries to call out and cannot. Since he was so industrious in his researches, he knew a lot about the private lives of his favourites. But he was never importunate, because his enthusiasm had a scientific and impersonal coolness. He was also as silent as a scientist who withholds the fruits of his researches until the day when he decides to construct his theory.

Since I knew of Arnold's interest in the theatre I was not surprised to miss him for several evenings in the coffee house. He must have looked in before the play, I thought. Probably there are actors who interest him playing this week. Probably he has an invitation.

When, however, he was missing for more than a week, even the card players became uneasy. They missed Arnold's tragic silence. For whom were they playing, then? Every time I passed by a table, someone would pull at my jacket and ask: 'What's Zipper doing all this time?' I asked, too. The waiters hadn't seen him, nor had the cashier. There was even post for him at the counter, uncalled for.

It was a long time since I had been to the Zippers. It was winter, and I knew the house was not heated.

Ah, I knew those winters in the Zipper household! There sat the old man in his winter overcoat. Frau Zipper, in the fashion of the peasant women of her part of the country, would wind a shawl back and forth about her body. The window panes were dim, little runnels of water trickled down them, they looked less like glass than clouded water; grey breaths issued from mouths, hands were red, fingers swollen, a dead fly hung here and there in a corner, for no known reason the light was a greenish grey, the whole place looked like the bottom of the sea, some sort of pool, an aquarium. Evening fell earlier in that house than it should have. If the lamps were lit, they burned in a grey fog, and one could not see their core. They reminded one of the midnight sun. Old Zipper blew his nose continually. He had suffered since his youth from a racking catarrh. I remember that year after year he had spoken of going to Kudowa. But since his stomach didn't function very well he hesitated as to whether he would not rather go to Karlsbad. It didn't occur to him that he would be going nowhere, since he had no money. He persuaded himself that he stayed at home because he had two complaints, each of which required a different watering place. He hawked, spat, drank slivovitz and sputtered.

As I entered the Zippers' house, I noticed that the old man was wearing his wife's shawl. He was a bit out of sorts, and could no longer go about his modest business affairs. It was a bit of luck that Wandl had come back safe from the war and was paying rent for the salon. This was now Zipper's only income. He treated me to morello schnaps and tea. He warmed up, and talked quite a lot, he was even optimistic. Listening to him, one could believe that he was heading for a happy, carefree old age. Arnold was well looked after. While a million young men were wandering about with nothing to eat, he was sitting in a job where he could grow and prosper, a plant in a well-placed flowerpot. Nothing could now stand in his way. Not only did he work on contracts but he was exceptionally well placed on the Order-in-Council side. In fact he had not been home for some days.

So as not to worry old Zipper, I lied, and said that I had seen Arnold in the coffee house two days previously. Why two days? It seemed to me to be a smaller lie if I placed our imaginary conversation further in the past.

I now knew that something had happened to Arnold. Oh, not an accident, not a catastrophe. For Fate could have no unforeseen influence over the lives of the Zippers. For them it had the slow, dreary persistence of a beetle boring. No thunderstorms broke out from the grey vault of the heavens which shrouded the Zippers, the clouds just drew closer about them. I could feel one of these irresolute clouds approaching now. But I did not raise the subject. I acted as though we were in full sunshine.

That evening, I decided to wait for Arnold in the coffee house. It did not seem to me to have its usual appearance. Arnold Zipper was missing. All the people who had previously asked themselves why Zipper was there now asked out loud: 'Why isn't Zipper here?' The players were missing him as much as the talkers. Some of them rose early from the tables because they were starved of Arnold's encouraging but melancholy approval. Some of the talkative ones were silent that evening, because of the absence of the one listener they always overlooked when he was present. From the symphony of faces, sounds and moods which gave the coffee house its value, Arnold's face and silence and the shadow of his tragedy were absent. Police closing time approached, and Arnold did not come.

Next day I went to his office. One of his colleagues said that Herr Zipper had reported sick and had already been away some days. I think it was Herr Kranich who told me this. I think, too, that he told me in that spiteful tone of voice which is affected by many unhappy civil servants after twenty-five years of service.

181

Nor was Zipper at his lodgings. I knew at once that he was not ill. Could he suddenly have left for Brazil? Sudden decisions of this sort were not consistent with his usual slowness. A Zipper never acted precipitately. Where should I look for him?

I decided to let a week go by. I would accept the fact that Arnold was not there. I struck him off the list of the living and acted as though he had never existed. I wouldn't give him a thought for a week.

But the week wasn't yet up when I met him. It was about noon. I went into the coffee house to check whether a letter had come for me. There he sat, in a corner, almost out of sight, obviously writing a letter. He hadn't seen me. I watched him, with his mouth half open, like a child or like someone sleeping. His head was bowed over the paper on which he was writing. He wasn't writing freely. He seemed to ponder, or to take breathers during which he would consider a host of thoughts, just as one follows a flock of birds on the horizon. Although his eyes were on me, he did not see me.

'Hello, Arnold!'

He put his elbow on the paper, remembered that this movement betrayed him, took his arm away, acted as though he had been writing something of no importance and moved over to make room for me. But I didn't sit down.

'Where have you been hiding?'

'I've so much work.'

'But you've reported sick at the office.'

'Ah, so you went there. Indeed! I'm working at something else.'

'Why don't you come here any more in the evenings?'

'Because I'm tired. Besides, it bores me. I don't feel like it.'

'Shall we eat together?'

'If it's on you.'

'Don't you want to finish your letter?'

'There's plenty of time for that!'

'Isn't it very important?'

'No, it's very important!'

'Then go ahead and write it.'

'I'm not in the mood now.'

'Why aren't you going to your office?'

'I can't stand it any more!'

Arnold picked up his letter, folded it into four and put it in his briefcase. In the street, I said: 'What if someone sees you?'

'All right with me.'

'Do you want to leave your job?'

'Actually, no. But I long for someone to force me to leave it. I should be happy, for instance, if Councillor Kronauer were to walk past. I haven't the strength to leave. I'm waiting for a *malheur*. It's in my power to conjure one up, but I don't have the strength to do it.'

At that moment I saw Councillor Kronauer in the distance. I seized Arnold by the arm.

'Look, it's Kronauer!'

'Where?' cried Arnold. A moment later he was hiding in the doorway of a house.

I pulled him out, like dragging him out of a drawer.

'Why did you hide?'

'I don't know.'

We ate in silence. When we'd finished, Arnold said: 'I'm going back to the office today. I'll come to the coffee house this evening.'

I waited for him that evening. He did not come.

People asked after him less pressingly. They seemed to be getting used to his absence. The players went back to sitting longer at the tables. The talkers began to resume their debates. Some empty but indefinable space had been filled again. A hole, left by Arnold, vanished in the ever thicker, more creative and self-renewing atmosphere.

Suddenly Arnold appeared. It was nearly midnight. Groups were beginning to break up. A couple of tables were already in darkness. The flickering carbide lamps were no longer being revived with the bellows. There were so few people present that Arnold's entrance made an even greater impression.

People pushed their chairs back. They gathered round him. It was as if he had returned from a long journey or had recovered from a long illness. The waiters were lurking in the background, waiting to congratulate Arnold when his friends released him.

This welcome delighted Arnold, as did anything which made him aware that someone valued him, even if it were only in his role as spectator. He, who always stood at the fringes, now found himself at the centre for a few minutes. That part of his personality which included his theatrical side, his repressed, dormant, passionate theatrical side, was awakened and stimulated. For five minutes Arnold was on stage. He acted and took his bows at the same time. Nothing moved me as much as this brief appearance, which concentrated the crucial moments of an entire role, an entire evening.

12

The regulars welcomed him heartily, not because they were really happy to see him back, but because his return was an event. Their life was short of events. They would sit in the coffee house like a besieged garrison in a castle. Nothing reached them from the outside world, and none of them reached it. They would have been equally pleased, at that moment, not to have seen Arnold again, but to have learned that he had committed suicide. They liked to sense that something important, something secret, had come into his life. For they had never known anyone to stay away from the coffee house for more than a week for any trivial reason.

And Arnold really had undergone a profound change: he had met Fräulein Erna Wilder.

Naturally, he didn't reveal this news in daylight. Arnold Zipper only spoke of her – and, in general, only when information had to be imparted – at night, as we walked home. He didn't tell the whole truth. All he said, after walking in silence for half an hour, during which time I sensed him searching for a suitable beginning, was: 'I've met Erna Wilder.'

'Met' was not the *mot juste*. Arnold had sought her out, as I was to learn later. As she had left her parents' house the previous year, he had been forced to enquire after her at the drama school. They wouldn't give him her address. So he waited in front of the school, as young men in love are wont to do. He saw her coming out. He followed her to the door, where her escort left her. Before she could climb the steps, Zipper greeted her and asked her how things were going.

But I found all this out later. For the time being Arnold confined himself to saying that Erna was 'a nice, sympathetic person'. She had greatly altered since the summer of the Silesian spa. This was hardly to be wondered at.

Arnold didn't go beyond such generalities.

I asked him whether he was going to the office again. He said that he had been working there for the last three days, but that he had by no means decided whether he would stay, become a civil servant and give up 'the world'.

It seemed to me, in any case, that whether or not Arnold stayed in his job, he was in love. That is, he found himself in that condition which since time immemorial has been called 'being in love'.

It was for the first time in his life. I wondered about this, because he had no bent for falling in love. He brought with him, in a manner of speaking, none of the prerequisites for love. If his intelligence was not particularly sharp or alert, his temperament was, even so, not strong enough to suppress it. If he was sentimental by nature, he had enought taste to combat this sentimentality. While he was sensitive, and capable of succumbing to outside influence, to charm, to an atmosphere, he was yet, in general, too indifferent to women to fall for one. I had by now known for a long time that Arnold was one of the few men who do not alter their attitude in the company of women. Card players were of more interest to him. Women made just enough impact on him for him to be aware that they were not of the male sex. For him, that was that. He had too little belief in himself to be vain, like all other men. For one must have a trifling opinion of oneself ever to fall in love.

I finally came to the conclusion that Arnold had fallen in love out of despair, like one of those people whose nature is to strive against alcohol, and who in despair become drinkers. To escape from the tragic monotony in which he lived – in which he almost had his very being – and to attain a more eventful life, he was forced to follow a long-established and dramatic formula. He was probably not really aware of what he was doing. (But even if one is unaware of the reasons for doing something, they are still one's own reasons.) Arnold had done exactly what I had suggested to him a few weeks previously. Incapable as he was of finding himself a woman, he struck on the convenient solution of recalling one he had found twelve years earlier. Too indifferent, perhaps also too idle to choose one, he went back to one whom he believed he knew well enough to spare him the bother of making a choice. Too weak to create a new love, he would awaken an old one. This was Fate, and no doubt about it. If he felt himself driven out of his indifference and towards passion, he proceeded to look for the most convenient of all passions; one in which he was already at home. After I had made this analysis, there was nothing for it but to make Erna's acquaintance.

He brought her to a small literary club. She was too clever to say anything intelligent herself – although she was certainly capable of doing so – and kept quiet. She was nevertheless too taken up with herself to listen to other people and, in her anxiety not to betray the fact that she was thinking only of herself, she played a masterly silent scene, during which any spectator would have sworn that her tireless, nervous brain was working away at the sentences which were being spoken. I recalled similar scenes which I myself had played, at school, where I had laid myself out to win the respect of the teacher, without actually wasting a moment on listening. I had more important things to think about, namely whatever concerned

me. Admittedly, I had never achieved Fräulein Erna's
standard. For not only could she give the impression of being
wrapped up in the conversation while being wrapped up only
in herself. Far from it. At a carefully chosen moment, when
she sensed that she could no longer keep silent, for fear of
being spotted, she would, with a single phrase, give a new
turn to the conversation. She had reached the stage where
everyone would then discuss her point for a quarter of an
hour. A priceless fifteen minutes for her, during which she
could think about herself.

There were several men at that table whom she had just
met. After some time, having grown tired of the fruitless and
demanding discussion that Fräulein Erna had imposed on us,
we began to make jokes and behave normally, whereupon she
called us all by our names. She had noted them all. She no
longer thought it worthwhile to use the prefix 'Herr'. She
treated us just as she did her colleagues, the young actors. She
simulated friendliness, because it was the simplest way of
appearing candid, sincere and straightforward. She played the
tomboy, which was bound to convince everyone that she was
genuine. She behaved like a young man, from which people
deduced that she would be easy to handle. She was tidy,
which indicated her character. She allowed a doubtful joke to
amuse her, she even encouraged it, and so seemed free of all
prejudice. She showed respect for actresses who were in the
news, an apparently frank admiration, and we judged her to
be free from professional jealousy. She made jokes about
acting. People, therefore, judged her to be untouched by
ambition. She saw good points in everyone's opinions. She
was therefore considered to be open-minded. She would even
ask one or another of us for his opinion, and we would feel
flattered. When she talked, she became beautiful. A glow
would come to her cheeks, a golden sparkle to her brown

eyes, she would move her small head with such artistic vigour that her hair would fall over her brow in disciplined confusion and share in her merriment. Thus, she often found an opportunity to lift her delicate hand, which seemed to have a mind of its own, to her hair – a gesture which makes every woman lovely. For it is an intimate movement. It is like beginning to undress.

I had no doubt that Arnold loved her. But neither did I doubt for a moment that she was entirely indifferent to him. Her dealings with him were only a few degrees warmer than were those with other people. She expected him to help her into her coat, to lend her a pencil, to hold her mirror for her, to pick up her handkerchief and to drive her home. And I had never seen Arnold happier. How well she knew that he – like most men – imagined that the small services demanded of him were but a prelude to rich rewards in the future; that a swift glance exchanged with him indicated a secret understanding, whereas in reality it was just a glance to keep him in check.

What need had she of him? He worked in the Ministry of Finance and watched cards over the players' shoulders. He was a man without wealth, without power, without prospects. If she needed a man at all, it wouldn't have been Arnold, who slowed her down. Why didn't she let him know that he meant nothing to her? I learned the answer later on. I saw that she was on the lookout not only for people to help her in her career, but also for servants she would not have to pay.

Arnold changed during that time. He still had no idea what lay ahead of him, but he gained in self-confidence. He no longer suffered from the conviction that he was superfluous. He joined in the conversations of people to whom he had previously just listened respectfully. He even took part in card games. It seemed that he wished to stop being a mere onlooker.

He gave up his job. He reported sick and then wrote a letter to Councillor Kronauer in which he informed him that he felt compelled to give up the career of civil servant. This was the letter which he had started to write some weeks earlier, the time I had met him in the coffee house. He was now looking for a private and, as he put it, 'provisional' position. As he failed to find one, he gave up his room and moved back in with his parents. With that cheerfulness which one can muster when in love, he told his father that he had no wish to be a civil servant.

Old Zipper was helped by his idiotic and eternal illusion that everything which happened to his son Arnold would turn out to be of value. If Arnold had sensed that he could not stay in the civil service, it was an indication that the service no longer held a future for him. If Arnold fancied himself in love, so much the better. That it was because he was in love that Arnold gave up his job did not occur to old Zipper. His gullibility lay, above all, in his inability to make the connection between causes and effects. He believed that Arnold thought in the same way that he did. Would he have left his job for any reason other than the prospect of never being rewarded according to his just deserts? No! So Arnold was right.

Any woman with whom Arnold fell in love had to be an exceptional woman. And old Zipper was burning to set eyes on her. He still remembered her from the Silesian spa and was in love with the memory.

'She's fair, isn't she?' he said. For he liked blondes.

'No,' answered Arnold, 'she's a brunette.' He did not want to say she was dark.

'But I remember clearly that she had light-coloured eyes.'

'Yes,' said Arnold, stretching a point. 'When she laughs her eyes do become light.'

190

'She must be tall and strong by now.'

'She's still small and delicate.'

'Well, well,' said old Zipper, 'it's fashionable these days for women to be delicate. Does she really want to be an actress?'

'Yes. Why not?'

'But then you couldn't marry.'

'Out of the question! Who's talking about marriage?'

'Certainly, out of the question,' old Zipper agreed. He had always favoured a relaxation of the moral code. He was no reactionary. He moved with the times.

Now and again Fräulein Erna came to the Zippers' home. Why not, after all? She was from the same sort of background, and was in the process of leaving it. She hated her father's clumsy affection, and her mother's petit-bourgeois pride, her constant touchiness, the scenes she made if her husband came back from a journey with inadequate presents, her fear that people might not pay her enough attention.

How fast could one escape from such a household? Fräulein Erna had discovered her 'true vocation', something no kindly father or vain mother can resist. And she subsequently proved to have been bright enough to possess talent, too. Nothing is impossible.

She was already 'leading her own life', as she had always longed to do. She was accountable to no one if she came back to her room late at night. She no longer had to listen to a thousand boring questions, which one could easily answer truthfully, so unimportant are they, but which one answers with a lie simply because the questioners are not worthy of the truth. To avoid the thousand complications which arise simply because one forgets tomorrow what one says today; to escape one's mother's foolish and persistent curiosity, which is merely an attempt to revive her own youth through her daughter's; to escape one's father's ridiculous pride, and his belief in the strong personality of his daughter, which nevertheless does not prevent him from treating her like an idiot child.

Nowadays Erna came home when she felt like it. The profession for which she was preparing herself led to such a remote world that her parents gave up trying to discover anything about it. This was no *lycée* for girls, such as her mother had attended. This was 'the stage'; reeking of sin, of distant, unknown riches, of glamour which could bring with it disaster or great wealth – both of which were so far from all bourgeois experience that one could hardly rejoice over the riches nor wring one's hands over the disaster. This world, for which Erna was equipping herself, lay far beyond her parents' control. She had already freed herself from their authority, their love, their pride and their silliness.

Because she was clever, she feared nothing so much as an unconscious relapse on her own part into one of the thousand detestable variants of her own home. She watched herself ceaselessly, for fear of finding in herself some resemblance to her mother. To strangers she transformed her parents into simple, unpretentious folk. She found this solution apt – the alternative, to pretend that her family was wealthy, was too banal, and every little actress did it.

'When one comes from a home as simple as mine,' she would often say, whether or not the remark was relevant. She would have liked best to have the world believe that her father was an illiterate woodcutter. After the revolution it had become fashionable for the young who dealt in art and literature and who wanted to keep close to the proletariat, because for a short time it looked as if it might win, to lower the level of their origins. (I knew the son of a wealthy jeweller who claimed that his father was a watch repairer.)

Arnold seemed not to notice this. While his father was incapable of distinguishing cause from effect, Arnold lacked the ability to tell truth from fiction. But then, what lover can?

13

The following season Erna succeeded in getting a small job in a theatre in Breslau. She knew well enough that this was not the road to fame, but was part of her own battle against the danger of losing her resolve. She knew that enmity, jealousy, meanness and discouragement were lying in wait for her, but no comfort, not a word to bolster her self-confidence, no recognition, never the disinterested love of a man. For that reason she was determined that Zipper should come with her. He, in his first enthusiasm, asked her if she would be his wife.

She would.

At the time this was beyond my comprehension. He would have followed her to the ends of the earth without demanding her love in return. It was incomprehensible to me that a woman of her type should pay for what she could have had for nothing. I realised later that in exchange for his loyalty, his work, his life and, perhaps, his happiness – for he could also have been happy – he took from her more than she gave. For centuries men have lived under the lunatic impressison – nourished by poets and novelists – that a woman bestows her greatest gift when she yields herself. Hence the bewilderment of a man of worth when he discovers that his wife has betrayed him with someone worthless. Hence the excessively gruesome significance given to a wedding night without love. Hence the frivolity of a 'seduction', and the exaggerated respect for Casanovas.

Erna did not greatly value her body – like many women. She would sleep with a man to whom she felt indifferent, because she was indifferent to love. She felt it more advantageous to undertake her first appointment as a young married woman. It was at least original. It meant something that she should have a man in tow, when jealousy surrounded her, for this doubled her desirability. She had no illusions, only intelligence.

Arnold was married and, although it was only a registrar's marriage and no reception followed, Frau Zipper, for the first time in many long years, wore her black spangled dress. Did she still put the fallen spangles into those red glasses? Was the blue inkwell still there? Did the sideboard stand where it used to? These, I recall, were the questions which preoccupied me at Arnold's wedding. Old Zipper stood there, stiffly and more solemnly than was warranted by the simplicity of the ceremony. Had he himself not once asked if they were going to be married? And, lo and behold, they really were marrying: his son and a young actress. Nothing remarkable about that. No need for a religious ceremony. A reception was basically only a convention. And old Zipper, who always went along with the young, said repeatedly that he regretted the money his own wedding had cost.

How Arnold was to live, nobody knew. Old Zipper again scraped up some money for him – whether he had saved it or borrowed it remained uncertain. Then Arnold set off for Breslau.

I lost track of him, heard little from him. I don't know how he made a living, but he must have worked hard. During the next two years he followed his wife to many provincial cities.

Finally she succeeded in getting involved with film people. Young Zipper and his wife came to Berlin.

The theatre took too long. Films must move faster. For the theatre had many centres, the films only one: Hollywood. One must get there to earn money, fame and power!

Erna had a triumph when she so appealed to the press in a film – *The Eternal Shadow* – in which she only had a secondary role, that she earned more praise than the leading lady.

Now her work began in earnest. For at that time the opinions of the press were not so much objective criticism as a sort of *quid pro quo* for advertising. Nevertheless the critics were useful to Erna in that her name acquired its first recognition and her personality its first outlines. With her innate adroitness, she began to work at her career.

For the time being she was dealing, in the film world, with people who resembled her father: small citizens with loud voices. These were the inflation years of the film industry. The people in it had come from every walk of life, every part of the country, every province. There were manufacturers and hoteliers, chemists and photographers, fashion designers and men from the horseracing world, publishers, journalists, travellers in ready-to-wear clothes and court photographers, unemployed officers and opportunists, people from Katowice and Budapest, from Galicia and Breslau, from Berlin and Slovakia. The film industry was a California. Former stockbrokers from Czernowitz sat down with German industrialists and invented patriotic films. Travellers in lampshades tore round the studios, swore at the mechanics and called themselves lighting artists. Mediocre portrait painters became architects. Students who had run academic dilettante societies became assistant producers. Furniture removers who had left their warehouses became scenic artists,

195

photographers became picture operatives, currency specula-
tors became producers, police spies became crime consultants,
roof repairers became set designers and anyone who was
shortsighted became a secretary. Many a sly owner of a
money-changing bureau made himself independent, rented an
office in the Friedrichstrasse and called it 'Direction', or a
corner on the Tempelhof and called it 'Atelier', wrote a script
and became an author, told a debutante to cry and her partner
to storm and became a director, glued bits of three-ply
together and became an architect, set fire to a magnesium
flare and became a lighting artist. And there he was and there
he stayed. He was his own man.

Cigarette vendors opened cinemas, from seven in the
evening onwards, after working hours, and sold three tickets
for every seat they had. The cinemas had few seats because
they had brought in so much fake marble, so many cubist
loges, and so many impressionistic galleries. The intellectuals
needed rare good fortune to get to the bosses of the
distributors and the studios. Now and then one would
succeed in outwaiting all the imaginary conferences during
which the great man could not be interviewed, would soften
the hearts of all the stenographers who sat like dogs and
barked before the offices of their owners, would outma-
noeuvre the secretaries who wished him ill because they
feared for their jobs, and would finally overcome their own
disgust at shaking this hand or that and 'changing one's
approach', as they used to say in those days. In spite of which,
the industry had but a single voice, and no words. What did
they know of business, or the public, or America?

Girls trained as statisticians sacrificed their virginity for a
vague promise from a third-rate assistant director that he
would make a star of them. Beside the heavenly white beds of
adolescent girls from bourgeois houses hung the postcard-size

portraits of their adored ones, signed by their own hand on the day of a première. To weave the beauties of the world into thrilling immediacy, film companies made long journeys, to maharajahs, geishas, toreros and fakirs. Empires collapsed and others rose upon their ruins. Directors became clerks, and clerks became stars.

It was a world for the shrewd, it was a world for Erna. This wasn't a provincial theatre, with its well-read secretaries, its sensitive, uneducated directors, its cunning, fearful, needy producers; here there was no longer the eternal fear of 'closing' – far from it: the constant cheerful excitement of opening. In the theatre it would be exceptional if a director 'knew' something and wasn't in Berlin already, if he loved her and hadn't yet slept with her, and if he still felt, after three hours of lovemaking, that she had 'a future'. In the theatre, which was beginning to die, her cleverness was no use. No tactics could be applied there, all her energy was wasted, every embrace, all the flirting with the theatrical agents, every false word of flattery to the director, every fine web of intrigue which one spun to entrap a fellow actress, every scene which one laid on, every bouquet of flowers which one allowed to be sent, all wasted. In the film world, however, everything was new and smelt of varnish; there was no tradition yet, there wasn't even slang – all the traditions were borrowed from theatre and were not yet well adapted to the new 'branch'. It was true that in films a promise was worth even less, an appointment was a joke, a signature was equivocal, a promise a trap and a contract a 'con'. But distrust inspired respect, slyness attracted attention, connections provoked fear and it was easier to keep going in perpetual motion than in a regular slow and inevitable death. If one looked on life as accurately and bitterly as Erna, it was easier to achieve a 'position' in films than in the theatre.

The primitive, small-town bourgeoisie of the film industry had to be impressed. By beauty? Their taste was peculiar. By conveying nobility of soul? They did not know what it was. By a distinguished tone of voice? They could not have heard it, for the noise they made themselves. By an unusual allure? They copied it. By a relationship with an 'authority'? That already existed. By debauchery? That was too obvious. By talent? Everyone had that. There was *one* solution: to mix every method, to blend them and use them according to the needs of the moment and – which could never do any harm – to become a trifle 'perverse'. This kept off the unspeakably boring men, but still gave them something to talk about. Last, but not least, it all led so far away from the family home, from mother, father, one's own blood, that one was almost assured of never again relapsing into one's past.

Thus Erna acquired a woman friend, two of them, three.

Former marriage brokers, who had ended up in the film business before they knew how they had come to be there, shook their heads and tried to work out how such a beautiful woman could have turned her back on normality. All the men thought about this, even the intellectuals, who were already familiar with the condition. They found Erna remarkably appealing, they liked her flirtatiousness, which seemed on the face of it to be wasted on men, and which for that reason charmed them; they liked her cleverness, which enabled her to follow complicated arguments; her undergraduate simplicity, which made no demands on them; her grace, which seemed so vulnerable and lost; her 'exceptional talent', which an 'unusual intellect' did nothing to diminish; Erna's endless willingness to give of herself – except to a man; the impossibility of being able to attract her, and yet her evident need to be surrounded by people. They treasured her, like all unattainable things before which nature herself has set up bars.

When Erna was with businessmen from the film world, she behaved differently: she poked fun at the intellectuals and their 'unworldliness'. She gave it as her opinion that the times had need of men of action, and that making money was a higher art than acting on a stage. She raved about America and told how she had already been there as a child. She created legends about her poverty-stricken origins and claimed that she had to earn money to support parents and brothers and sisters who were still living in the darkest slums of Vienna. Admittedly, this did not prevent her from being acquainted with Hungarian counts. She never for a moment lost the superiority of the artist, although she professed not to value talent, least of all her own. She behaved as though she were an aristocrat totally devoid of prejudice, moving among the bourgeoisie which respected her – not simply because she was free of prejudice, but because she was free of it *and* an aristocrat.

She spoke *de haut en bas*, but as among equals.

'She is charming!' said Herr Prinz, of Alga, Inc.

'Is she ever charming!' echoed Herr Direktor Natanson.

And each – without the knowledge of the other – invited her for a little run in the car.

She went with one, she went with the other, she allowed each of them to make the most of her apparent defenceless-ness and allowed each of them to nurture the hope that he, and he alone, might be in a position to bring her back to a 'normal life', if one or two more intimate trips were to follow this one; and from both she received propositions.

She no longer took on minor roles. She put her affairs in the hands of an important lawyer, to whom, for the moment, she paid no fees. She let producers wait, learned to ride, fence, swim, climb, jump, perform on the trapeze, all the things required for Wild West pictures in Hollywood. Sometimes she would suddenly fall ill, have accidents; each Wednesday she would invite influential men; she took on a secretary and hardly accepted any invitations. She bought Buddhas from antique dealers, had her picture in the illustrated magazines, gave 'basically' no interviews, flew in aeroplanes instead of taking trains, exposed herself to real dangers in order to win celebrity, supported strike committees, read radical poems in public, called people she despised 'Comrade', but also allowed herself to meet high-ranking officers and 'could see their point of view'. In the end she reached the stage where they paid her a high salary, and she ran up debts, won success, honours and every advantage which could be won by the art of pushing oneself forward.

She began to put out feelers in the direction of Hollywood.

14

I had no desire to see Erna, who was at that time still acting, if temporarily, on stage. I could perhaps more truthfully say that I had an urge to see her not in those parts which were allotted to her by her profession, but in those other parts, of her own choosing, which she played better by day than she did the official ones on stage in the evening. In the case of Erna, there was allied to my natural contempt for the theatre, inborn, I believe, the fear that I might lose the clear-sightedness with which I observed her and saw through her, the fear that, confused by the art of the professional actress, I might fall victim to that of the private person. This happens not infrequently. It seems to me that actors, and particularly actresses, must be excepted from moral judgements, as they expose themselves to artistic ones, and whenever someone succumbs to them with love, devotion and worship, they turn out to have been conquered not by the honest, as it were primitive, weapons of a woman, but because of the tolerance with which, for example, their cheap conquetterie is accepted as being part of a professional need, in many instances, to be cheap in order to be effective. For that reason we will forgive a lack of taste in a woman of the theatre more easily than in another. In many actresses we turn a blind eye to moral inadequacy, even if we are moralists, not out of 'respect for art', but from an unconscious respect for the effort it must demand to simultaneously please the multitude and yet not repel a single individual. I was biased against Erna.

But because I knew that any opinion, and therefore any prejudice, was liable to be more or less right, and because I believed my own prejudice to be justified, I did not consider it necessary, despite my curiosity and my interest in everything which concerned my friend Arnold, to form a second opinion, which might perhaps have turned out less favourable, of the stage artiste, Erna. Even so, one day I was unable to resist Arnold's urging. I went with him to the theatre. I saw Erna in a role in which she pleased the public. It was an indifferent play; I have forgotten its name, and the author's, and the plot. Erna played the supposedly misunderstood wife of a good-hearted, uncultured husband. I was at once irritated by the shameless pretentiousness of the piece. For apart from the cheapness of these stock characters, the misunderstood wife and the philistine husband, boring to my taste, the impression the author's arguments made upon the audience seemed to me physically too close, like their sweat and their smell. It was as if the secretions of the human body were dependent on the artistic or spiritual impressions received. People laugh differently at a blue joke and a witty joke. The tears shed by a woman of the people over a thumping great tragedy are of a grosser nature than those she would shed at the sight of a real, and therefore less public, sorrow. In this play Erna was unquestionably setting the mood which was dominating the public. She certainly played the part more believably than the author had written it. But just because she was so remarkably adept at refining the vulgar views of a vulgar writer to the point at which they almost appeared artistic, I was able to recognise the Erna of the literary cafés, and spotted her right away. She had something of the ability of a clever suburban dressmaker to achieve with cheap material something which in her window will look very nearly elegant. A two-pronged attraction. People are drawn to the cheapness of the material, and to the false impression that, in spite of its cheapness, it can look elegant.

In private life Erna was fastidious. On stage, she was disgusting, but with a certain grace. In private she was malleable and tough. On stage she was wilting and helpless. In the company of men she behaved in such a way that everyone felt he had to look after her, and each of them believed she had some job for him to do. On stage she looked so much as if all men would desert her that every man in the stalls was on the point of rushing onto the stage to her assistance. In the afternoon she would talk in a deep voice which seemed to come from her boots, in the evening in a high, clear one, fraught with anxiety. The well composed coquetterie, with which in the daytime she created her impression of cleverness and wit, changed in the evening to a different aura, from which radiated a noble, tranquil, modest simplicity. In conversation, if the talk touched on a subject which was distasteful to her, she would edge aside with the elasticity of a balloon, which seems to give way to pressure yet retains the air, which is the substance of its resistance, without noticeably changing. When she was on stage, however, it seemed that she was happily exposing herself, without a second thought, to precisely those perils from which she so scrupulously protected herself in the daytime. The audience feared for her. They wanted to call out: 'Don't go! Don't say it! Watch out! Don't give it away!' All this to her, who always watched her step and generally lied, not because she had much to conceal, but because she knew that a lie has more charm than the truth, even when one knows the truth and does not believe the lie.

Despite her cleverness, it still seemed to me that other people – not just I, who knew her – but critics, for example (supposing that they knew half as much about women as they did about theatre), would spot that there existed an inexplicable contradiction between this brittleness, which threatened at every moment to shatter her, and the serpentine, tense, almost muscular elasticity with which she moved her body, her arms, her neck. During dialogue she would raise her eyes, as if in prayer. But it was in the end bound to strike one that this look, eternally turned heavenwards, even if the line she was speaking was: 'A glass of water, please,' had its base in complete indifference, from the soul of a person who could mistake heaven for a neat garden with a railing. One's ears had to register in the end that this gift of constant supplication ruled out all aptitude for prayer. One had finally to recognise that this elegance, which deceived the wives of master butchers, derived from some sort of conscious artifice and was not aimless, as was the play itself, but was designed both to prop up the play and to edify the spectator.

Although we were sitting close to the stage, Arnold watched her through his opera-glasses, which seemed a natural extension of his eyes. 'She doesn't like it,' he said, 'if I don't look at her through glass. She says my naked eye could bring her bad luck. I don't watch through these glasses so as to see her better, but so that she doesn't see my face.'

I sensed, however, in fact I thought I knew, that Erna had no fear of his eye; that she attached importance to being clearly seen by Arnold, clearly seen but unattainable, so as to inflame his fantasy through a trumpery proximity, which yet maintained its distance. I could also see very well that Arnold suffered, seeing her so near but yet beyond his grasp.

Why did she torture him? I could find no answer, and I still cannot. I believe that Erna fed on Arnold's pain, that she needed the suffering of her lover, where other women just need the lover. It is not true that there are women who torture for torture's sake. They need the other's pain as an aid to their own health and beauty. I also believe that the superstitions to which actresses are so prone do not stem from pure fear, but have a sensible basis and conceal a premeditated purpose, as did Erna's.

15

Arnold Zipper sang the praises of his wife. At last, through all sorts of contacts, through a combination of flukes which closely resembled Fate, he had become the film editor of a midday paper.

It seemed to me that he had at last discovered the profession which suited him. He possessed just that conciliatory skill without which it is impossible to criticise something in which one has a financial interest. In his position it was necessary to disguise his lack of bias so cleverly that he did not wound the susceptibilities of his advertisers. One must not praise bad pictures, but one must still find in them enough of interest for the public not to decide at once never to see them. It was hard to find one's way in the dark and opaque web into which the newspaper and film industries had interwoven each other.

There were weighty news items which had to be set aside until whoever had supplied them was ready to pay to have them published. There were other, unimportant, items, of no interest to readers, which were published because they came from a source which spent money regularly every six months. There were items from enemy companies, which one immediately threw into the wastepaper basket. There were disguised items from rivals who tried with the utmost cunning and extreme secrecy to smuggle them in, which had at once to be unmasked and refused. There were newspapers from which one was supposed to 'take clippings', and others which were on the publisher's 'Index'. There were interviews with financiers from the film world, which one had to bring out to a precise deadline, on just the day when the international 'Constellation' was receptive to an interview. There were mergers which one knew about a fortnight before they came to pass and about which Arnold was anxious to inform the world. But no! The publisher ordered patience, even to the point where a competitor might come out with the news first. One often had to worry about the competition, about the unfortunate consequences of an announcement.

But Arnold worried about the publisher all the time.

Arnold worried about the publisher all the time. What he was doing seemed to him so important, and he took his profession so seriously, that he did not want to lose his job at any price. He had no fear of unemployment or hunger. But there, at his desk, was the only place where he could work for his wife – insofar as he could, indeed, work for his wife. There he would hear about favourable opportunities which she could exploit, of dangers looming, which she could avoid, of personalities who were 'still in power' or had just lost it, of roles which had not been filled, of rivals on the make and intrigues threatening. Oh, how sacred to Arnold was this profession. He now sat almost as an equal at the writers' tables – several in fact needed his support and even flattered him – not as in his old café in Vienna, in which he would have been so happy to live his triumph, but at least it was still a literary café. From time to time someone would come up from Vienna, see Arnold moving in important circles and think to himself: 'Well, well! In Berlin even our Zipper has become someone!'

This bearer of tidings would return to Vienna, surround himself with the regulars and call out: 'Our Zipper isn't an idler any more!'

Arnold Zipper was now a member of several associations, none of them charitable, like the ones his father had frequented! There was an association to promote the erection of an Asta-Nielsen memorial, one or two newspaper clubs, an association which promoted annual film festivals with beauty contests and female boxers. Arnold was an active member everywhere.

He felt not the least compunction about the shady stories which he edited. I do not believe that he noticed even once that he was paid to disseminate lies and half-lies. He never allowed himself to be involved, he would not accept the smallest present, not even a harmless invitation, if he sensed a hidden motive. He lied only for his boss. He was like most of the honest drudges among breadwinners.

206

He had only one aim: to be of service to his wife. Far removed from her, on the periphery of her life, he was at a loose end. They did not live together, eat together, sleep together, and never met. But since everyone knew that Arnold Zipper was the husband of the enchanting, if man-shy film actress, this was enough for him, or it seemed to be enough. For I was to learn later that he was one of the unhappiest men who ever lived between the film and newspaper worlds, although even so he looked happier than he had two years before in Vienna without a wife.

For her, he bowed his back when his publisher stormed at him, for her he spread false rumours, went to interviews, had a thousand brainwaves, and for her he became a 'serviceable film newspaperman'. For her he would talk for hours with advertising agents, and because in the film world dirty linen is washed in public – one of that world's few virtues – Zipper was not ashamed to tell people in coffee houses or clubs that he had brought off a coup or wangled a favour for his wife, however little interest she might take in Arnold's doings.

For she paid no attention to him. She lived outside the city, in the west end, naturally, in an elegant neighbourhood where a colony of well-paid artists lived among the bankers, politicians and industrialists. She lived with three women friends, two Afghan dogs (which were very fashionable at that time, as they reminded people of Potsdam and made an impression with their silly, delicate grace), a chauffeur and a gardener in a villa; naturally it had to be a villa. Statues of Buddha began in the hall and went on up into her bedroom. One of her friends was a morphine addict – to lend a bit of tone – and owned a gramophone, which lullabied her to sleep. It played all day long, and one could hear its distant wheezing accompanying the melodies it played through every door, and the gentle squeaking of the handle as it was wound up. Above, in a room which contained only Afghans, sofas and Buddhas, lived Arnold's wife, when she wasn't at the studios.

At home she wore a kimono in the morning; for her 'second breakfast', which she took at about four in the afternoon, she affected a so-called '*déshabillé*' of transparent, pleated silk, and slipped out of this, her daytime ensemble, straight into her evening, which is to say into her 'toilette'. She would then receive guests.

These would be her colleagues from the neighbouring villas, all beloved of the public, demonic, sarcastic, lyrical seducers – and plebeian types, go-getters and irresistible forces of Fate. Ah! How very alike they all looked, and how harmless they all were! They were not made up, there were no lights, no orders from the director. They had no one whom they had to obey; only the custom that they had to marry twice every five years and be burgled every four months. When one looked at them as they played cards or dominoes, or as they ate *schnitzel* and snapped at fluttering salad leaves, or as they mixed liqueurs and danced to the gramophone, one could not understand what actually drove them to become actors, to bustle about desolate, noisy studios in remarkable costumes which entitled them to gush tears and sit on three-ply thrones, to gallop about on horses and go down with ships; nor why, furthermore, they placed their private lives on show in plate-glass windows, had them printed in the papers, shared them with biographers, organised gossip about themselves, lied and denied, fell in love – without believing in love – and separated, without believing in the separation. Oh, why were they not like their fathers, cigar merchants, stockbrokers, sensible watchmakers and bank officers? Why did they pretend to be a merry band of artists, causing trouble to their neighbours, the bank directors, manufacturers, and property owners? Had they all come to the stage for the same reasons as Fräulein Erna Wilder?

Once a week, on Sunday afternoon, Arnold was allowed to visit his wife. 'I can't stand Sundays!' said Erna: 'People are quite a good idea, but people on Sundays get on my nerves! It's a good thing most of them work then.' As a result of this, she did not go out on Sundays. 'I only stay home on Sunday!' she told people who wanted to see her at other times than her official receptions on Wednesdays. So Arnold called on her every Sunday afternoon.

It was the one time in the week when he drove his car; for he brought his wife flowers, and he was too shy to let anyone see him carrying flowers. He wore a smart suit – he now had a few of them. For in the worldly circles which he now frequented one had to dress better than one ate. Arnold even carried a monocle in his waistcoat pocket. When he wore it, it lay in his melancholy face like a frozen lake in an autumn landscape. But he had to wear it, at beauty contests, and also because he was short-sighted.

His clothes came from one of those small, expensive places which are not yet known to the world at large. A year earlier, they had been making suits for postmen, but suddenly had an order from an actor, and now they had nothing more to worry about. Someone or other said in the artists' nightclub: 'I owe Tschipek a thousand marks.'

'Who is Tschipek?' asked someone.

'You don't know who Tschipek is?'

And the other began to wonder if it would be possible to say he had heard of him, before having to admit that he had not.

'Tschipek is the best tailor in Europe!' said the debtor (when he was in a witty mood he would say: 'In Europe and points west!') Then everyone pulled up their chairs and examined the suit.

There were a number of scarcely noticeable and subtle points about it, which only the connoisseur could appreciate, and which at first could not be divined. One was therefore informed by the knowledgeable that the buttonholes were virginally sealed, although they looked as if one could stick a flower into them. The pockets were lined in grey, not white. The trousers stayed up without belt or braces, and the waistcoat had no strap at the back. The inside pockets of the jacket had flaps, and the inner lining had a tuck, so that the material would not be 'drawn', as the technical phrase went.

Zipper, too, had Tschipek 'make' for him. For some years the man had been recommended by word of mouth. 'Everybody's sewing down at Tschipek's,' said Zipper. He showed me several invisible refinements, unknown to other customers and which may well have stayed unknown for ever. I thus remember a waistcoat which was so magically cut that one could wear it 'deep' or 'shallow', which meant that it could be worn with a wide or a narrow cut-out, according to the colour of the shirt one was wearing.

What a long time ago it seemed, that Arnold was wearing a shabby suit of dyed army cloth! My friend Arnold Zipper had taken a fancy to a number of costly toys. His ties set a standard, even people who wished him ill had to admit that. His shoes were hand-sewn to measure and Zipper had as great a hatred of the mass-produced as I had for a knacker's yard.

Many people racked their brains over his relationship with his wife.

'What is she doing with a husband?' asked the ill-intentioned.

'What is he doing with this woman?' asked the kindly ones.

'Why don't they get divorced, like everybody else?' asked the neutrals.

But Erna held that it set a special tone, to be married in this unusual way. If someone asked her, she would explain: 'The worthy Arnold and I were married as Catholics. We cannot be freed from one another.'

And even though I had been their witness at the registrar's, Erna would say this in my presence.

That she should call him the 'worthy' Arnold seemed to me a trifle unworthy, even of her. Why? She had no need to use such an outdated adjective. She might have taken a little trouble to find a more original description. But Arnold only smiled when she called him 'worthy'. When speaking directly to him, she addressed him as 'Dearest'. He smiled, like someone who knows better and who, even if others do believe him to be only worthy, has his moments when other adjectives are applied to him.

I, too, ask myself why she held on to Arnold. But she was clever enough, and bitter enough, to think of the times of misfortune which could come one day. From much of her conversation I thought I detected that she was superstitious, and that she held on to her man, just as some people place some kind of mascot on the bonnet of their car, to ward off accidents. But behind this superstition lay her homesickness, of which she herself was unaware, that icy little bit of soul that a person is not aware of when the room is warm, that hidden fragment of poverty which one reveals to no one and which one does not see oneself when one is wealthy, the tremulous longing which only begins to sing in the last hours of life.

16

On one Sunday afternoon, when Erna had also invited me, I persuaded Arnold not to drive to his wife but to walk there with me.

It was a warm Sunday, the first for a long time. The populace, the 'worthy folk' from whom Erna shut herself away, were wandering about in droves outside. It was late summer, a last, golden gaiety was about in the streets. The trees which stood at their edges were shedding golden leaves. 'I'm grateful,' said Arnold, 'that you persuaded me to come with you. I haven't strolled so contentedly for years. Do you still remember our excursions with my father?'

'Yes,' I said, 'I remember them as if it were yesterday. Your father used to wear a pale grey stiff hat, with an even paler, unusually broad, watered-silk ribbon. It hid amost half the hat.'

'A genuine Habig!' said Arnold.

'Yes, a genuine Habig hat. Your father also had a stick with a real ivory handle. The handle had fallen off a few times, it had a loose screw top. He used to slide paper between the handle and the stick, to hold it more firmly. We used to go into the Krapfenwaldl and stand in front of the Sobieski church, and your father would say: "That Sobieski has been greatly overrated. The Viennese would have seen off the Turks anyway." King Sobieski did not appeal to him.

Basically, your father was a patriot, but he wouldn't admit it – even in wartime.'

'I had a letter from my father yesterday,' said Arnold. 'Do read it.'

I read it.

'My deeply loved son,' I turned over the page to the same old ending: 'Nothing else in particular. Your loving father.' Old Zipper informed his son that he was in good health, and that he went to the cinema three times a week. Thanks to his old contacts, he had free passes, which were valid every day except Sundays and holidays. Not he himself – wrote old Zipper – but, actually, Frau Zipper would appreciate just one note from their celebrated daughter-in-law. 'I still haven't set eyes on her handwriting.' But as long as he knew that his son was happy, he would not think twice about the silence of very busy people. Since he knew, and very well, what intensive work meant.

I gave Arnold back his letter. As was his wont, he folded it in four and placed it in his wallet. We were silent for a few minutes. Suddenly Arnold said: 'Fathers sense how it goes with their sons. If he knew what my marriage looks like!'

I tried a joke: 'What do you expect? You still get along!'

'Don't joke,' said Arnold, 'I've never been happy in my life, but I was never as unhappy as I am now. If you knew what these years have been like. It began in Breslau. We lived in a hotel, in adjoining rooms. The porter left the communicating door open when we arrived and he'd brought up the luggage. She showed me out. She changed. Then we ate. "I want to sleep by myself," she said. "Of course," I said.

'I went to my room and read. I read a play in which she was to perform, made notes, imagined her, and I loved her in those days – not like now. I loved her in a childish way, I was crazy about her, I wanted to devote my life to her, and one life

213

didn't seem enough. I dreamed of dying, to make her happy. I went on reading, and all of a sudden I heard her very quietly sliding the bolt into position. How carefully it was done! But she didn't want me to hear – and that, you see, was the great hurt.

'I didn't sleep at all that night. I found my consolation. I thought: she slid the bolt so softly so as not to disturb me. She didn't know if I had gone to sleep yet. I hung on to this consolation so hard that I was afraid of going to sleep. I was happy, and I was kept awake by my happiness.

'But in the morning I knocked and she answered: "Coming," and then – then she slid the bolt softly back again. I had been so happy as I got up. I found it quite natural that we should not sleep together. But now the door opened and suddenly I hated Erna. She must have seen it. But she never gets excited. She's always calm, so much cleverer than me, and so charming. Isn't she?'

'I'm sorry you're in love,' I said.

'You don't like her,' said Arnold. 'I've known that for a long time. You think she's wicked. If one didn't love her, one might think her wicked. But I'm the only one who understands her. No one knows her.'

After a while, he went on: 'When this thing with girls started, I had no idea. I thought these were harmless friendships. We were still living together at the time, my room was next to hers. I was fast asleep, and suddenly I woke up. It seemed to me that someone had cried out. I knocked on her door. Nobody seemed to hear. I opened the door. They jumped. That little Anny was with her. "What are you doing here?" asked Erna. I apologised. "I heard someone call," I said. And when I returned to my room, Anny was lying in my bed.

'Next day I moved into the Pension.'

214

He was silent again. He walked into a big heap of leaves and kicked them.

Then he began: 'All the same, I do understand her. No one can understand her as I do – and I wait.'

'For what?'

'I wait for the day when she'll send for me. Every day I believe: now she'll come. Every time the phone rings in my office, I hesitate for a moment before lifting the receiver. I've lived under this strain for a year. When I go home, my heart stands still when I'm on the stairs. This time, I think, she'll be waiting inside. And then I see the empty room. I look again, carefully, in every corner, pull the curtains back, because I remember that once, just once, one night she played a game with me. She had hidden, then, behind the curtains.'

'And suppose this day never comes?'

'Out of the question. I really know her. She herself is waiting for this day. She has no idea of it. I know her better than she knows herself.'

We arrived at the house. The maid said: 'The *gnädige Frau* left last night. Here is a letter.' Arnold stuck the letter in his pocket without looking at it. We walked halfway back in silence. We then turned in to a coffee house. There Arnold began to read.

'She's had to leave suddenly,' he said. 'They're shooting a film in Ischl. I know nothing about this. Could it be *The Deadly Mountain*? Or *In the Shadow of the Giant*? There's some sort of fairy-tale film in which she is to be the Princess.'

What else was there to talk about? We went our separate ways. A few days later, in the *Illustrierte Zeitung*, I saw Erna at the side of a well-known actor who specialised in demons on the screen, but who was wearing mountaineering clothes in the photograph.

'Art in the Mountains,' ran the caption. All these young

people from all the arts were carrying alpenstocks and falling about with laughter.

For the next two months Arnold was not to be seen. He did not come to the coffee house, nor did he come into the club. I looked him up at his paper.

'She could have done anything,' he said, 'but to go away with that idiot, no! The shooting of that film, *In the Shadow of the Giant*, doesn't begin for another six weeks. If she has her little ways with the girls, well and good. But what's it going to lead to if she starts going off with men? Everyone will think she's just a little tart now. With that fellow! He is the dumbest! Even among actors, he is the dumbest!'

He went on: 'I could understand it if she'd taken advantage of some exceptional opportunity. Director-General Hartwig, for example. He's been after her for years. He wanted to set up a complete film company for her, the lot. He wanted to make her a present of the big Alga Studios. I would have let her divorce me at once if I'd felt that it was necessary for her. If nothing happens in the next week from now I'll take leave and go to her.'

Arnold went to the desk, riffled through the calendar and underlined a date in red.

'I shall go,' he said.

On his desk stood six photographs of his wife. Erna in different costumes and parts. Erna, Erna, Erna.

As Arnold was about to go out, he put the photographs into a big briefcase and shut them into a drawer.

'I never leave those pictures lying around,' he said.

At that moment Arnold was brought a telegram. He let the overcoat, which was hanging over his arm, fall to the floor, along with his hat and stick. His hands were trembling. He went to the window, as if to read by better light. (It was dusk already.) He thought for a minute, went to the door, turned on the light, then the reading lamp on the desk, sat down as if to begin work on some major project, and opened the telegram.

'I'm off this minute,' he cried, and shot out of the room.

17

It was at about that time that old Zipper came to Berlin. A lawsuit, in which he had been involved for many years, and which he liked to talk about with a certain pride, as if it concerned a considerable sum of money, the payment of which would be expedited by the result of the case – whereas at best it could only lead to a verdict against Zipper – was at last due to come to trial. And although in due process of law, as the jurists put it, it would have been more usual to hold the trial in the city in which old Zipper lived, he had managed, by all sorts of tricks and stratagems – which would never have succeeded had they not been to his own disadvantage – and after the passage of many years, to have the case heard in a Berlin court, because Zipper had the impression that 'the thing would be dealt with more rapidly' than in Austria, where 'the judges sit about biting their nails.' Old Zipper, who had for a long time wanted to come to Berlin, now had an excuse which would have been justified even in the eyes of his wife, had she not long since grown tired of asking her husband to account for himself. 'This lawsuit has already cost me a small fortune,' Old Zipper used to like saying. But what lawsuit does not? And when he was asked: 'Do you really have a chance of winning?' Zipper would smile a weary, knowledgeable smile, as one who has discovered the secrets of creation might smile when asked whether God really has a long white beard. Zipper's eyes would be lost for some time in unknown, perhaps unearthly, regions, returning from which, shining and illuminated, they would resume their questioning gaze. And, as if from some world which his questioner would never attain, Zipper's answer would come: 'Will I win my case? My dear friend, cases do not depend on laws, but on Fate. It is my firm conviction that all those thick volumes were written in vain and have been studied in vain. The judge has no idea, nor have the plaintiff or the lawyer. Only the defendant has some vague clue, and in this case I am the defendant,' and Zipper laid his right hand, with fingers outspread, on the broad cravat which flourished above his waistcoat. 'Yes, just look at me,' he went on, 'I am the defendant. And, as I live and breathe, the verdict will go against me! It's true that my lawyers tell me there are ways round this. But I'm not in favour of ways round. True, I do not believe in justice, but I do believe in Fate. Let it take its course!'

On the day Arnold received his telegram, I also received one, from Arnold's father: 'Arriving Wednesday, 11 a.m. Excuse inconvenience. Details verbally,' ran the text. I must expect old Zipper – I was in any case curious to see him. He arrived with an elegant leather trunk, which he had borrowed from a business friend for this trip. He wore an English travelling cap with large checks, and he brought the stick with the genuine ivory handle, along with an umbrella in its case.

He stepped out of his compartment, chronometer in hand, and I had hardly greeted him before he said, tapping the glass of the watch: 'Exactly one minute and ten seconds late! Furthermore, I've noticed that the electrical clocks on these stations all tell different times. I ask myself what point there is in this electricity!' As we entered the taxi he said: 'To Arnold's house,' in tones from which it was to be deduced that old Zipper assumed that every taxi driver must know Arnold's address.

'I would have telegraphed Arnold himself,' said the old man, 'but I think it's better to surprise him. He wrote to me that his wife is away, so we need fear no disturbance.'

I did not tell old Zipper that Arnold had never lived with his wife. It would have been an effort to resist or deflect his questions. I managed not to talk to Zipper at all. I just let him talk and meditated about him. He hadn't altered at all. He had become younger. The war, the death of his elder son, the ill-fortune of the younger – which he must sense – worries, debts, the burdens of age had only laid sorrow about him as though it were a covering, a cloak which one puts on because it is cold outside, not because one is freezing oneself. Just as to some people a change of climate means nothing and winter seems just as warm as summer, even if they follow the prevailing custom and wear an overcoat in winter and leave off their waistcoat in summer, so there may be people who carry inside them an unthinking cheerfulness just as they do their own temperature, and who merely wrap themselves in a chilly atmosphere of mourning when something tragic happens to them. So I had been mistaken! I had mistaken the old man for a has-been, perhaps because I had been concentrating on the son with the intensity I had formerly devoted to his father. But the father was still well worth studying!

We arrived. Arnold had just eaten. He was packing. His bags were standing on chairs, his vivid ties hung over their backs, a kind of mundane art. There was hardly anywhere to sit.

Arnold was by no means as surprised as the old man might have expected. His head was full to bursting with quite different thoughts. He was thinking about his wife. 'Sit down!' he said, after briefly embracing his father, and without noticing that there was nowhere to sit. 'What will you eat?' he asked, almost grumpily. 'Two eggs in a glass, soft-boiled, timed by the hour-glass, not the way your mother cooks them!' replied old Zipper, still very precise and not noticing that he had arrived at an awkward moment. By the time coffee was ready, Arnold's bags were packed. He had calmed down, obviously because, like many another, he suffered from the happy delusion that packed bags mean a journey already accomplished.

They sat facing each other, the old man and the young one. For the first time, they sat facing each other, not in their own house, not surrounded by the familiar furniture, not with Frau Zipper in the offing. No longer as father and son. Like an example from history, I thought. Representation of two generations of the same race. Each had the job of representing his time.

'Your wife is away, of course!' began the old man in the tone of voice which he used at home to say: 'The tea is lukewarm, of course!'

'She has unfortunately had an accident and I'm just about to go to her!' replied Arnold. 'And I don't like you taking that tone when you speak of her.'

'I meant no harm. What sort of accident, incidentally?'

'I don't know yet. I'm on my way there.'

'Now,' said the old man, 'an accident is only publicity for an artiste. They say that Sarah Bernhardt earned twice as much after having her leg cut off.'

'For God's sake!' yelled Arnold.

'I'm not saying that your wife will have her leg amputated. And she won't earn a third of what Sarah Bernhardt does.'

'In the circumstances, who's talking about money?'

'I've often had to give you a hand, my son, since you married her. And you know my affairs aren't in the best shape. My lawsuit is costing me a pretty penny, and now I've had to pay for this expensive journey.'

'How can you reproach me about money in this situation? You know I married an artist.'

'Bread comes before art,' old Zipper asserted.

'And I may as well tell you right away that you will have to raise the cost of my journey here and now,' continued Arnold. 'It's a good thing you came. If Erna has really had an accident I must get her into the very best hospital. She mustn't think of taking advance payments which will tie her up for years. I have to secure her financial independence.'

'How much money do you need?' asked the old man. At that moment he was imitating one of the American billionaires he had seen at the cinema, one of those who always have a chequebook handy to help their sons out of awkward situations.

'As much as you can raise!' said Arnold.

'That's going too far!' the old man said furiously. Every month he had to try in vain to postpone one debt with another.

'If only one could be sure that it was only art which occupies her time,' said old Zipper more calmly, in the tones of an expert smugly confirming his own expertise by the use of such a precious expression.

'She is the most passionate actress I have ever seen,' said Arnold, 'and for one gesture of her hand I would give all the monologues of the great tragediennes.'

'She's not strongly enough built to make a tragedienne,' contradicted old Zipper. 'Besides which I have yet to see her act.'

'Ah, if only she were well, you'd see her this evening and admit I'm right.'

'So, does she convince you, too?' the old man asked me.

'I believe her to be capable of a great deal.'

'Yes, yes! Capable of a great deal!' repeated old Zipper.

And I noticed how pride in his daughter-in-law woke again in the old man. He had only suppressed it in order to simultaneously promote himself and his wounded vanity. Full of the circumstances attending his case, and preparing the part which he would play before the court next day – a Berlin court at that, where everything always worked out – he had felt himself obliged to give less importance to Erna than he would have in quiet times. Now, however, because of this accident, she had come to have greater significance, not only as a person but also as an actress. In fact, old Zipper only contradicted his son for dramatic motives, so as to have a chance to say his piece, to keep the dialogue going, and because he liked to give the impression that he could only ever be persuaded with great difficulty and after a long while.

For these reasons, they quarrelled about Erna's genius for a bit longer.

I wasn't surprised at the old man, but I was to some extent taken aback by Arnold. It seemed to me that only now, for the first time, had I established the similarity between father and son, now that they were quarrelling over a subject about which they were really in agreement. I noticed in Arnold's expression the same mark of a lost and childlike happiness which had so fatally branded the old man's face. Except that in Arnold's case it was veiled in melancholy. It was as though the son were already aware of being a figure of fun, and had thus attained tragic stature, while his father exhibited the same characteristic with the victorious pride of a man who believes that, precisely because of it, he will ultimately triumph.

We sat like this for a long while – Arnold's train didn't

leave till evening – drinking many cups of coffee and talking about Erna. Finally – twilight was coming on – old Zipper raised his voice and said, 'Right is right! Honour the truth! Show me a picture of Erna!'

Arnold brought a dozen photographs of Erna in various roles. Old Zipper brought a magnifying glass out of his pocket, closed one eye, bent over the table and studied the photographs.

Finally, he said: 'You seem to be right! She holds herself nobly, I must say! I can almost hear her declaim! Medea! At the end, when she sends over the poisoned garments, you remember! It's a shame that I go so seldom to the *Burgtheater*. It isn't easy to get free passes there, and besides I don't like to make myself unhappy. But this woman does hold herself nobly. If ever she comes to the *Burgtheater*, I shall go and see her!'

And Arnold, Arnold who knew his father as well as I did, Arnold cried: 'Isn't it true that she's a great actress?' as if he were receiving the verdict from the mouth of the greatest connoisseur.

Evening drifted into the room and softened the lines in both their faces. Now they were sitting there as alike as two brothers. One could see neither the white hair of the old man, nor the brown hair of the young one.

They sat there in the evening as if they were in a ship, sailing slowly, foolishly and happily towards the same destination.

18

The following morning Zipper's court case began. And although this case represented no more than an unimportant episode in the lives of the two Zippers and no more than a minor detail in the account on which I am engaged, yet I must not fail to report as much of the legal proceedings as I believe I know. For I was not present throughout. Besides, I had neither the time nor the wish to immerse myself, as the jurists say, in the substance of the case. Generally speaking, I only know that old Zipper was, of course, in the wrong and that only out of folly and a certain pleasure in unsavoury business had he allowed the matter to come to court. The case concerned contracts to deliver paper in Germany; so much for the broad outline, but the particulars of the business bothered me less than the principal actor.

I came into the court two hours after the opening of the proceedings. There was still a very small public attendance. Old Zipper spotted me at once. He sat beside his lawyer, and although the latter wore the usual legal robes, old Zipper looked far more ceremonious and to some extent more juristic. He was wearing a black suit, a top hat lay in front of him, he was leafing through papers in a briefcase, drinking a gulp of water now and again and looking about from side to side although there were so few people to look at him. He saw me as soon as I came in, waved cheerfully to me, and pointed me towards a place on the front bench. He smiled in my direction. He was playing with a pencil, sharpening it and making a regular, swishing sound which caused the judge to pause for a moment, although he was on the point of delivering a very long and important sounding sentence. It seemed as if no one in the courtroom noticed anything odd about old Zipper. It seemed rather that they were all taken in by his air of respectability. Probably, since they did not know him as well as I did, they thought that he was following the progress of the case with acute attention, and that he was so confident of the justice of his cause that he was only waiting till the last moment to pull some great surprise from his briefcase, to the consternation of the plaintiff. Whenever Zipper's lawyer addressed the court the old man would listen, only to shake his head a moment later. Indeed, this unusual defendant would go so far, in full view of his counsel, as to make confidential grimaces at the judge which gave the impression of making fun of his lawyer's naivety. His defender would sit down again, somewhat confused, and enquire of old Zipper whether he had been under a misapprehension. The defendant would begin a whispered explanation of the case with his lawyer. The lawyer, who could be assumed to know something of the business in hand, and who had only been trying to give a subtly slanted exposition, would again rise to his feet. He would hardly have uttered a sentence before old Zipper began to disclaim what he said with more vigorous shaking of the head. Eventually the judge urged Zipper to speak for himself. Whereupon he began to repeat word for word what his lawyer had said. For he also was clever enough to put the circumstances in a more favourable light than the judge or the plaintiff's lawyer would have done. But, being incapable of keeping silence while his position was being discussed, and feeling a bit put out by the silent role allotted to him by his defender, old Zipper denied, while seated, the very facts he himself proclaimed when he was on his feet. And each time the judge saw him shake his head and asked him: 'Well, Herr Zipper, you will agree –' he would rise to his feet and, to everybody's surprise, declare: 'By no means! I am in complete agreement with my lawyer!' He would then bow to the judge, nod to his lawyer, sit down, look across at me and smile. It looked as if, because of this unusual behaviour by the defendant, the case might become even more complicated than it was already. As a result a slight air of fatigue became noticeable on the faces of all the participants. Only old Zipper's face was fresh and beaming, as if he had just stepped out of his bath. I doubt if he would have worn such an air of triumph if he'd just won his case. The lawyer for the defence, who wanted to gain some advantage for his lost cause from this general weariness, proposed an indefinite adjournment for the summoning of fresh witnesses, and explained that he wished to procure new evidence. The court consented to this proposal with alacrity. Zipper made a deep obeisance, closed his briefcase, which emitted a loud creak, and left the courtroom with such a measured tread, top hat in gloved right hand, that the beadle, probably unconsciously, bowed before him as to an Attorney-General.

I had expected Herr Zipper to talk to me about the case, but he greeted me with the question: 'Has Arnold left already?' And when I answered that he had, Zipper said: 'Then I'll send him the money. I'll get my deposit back from my lawyer. In any case he's quite incompetent. I just wouldn't want to blame him. Do you know what I was thinking about during the whole proceeding? I was telling myself that it would have been better to let my son take up the law. Arnold has a markedly legalistic brain.'

That evening old Zipper went home. As I gave him my hand at the station, he said, right out: 'Shall we see each other again?' It was as if a cloud had suddenly come sailing over his sunny foolishness. Perhaps Death, which already stood behind him, had given him a gentle tap on the shoulder. I meant to answer him with some banal word of comfort, but the train slid away as I stood, open-mouthed, and there was nothing I could do but wave farewell to my old friend. I could pick out his handkerchief for a long time. It seemed to wave more busily than the others.

19

That very same evening I saw the demoniac actor in a nightclub. He told me how Erna had been thrown from a horse and had hurt herself. He had had to come back because his money had run out, they still hadn't begun shooting and nobody from the management had been seen at all. Consequently Erna had wired her husband.

It turned out that Erna was seriously ill. She was brought to a hospital in Berlin.

That was Arnold's finest hour, for he could spend all night with her, and lived in the hospital.

During the day she received the visits which are the due of an actress who has had an accident. She enjoyed the gratification which is customary on these occasions. She wallowed in the appreciation which was her due. Nothing is more agreeable than to read a set of obituaries, of a sort, and yet to know that you are still alive.

Shooting was postponed. In reports of parties and balls it was said that she was 'missed'. Ah, the delicious décor of the flower-strewn sickbed! Happy returns from an unhappy accident! At once sought after and missed!

She had to have an operation. It turned out that she would limp for some time.

Her name gradually slipped out of the papers. The film was made without her. Her replacement received good notices. Her advances shrank. She left the hospital. Arnold moved into her villa.

She sold the car and let the gardener go. The girls moved out. Only the gramophone stayed in the house. Visitors became rare. It looked as if the young Zippers were living on Arnold's salary alone. They sold the house, moved into town and rented a large apartment in a smart building. Then Arnold discovered one just as big but at the back of a house, for half the rent. They moved into these back premises. Before one reached them one passed through a long paved courtyard where hens were clucking. The porter kept his kitchen windows open. One could smell what he was eating. Arnold now had a salon. But it wasn't like the one he had had at home, that dark, damp room. It was warm and dry. On the sideboard stood little Buddhas, with tiny drawers in their tiny bellies. In these drawers lay knick-knacks, cuttings, bits of Erna's make-up.

They had a servant, a stern woman with a face like the roots of a tree, knobbly and dark. She wore a long blue apron, the size of which reminded me of Frau Zipper's aprons.

One ate in a room adjoining the kitchen, at a small, round table, and each day Erna had fresh flowers brought in. She read with great care newspapers the names of which she would not have know before. Since fame had deserted her, she now looked to the world for novelty, the unknown world, with horror and curiosity. Since for the time being she had no goal to aim at, it seemed that her intelligence diminished. It was an apparatus which only operated in certain conditions.

Erna became sensitive, mistrustful, weepy, a pitiful little woman. She was still an intrigue, but she played her cards wrong. She suspected Arnold of not working hard enough on her behalf. 'It ought to be his job to remind the world of me every day. But he's happy that I'm not working.' If he came home and said he had been in company, she would ask: 'Did they talk about me?' Arnold had to recount in the most minute detail when, why and how the talk had turned to Erna. He had to describe the women's clothes and repeat their conversation word by word. Had she not in her time been taxed by her own mother?

Her fracture did not heal. It became worse when the weather was cold. They sent her to Nice for the winter. She would not travel alone. Arnold had to go with her. He took six weeks' leave. When his leave was over, she forced him to stay with her. She ran up debts. Old Zipper sent more money.

Six months later I ran into Arnold in Monte Carlo. He was gambling, and winning. Not big sums, but he and his wife were living off his winnings. Every day he would win a couple of hundred francs.

'I've no system whatever,' said Arnold. 'I win simply because I don't set my sights high. I wander up there every morning, slowly and without a thought in my head, just as one goes to some boring job where nothing can happen to one. Every evening at six I cash in my chips. I've never won more than a thousand francs. Sometimes it's a hundred, sometimes three hundred, sometimes seven hundred and fifty.'

'What does Erna do?'

'Gets better and better. She's putting on weight and

beginning to worry about slimming. She's determined to act again. But I don't believe she will. In any case I'm quite indifferent to her.'

'Indifferent?'

'Yes. Why not? I'm not in love. We live like an old married couple. It's just that I'm too lazy to leave her. By now I'm used to these gambling rooms, to the daily bus to and from Nice, to Erna who will be sitting in the window or by the water. It's not a bad life.'

I went on my way. Arnold promised to write. He did not write during the months which followed.

At one time I read in the paper that Erna had gone back to films. She was to go to America.

A few months later I saw an American film in which she appeared. It was a feature film, as they call it in the trade. Erna played a mature woman, the rival of a sixteen-year-old in a struggle for a man in his forties. The sixteen-year-old was her niece. She had the best chance, so Erna won sympathy. She won the man in the end. She had to be clever, honourable and thoughtful, rather hard, full of bitter experience of life, sceptical as far as men were concerned, endowed with enough good heart to seem sad when she was alone, but not so sentimental that she might cry. One was meant, rather, to suppose that anyone else in her position would have cried. She was one of those who bravely choke back their tears, as the saying goes. In real life she would of course have been seen off by the sixteen-year-old. For life is fair, and grudges success to those who have shown that they can survive without visible happiness. The special sense of justice of American films, however, rewarded Erna's efforts.

I could spot that she still limped slightly. The public certainly would not have noticed it. Probably, I thought, in that magical Hollywood, she would be given a new hip of platinum or even of alabaster, so that the weak leg would be gripped by a reliable joint. In America nothing was impossible.

I was sorry not to be able to watch how she pursued her career over there. The film I saw gave me only a remote inkling of all the experiments which must have preceded it.

I went again, and a third time, to that film. Each time it seemed to me that I could understand more from a scene, a look, a movement, than was really to be found in the plot. But I learned nothing new. Her face simply impressed itself on my mind. She looked beautiful in that film, beautiful as people can be only in America. She was noble in a way which only the victorious can be in America. She was so womanly, so helpless, so touching, during the few minutes that external loneliness threatened her, that one took her for a whole woman.

Suddenly a postcard arrived from Arnold, a picture postcard from Lisbon, with greetings. After a few weeks another card turned up, this time from Boston. After a rather longer pause I received a third one, from Amsterdam. What had happened to him? What kind of fate was tossing him about the world like this?

I was soon to learn.

20

A few months after I received this last card from Arnold, I travelled to Vienna. I decided to call on the Zippers, not only because Arnold's fate interested me, but also because I wanted to talk to old Zipper. I could see in my mind's eye the noisy street in which they lived, the broad house with the imitation marble front, to the right of the *Elegalanterie* shop, everything in the windows of which belonged to the 'Luxury' class, and was made of a different material from what one would at first glance have supposed. What looked like crocodile skin was artistically fiddled calf, snakeskin came from lizards, silk was artificial, sapphires were glass, gold rings were *doublé*, silver cutlery was plated, steel was nickel, and even iron was not genuine. I could see the old photographic display to the left of the entrance, the bridal couples constantly being replaced. The last time I had looked in, there was still a photograph of old Zipper disguised as a sergeant hanging there, the last picture left from the war – the photographer had swept away all other uniforms. Old Zipper had probably been allowed to stay because the photographer was mindful of such a worthy and close neighbour.

I could see the cold, stone steps, the worn green carpet which only went up one floor, the iron banisters, the cheerful window panes in the corridors engraved with naked women, allegedly 'symbolic' figures. I smelt the houses one passed on the way to the Zippers'; onions, people, beds. I saw the note on the Zippers' door – 'Please knock loudly, bell out of order' – for how many years had it been out of order? And that dark entrance hall in which, since my earliest youth, an umbrella had leant in a stand, and no one knew who had forgotten it. We used to play with it. Gradually, it had lost all its skin and one saw its hard, iron skeleton.

Finally I conjured up old Zipper – *old* Zipper. He had always been old for me, even when he had thought of himself as young. How old he was now! How green must his black suit have become, how grey that white cravat, how loose the ivory grip of his stick; how gently must he deal with his wife nowadays, perhaps they lived together like a couple of old doves. They couldn't still be shooting poisoned arrows at one another, the poison must have become harmless, or their bodies immune to it. Did Zipper's brother still come at Easter and did Secretary Wandl still inhabit the salon?

When I thought that I should shortly be sitting with the Zippers in the 'dining room', it seemed like calling back to mind an old, tedious, pain which had been with one all one's childhood, something like swollen tonsils, which one had to thank for a few carefree hours in bed. I could measure the years which had rolled over me by the many changes which had happened in the Zippers' house, the unfortunate results of unfortunate efforts which had always encouraged a false gaiety, by the hopes gone astray, their glitter always false, as if they were green not by nature, but from paint. I would soon be reaching the age at which old Zipper had become a father. It seemed to me, though, that I was still going to school with Arnold. There he sat, at the right-hand end of the third bench.

I had a certain tenderness for old Zipper. He had been good to me, and had sometimes been merry. He had said: 'Show me that hand of yours; you've hurt yourself, we'll go across to the

233

chemist and have something put on it.' And as our infantry company was pulling out, he had shouted: 'Victory at Lublin!' Everything he had undertaken had gone wrong. At the chemist, he bought the wrong thing for my hand, and he consoled us with a victory which was no use to us. His jokes were not cheerful, when he was serious he was laughable, his ambition missed its target, he was a speaker with a poor memory, a carpenter who could make nothing, a violin maker with only one tune – a sad tune, but one that made him happy. But he had nonetheless filled my days. Arnold had lent him to me, often.

I went to Zipper's quite early in the morning, because I knew his old custom of going for a walk about the streets at eleven, and that after lunch he would be sitting in a coffee house, and that in the evening he would use his free pass to go to the cinema. I was about ten paces from the house, the sun's rays lay clear and golden across the street, when I saw a black box being loaded into a black coach. Two men in black top hats then climbed on to the coach, the reins tightened and the hearse rolled away through the bright sunshine.

Zipper, none other, was dead.

The shopkeeper told me the story. A week previously Frau Zipper had travelled to Brunn, to her brother's. Only yesterday the old man had said to him, the shopkeeper, that his wife was staying away too long. After such a happy marriage one cannot bear to be alone, even for ten days. He died that evening. The housekeeper had telephoned the cemetery at six in the morning. Zipper had died at the moment – and how well I remembered it – that he was winding his watch, as he did every evening. He had dropped it and fallen himself. And so the maid had found him.

Three days later I read that they were burying him. Frau Zipper stood by the grave. She did not cry. I thought, all her tears are long since shed. Representatives of many associations made speeches. Arnold was not there.

After a couple of days I determined to call on his mother and ask after him.

21

The next morning I met a mutual friend of Arnold's and mine, one Eduard P.

Haggard and stealthy, always keeping to the wall or to the edge of the pavement, never to be seen walking about the middle of a room, P made one think of a shadow which, shaken loose from its body, no longer looks for it and has resigned itself from any bodily existence. He not only drifted along the edges of streets, but also on the margins of events. To some extent he neglected them. He was an outsider, and he adopted an attitude towards the world and its goings on as if he was not himself part of it.

Indeed, he did so with a passion. Although he could become enraged by the detestable, scornful of the mediocre and admiring of the beautiful, even then he was more of an ardent spirit than an ardent person. His passion came from the beyond, the measure by which he judged men and their actions was not of this world, and was therefore unjust. His sense of justice was either divine or infernal, in any event not human. Of all the people I knew, he seemed the most likely to understand the imcomprehensible destinies which are handed down by the unknown.

He was coming out of the authors' and artists' coffee house. But in that establishment he was not a guest, like the others, but a sort of *genius loci*, a ghost perhaps, the spirit of some long-departed writer, who had left no books behind him and who found no inclination to join the habitués of the beyond in their usual pastime of haunting, but preferred to converse with the living. He read no books, and never went to the theatre, but he always knew what was being played and written. He offered no opinions. It seemed to him frivolous, demeaning, even, to give an opinion about an individual work. He placed each event in the context of the century, and from his lofty viewpoint, from which he looked down over three hundred or six hundred years, he would talk about some forgotten book which had found its place and its oblivion in its own decade.

I had always previously avoided P, for fear of the altitude at which he lived and the icy blast which might descend on me. After all, one is alive, has one's hopes, may even be immortal, but nevertheless feels happy within the limited horizons of the few decades which circumscribe human life. One would rather not know about the insignificance, the triviality, of a phrase one coins, an action one undertakes, a pain one feels. When P was talking it was like peering into the milky way and experiencing, to the power of a hundred thousand suns and a million planets, what is apportioned to our single sun and earth. His relentlessness was neither unfair or cruel, for some felt that it was necessary. But one probably had to have reached a great age before one could talk at all with P.

P had never left the city. He was ill, he had not gone to the war, he was waiting to die. Since it was certain that he was going to die, everyone kept wondering at his still being alive. A number of people held it against him that he had not kept his word. Perhaps they were nervous of him, as I was.

In any case, I had never supposed that he would outlive old Zipper. For although Zipper was far older than P, it still seemed to me that, despite all his peculiar characteristics, he ought to last indefinitely. It was as if old Zipper had not existed in ordinary life, but in another realm, not subject to death and decay, whereas young Eduard P, despite being a spirit already, was nonetheless embodied as a weakly member of this world over which, hour by hour, death was scattered down like snow in winter.

'I see from today's paper that old Zipper is dead,' said P. 'Did you know him? He was the perfect example of a certain type of Viennese. The paragon of petit bourgeois liberalism, a philistine whom I would have abominated, had his muddled head not been his excuse.'

'Do you, by any chance, know where Arnold is?'

'Ah, you don't know about Arnold's fate? If I remember correctly, you've always held that life was never as eccentric as are writers. As I recall it, the text of your sermon in the coffee house, in the evening, on the sofa, at the *Rote Ecke*, used to be that it was the author's duty to write down what he saw. Am I right? Now, if you were a novelist of the good old school, you would have in Arnold's life a lode of remarkable ore. You know that in Monte Carlo he and Frau Erna lived off his daily winnings? Isn't that romantic enough? But, just you wait! That sly Erna (who once fooled you, you too!) managed to get to Hollywood from Nice, where she met an American film man. You've probably seen her latest film. An outstanding role. There, at last, is a good actress without a grain of talent. The day she left Monte Carlo, Arnold began to lose. He had to eat. But what did he know? His father had brought him up to be a genius, as my father did me, but it did me no harm because I was not in any case cut out for living. Arnold has his father to thank for just one trade: he can play,

ZIPPER AND HIS FATHER

as you known, the fiddle and the piano. In these circumstances, what does one do? Perhaps you remember how
Arnold played? No God-given talent, that goes without
saying! But old Zipper used to say: "He goes straight to the
heart." Perhaps after all he should have been a musician. Do
you remember what an idler he was? How he used to always
sit at our table and never say a word? But that's by the way.
Back to your novel.

'So Arnold went into some café-concert, and they didn't
need a pianist, but they could use a first violin. A solo piece
once an evening, with piano accompaniment, "*Ave Maria*" or
some such. You know those pauses for reflection, when the
society people feel awkward and the petits bourgeois chew the
cud. Have you noticed how people slurp their coffee during
the solo? Then a few people clap, to the annoyance of the
socialites. The solo violin bows but doesn't play any more.
He's not paid for two solos. But the leader of the orchestra
makes a sign, whereupon he stands up and begins again. And
after the encore nobody claps anymore. It is too much even
for the petits bourgeois. So the soloist sits down, somewhat
mortified.

'Zipper was one of those soloists.

'But it becomes even more novelettish. Come on, we must
have a coffee, I can't talk so much any more. Old Johann,
Markor, has gone on leave for the first time in forty years. So I
have no credit. But you'll invite me.'

P went on with his story: 'One evening Lock, the famous
clown, comes to Nice and into the café, just in the middle of
the solo. During the interval he goes up to Arnold and takes
him on as his partner. Now Arnold really is a musician. I
never did know where his face would fit. Now I know:
unquestionably in a variety show.'

P drew out his wallet and took a photograph from it. It was

238

Arnold. He was wearing baggy trousers, a tight-fitting jacket, and a light-coloured top hat with a wide ribbon.

'A genuine clown!' I cried.

'Just look!' continued P. 'Take a look at this face! This face has had twenty thousand thick ears! It has a dog-like melancholy. It looks so sad because it cannot say how sad it is. Think of his entrance. He comes on stage, unsuspecting, has no idea that the public is sitting in the stalls. He is a fathead, and he looks like one, like someone who only needs a meal and a drink to put him in a good humour. He wants to play a piece on his violin. But as soon as he is ready to play another clown comes on, a self-confident one, also a fathead, but a fathead with ambitions, who knows very well that there is a public, a director, wages. This clever one gives our Arnold a thick ear. Arnold has played precisely two notes. But these two notes, which he plays before the other one notices, are so clear, so heavenly, that all the audience is sorry that Arnold doesn't play on. Do you know this one? Of course. You've already spotted it, and now you know that Arnold's musical gift is just sufficient to play those two notes divinely. There's your novel!'

'I don't see anything there that would make a novel,' I said, 'even if I were to write the life of Arnold, it wouldn't be a novel in the true sense of the word. Moreover, I have to protest that to me this conclusion seems a bit precious. I would have left Arnold as solo violinist in the café-concert. And I couldn't have dealt with him apart from his father.'

'Now there you're right!' cried P. 'The Zippers belong together. Look at the father. He is responsible for Arnold's misfortune, and for the fact that Arnold is always unlucky. But that's beside the point. All our fathers are responsible for our bad luck. Our fathers belong to the generation which made the war. They gave their watch-chains and their wedding rings in exchange for iron ones. Ah! What patriots they were! Nothing upset my father so much as my illness, which prevented me from going to the war. Just think: who was it who in the summer of 1914 demonstrated before the Serbian Embassy; us or our fathers? Who had "encircled" the enemy – at least in the Mess? That afternoon with the sixty-sixth? *You* were loaded down like an ox and it was your father who said to your mother: "Every bullet doesn't find its target." Even though your father did join up again, all he did was to guard a bridge at Floridsdorf.

'Just think back: you came back, you, the unluckiest generation of the modern era. What had happened? Your fathers had had time to get new children on the girls who were actually meant for you. You'd hardly come home before your fathers were sitting again in the chairs they had had at the outbreak of war. They made the newspapers, public opinion, the peace treaties, politics. You young people were a thousand times more competent, but exhausted, half dead and needing to rest. You had no means of earning a living. It made no difference whether you had lived or died. And to *what* did you come home? To your parents' houses!

'Do you recall those sinister parental homes? Did you ever see the Zippers' bookshelves? I often played with those books. There were three sets of a year's issues, splendidly bound, of *Moderne Zeit*, *Deutsche Knabenbuch* and *Der Trompeter von Säckingen* – what literature! Do you remember that sideboard? We have one like it at home. I'm scared of its corners at a metre's distance. What mortally dangerous furniture! Those tinkling chandeliers with porcelain electric candles made to look like wax! Those calendars, which were hung once a year above the desk! And those papers with leading articles, which they subscribed to. Nowadays my father cannot go to sleep without knowing what "He" has said. "He" is the absolute He behind the leading article. "He"

240

lives there, where everything is known. "He" is basically a stupid little burgher like his readers.

'Arnold is the young man of the wartime generation. Come on, let's walk for a bit.'

We turned into the park. P spoke at length. He tried to trace back to his upbringing and the war all the indifference, melancholy, indecision, weakness, and lack of critical faculty in Arnold's nature.

The sun was high, the nursemaids were getting ready to go home, the hour of noon was approaching. I heard how harshly P analysed the people of our time. Perhaps he had more right than I did to this decisiveness, more than anyone else, for he was a dying man. He had to be ready at every instant with a judgement on everything that happened, for at any moment, today even, he expected to die.

I did not contradict him, I did not agree with him. I simply said: 'Had I had a father, I would not have blamed him.' Furthermore, to some small extent, old Zipper had been a father to me.

'You place yourself so far above people that you only see them in black and white, guilty or not guilty. You sit like a god in judgement, by motive and by deed. But we who were in the war judge by the stuff that men are made of.

'We were not just tired and half dead when we came home, we were indifferent, too. We still are. We did not forgive our fathers, any more than we forgive the younger generations who were bustling us before we found our feet. We do not forgive, we forget. Or, to put it better: we do not see. We do not pay attention. We do not care. What have mankind's destiny, or the country's, or the world's, to do with us? We are not starting revolutions, we are passive resisters. We don't become angry, we don't lament, we don't defend ourselves, we don't expect anything, don't fear anything – that we won't

ZIPPER AND HIS FATHER

die by our own hand is everything. We know that another generation will come which will be just like our father's. Yet again there will be war. We observe the laughable pretensions of those who are distressed by the world's sorrows – such as yourself – of those who were not in the war, of the young who suffer from the urge to remedy things, to change them. If scepticism did not also imply participation, I should say that we were sceptics. But we do not participate. *You* despise pathos. But *we* do not even believe in wit. *You* hate reaction. *We* doubt even the benefits of revolution. What do you expect? – *We made the mistake of coming back.*'

P was silent.

I watched the children who were excitedly collecting their toys; they had no intention of forgetting anything, and relentlessly extracted from their playmates anything which was theirs. But the green peace of noonday in the park, the gentle, fair faces of the nursemaids and the deep song of the bells reconciled me to everything about me – even to the gloomy instincts of the little man and the apathy of the old.

Even the flies were buzzing, as if in imitation of the bells . . .

Letter from the author to Arnold Zipper

Dear Arnold,

Perhaps, indeed probably, this, my modest report of your father's and your own modest life may reach you. It is possible that you have given up any idea of renewing by correspondence your connection with me, and that you embarked on your new life with the probably sensible decision never more to stir up the past. In any case, the letter I am writing to you now will be the only sign of my friendship which you will have received for a long time, and an assurance that the foregoing account means neither the end, nor even a diminution, of that friendship. For, as you will see when you have read all this, I have no more exhausted our friendship than I have your destiny. Indeed, I had hardly placed the last full stop to what I had written before it seemed to me that I had written too little rather than too much about you. The reason for this seems to me to be that there is not as much distance between you and me as there was between your father and me. Perhaps, too, I was justifiably afraid that, if I were to write more about you, I should be forced at the same time to mention a number of unimportant things about myself – and that might have broken the framework of what I had set myself to do. As I have already said, it would have been impossible to describe you with the clarity which only comes with distance. Yet your father's life seemed to me so necessarily bound up with your own that, had I eliminated you, a great deal would have had to be omitted. And, in writing, omission is where the lie begins.

I have to tell you all this directly, to some extent face to face, despite the fact that there is a danger that this letter may never reach you. I felt the need to make my excuses to you, not because I have made your life the subject of my book, quite the reverse; because I have not been able to give a sufficient account of you. You are one of those people to whom it is superfluous to explain the difference between an indiscretion and a first-rate performance. I, therefore, know already that you, being far away, will be angry or pleased with this book in the measure that my attempt will seem to you to have succeeded: the attempt to present through two men the differences and similarities of two generations, in such a way that the presentation cannot be considered a mere reporting of two private lives.

For, although your father's individuality was marked and, one might say, unusual, his characteristics were still more than typical of our fathers' generation, and I cherish the hope that many readers of our age will recognise in Herr Zipper, or at least in many of his peculiarities, those of their own fathers, just as they must recognise themselves in you, just as I believe I recognise myself in you. Indeed, I must confess to you that it often seems to me that I might be you, might myself stand on the stage of a variety theatre, desperately trying to start playing my fiddle. Perhaps I could better express in this way the unhappy relationship I have with the public, rather than through the laborious sentences in which I vainly attempt to make myself clear, as vainly as do you with your violin playing. Your profession has a clumsier, but for that reason more evident, symbolism. It is symbolic of our generation of returned soldiers, whom

244

everyone hinders in our attempts to play a part, make a decision, play a violin. We shall never be able to make ourselves understood, my dear Arnold, in the way that your father still could. We have been decimated. There are not enough of us. Not enough of us for this world, in which nothing but the sheer physical weight of the masses can make a breakthrough, and not the spiritual energy of an individual person.

Nevertheless, I wish you well in your new profession. Just carry on trying in vain to play, just as I shall never give up writing in vain. 'In vain', which means: *apparently* in vain. For, as you know yourself, there does exist somewhere a region in which the traces of our playing are recorded, illegibly, but in some strange way effectively, if not today, then years hence, and if not years hence, then millennia hence. Probably it will not be known whether I wrote or you played, or vice versa. But in the spiritual content of the atmosphere, which is more powerful than its content of electricity, there will float the distant echo of your single notes, beside the equally distant echo of a thought which I must once have written down. Assuredly, too, the frustrated longing of our whole generation will remain as immortal as it was unfulfilled.

I salute you, my old friend.
Joseph Roth.